"... It's obvious I'm attracted to you, and you've given me two of the most mind-blowing orgasms of my life, but I want more than sex. I want *you*. All of you. Heart, body, and soul. The total Toby package."

HE OWNS MY HEART

Evie Drae

Published by

 clandesdyne

Published by
CLANDESDYNE
PO Box 621
Barberton, OH 44203-0521
www.clandesdyne.com

He Owns My Heart
Copyright © 2020 Evie Drae
Edited by Blue Ink Editing, LLC

Cover Art
Copyright © 2020 Clandesdyne
www.clandesdyne.com
Cover content is for illustrative purposes only and any person depicted on the cover is a model.

Paperback ISBN: 978-1-952695-02-5
Digital ISBN: 978-1-952695-03-2 / ASIN: B088SYNN1S
Library of Congress Control Number: 2020912166
Paperback published August 2020

To the best bestie anyone could ever ask for—my person—Lily Michaels. You're the only reason I found the courage to release my words into the world. Without you, I wouldn't be where I am today. Thank you, my love.

Acknowledgments

Every story follows its own journey, and this one is no different. From the moment of inception to its final release, He Owns My Heart has been touched by countless hearts aside from my own. I'd like to extend all the "thank-yous" and well-wishes to the following:

First and always foremost, to Benjamin, my life partner and spouse, who continues to go above and beyond to support me as I reach for my dreams. To my family, who have supported my writing journey from day one, even when it meant accepting I'd never be who they thought I'd be.

To Meka, one of my staunchest supporters and writing buddies, who pushed me to write this story in the first place. It started as a joint venture to write a novella-length story in hopes of curing our mutual writer's block and turned into the massive trilogy-length story it is today. To my invaluable beta readers—including Meka, Marit, Kat, and Sarah—who put their blood, sweat, and readerly tears into this book's first drafts to help it become the final product it is today.

To my brilliant and beautiful agent Eva Scalzo, who accepted my pouty author decision to self-pub this story instead of subbing to publishers following a negative experience with my first traditionally published novel. I know I was a grouchy pain during all of that, and I can't thank you enough for standing behind me despite my decision to go off on my own for a bit to take a "breather" from the trad drama.

To my amazeballs editing team at Blue Ink Editing, LLC, I can't thank you ladies enough for your hard work, honesty, and dedication to helping me mold my book baby into a final product worthy of publication.

To the endlessly supportive and positive Twitter #am-writing #writingcommunity—most especially my #writeLGBTQ lovelies—who manage to be a constant form of personal and writerly support despite their physical distance.

And, last only because she deserves a spotlight, to my alpha reader and bestie, Lily, who has been there for me from the beginning of my writing journey and holds me up in a way incomparable to anyone else. Without her in my life, I'm not sure where I'd be today.

A CONTEMPORARY MM ROMANCE

HE OWNS MY HEART

OWNED HEART, BODY, & SOUL
TRILOGY

Chapter One

Landon stood outside a dilapidated motel off I-55 on the outskirts of Chicago. He held a rusted metal key, its edges dulled from years of use. The cracked red plastic of the key ring had the numbers 103 etched into its surface. A couple flecks of gold trapped in the sharp corners of the 1 and 3 were the only telltale sign the indented numbers used to bear a cheap inlay. His gaze drifted from the key in his hand to the chipped robin's-egg blue door bearing the same number.

On the other side of that worn, weathered piece of wood, a man waited for him. A man Landon had never met before, and a man he would never meet again.

Which was exactly how he wanted it... right?

Landon huffed out a breath and rolled his neck until it cracked, twice. "All right, asshole, you're the one who asked for this. Don't puss out now."

Nodding at his lackluster attempt at self-encouragement, he took the few steps necessary to reach the door and jammed the key into the lock without allowing his body time to catch up to his mental reluctance.

When the door popped open, he swallowed to soothe a dry throat and walked into the dimly lit room. A single lamp positioned on the peeling laminate wood of the nightstand between two double beds threw an eerie copper glow into the space. Its flickering bulb did little to calm his raging nerves. He licked his lips and looked around the room, a mixture of relief and regret sinking heavily into his gut.

He was alone.

Landon eased the door shut and stood inside, still gripping that damn key as if it held all the answers. What had he expected to find when he walked in here? A welcoming committee?

He nearly jumped out of his own skin when a clunking bang broke the silence in tandem with the sound of water. Landon's attention shifted to a door on the opposite side of the room as he ran a shaking hand through his long bangs, shoving them out of his face in the process. "Get a grip, Jenks. He's just using the john."

That phrase rattled through Landon's brain a moment before a bubble of hysterical laughter slipped past his lips. *Using the john.* Talk about an apropos innuendo. Wasn't a *john* the term used for guys in Landon's current position? And wasn't he hoping to be just that... *Used?*

The bathroom door clicked open, and Landon retreated a step as his mystery guest filled the frame, propping a shoulder against the warped wood. Black boxer briefs hugged his narrow hips and accentuated the cut of hard thighs. His chiseled, tanned chest was bare, his pec muscles flexing as he crossed his arms and committed further to his casual lean.

As Landon's hesitant gaze moved up, he bit back the slew of profanity threatening to tumble from his lips. If possible, the face attached to that Adonis body was even more beautiful. The jaw was strong and angular, dusted with a five-o'clock shadow a shade darker than his sandy-brown hair, and a smile befitting an A-list model stretched a set of lush, full lips.

But it was those eyes that drew a low-grade whimper up Landon's throat. Their color wasn't distinguishable in the dim lighting, but they sparkled with humor and a hint of something else. Something darker, somehow tragic, yet hidden well behind a mask of cocky confidence.

Jesus fuck. What had he gotten himself into?

"Enjoying the view?"

Those words dripped into the silence like honeyed whiskey—smooth, deep, and sinful as hell.

"I..." Landon clenched his jaw. What was he supposed to say to that? Yes? "Ah..."

A chuckle rumbled up the Adonis's ripped chest, its warmth filling the stale air and sparking electricity over Landon's skin. "Am I making you nervous?"

"Ah, you could say that." Landon dropped his chin with a groan. "I'm sorry."

"No need to apologize." A hint of empathy softened the man's voice. "This your first time?"

Landon squeezed his eyes shut as heat crept up his throat, burning his cheeks. "That obvious, huh?"

That chuckle rolled through the room again, but this time it was closer. Landon peeked open an eye and drew back in surprise when his stare locked on to a pair of gorgeous hazel irises, perfectly on level with his own. The younger man—easily a decade if not more below Landon's own thirty-five years—ran a lazy hand through his styled-back locks before closing the distance between them even further.

"This your first time ever, first time with a guy, or first time with someone like me?"

Oh god, oh fuck. The flush kept climbing until the very tips of Landon's ears were aflame. "No, I mean, this isn't my *actual* first time. I-I've done it... I mean, *this*... before. I mean, shit, not *this*, but you know... with a guy.

Jesus. I'm sorry. I should leave."

The Adonis's radiant smile returned, nearly blinding Landon with its bright white brilliance. "You're adorable, you know that?"

Adorable. *Great.* Just what every guy wanted to be called when he stood in front of a nearly naked Greek god. A nearly naked Greek god he'd paid to have sex with him.

Shit.

Landon puffed out his cheeks on a heavy exhale. "I don't know what I'm doing here. This was a mistake. I should really go. I'm so sorry for wasting your time. I..." He scrunched up his face on a low groan. "Jesus, I'm sorry. I'm such an ass."

The man took a step back, offering a weak smirk. "I didn't mean to weird you out. I should be the one apologizing. I'm used to clients wanting that brash behavior. Didn't read the room right, I guess."

"It isn't your fault." Landon scraped his teeth over his lower lip and let out a shaky sigh. "This was a stupid idea. I-I don't know what I was thinking."

Quirking a brow, the guy folded those cut arms over his muscled chest, sending a ridiculous punch of lust straight into Landon's groin. "I assume you were thinking you'd get laid. That's what most of my clients are looking for. Nothing wrong with that."

"No, it wasn't..." Landon groaned and pressed a fist between his eyes. "I thought I could be something... some-*one*... I'm not. For one night. But I can't. This isn't me. I don't do crazy shit like this."

When Landon glanced up, his heart squeezed. The man stood rigid, staring at the floor, his tongue running over that full bottom lip in a slow, repetitious rhythm. He looked about as lost as Landon felt, and wasn't that un-fucking-ex-pected?

Then again, how else would he react to those harsh words? Landon had all but denounced his profession as something, what, beneath him? *Idiot.*

"I didn't mean to say there's anything wrong with doing this, because there isn't. It just isn't something I've ever done or thought I'd do. I'm... boring. Unadventurous. Not really the one-night stand kinda guy, you know? Not that I'm saying this would be a one-night stand. I mean, I know that's not what it means to you. Not that one-night stands *mean* anything. I... Oh my god." He covered his face with both hands. "I'm having some sort of malfunction. Feel free to go and leave me alone to drown in my humiliation."

That spine-tingling laugh filled the room again. "Why don't we take this slow? We have all night, after all."

Landon let his hands fall as his shoulders slumped with relief. Sure, he'd been the one to initiate this whole thing, but he was terrible at sex, even when he was in an established relationship. How in the hell was he supposed to do it with a man he'd never met? A *professional*, even?

Maybe he could take things so slow they wouldn't happen at all?

Resolved to shift the awkward tension away from his sexual ineptitude, Landon cracked his knuckles. "Are you, ah, hungry by any chance?"

The Adonis tilted his head, a grin pulling at his lips. "I can always eat."

Landon yanked his cell free of his back pocket. "I saw a Chinese restaurant down the street advertising delivery. Does that... I mean... are you okay with that? We can do whatever. I just thought it'd be easiest."

"Chinese sounds amazing." His smile softened, treading carefully over Landon's disastrous nerves. "I'm happy with anything, but unfortunately, I don't carry money on jobs."

"Oh, yeah, no, of course. I've totally got this. Not a, ah, not a problem." Landon swallowed and ducked his head, cursing himself as he located the Chinese restaurant on his phone. "Do you know what you want, or—"

"I'm the opposite of picky. Order two of whatever you're getting."

Landon nodded and turned away, putting the phone to his ear. He placed identical orders for beef and broccoli with fried rice and an egg roll on the side. At the last minute, he added a two liter of soda before giving the motel name and their room number. They took his card over the phone, and then he hung up and shifted his gaze to the Greek god.

He'd slipped into a pair of black dress pants and a skintight ribbed tank in a dark-charcoal gray. Part of Landon missed the delicious view, but a much bigger part of him appreciated the clothing provided a step away from painful awkwardness.

The Adonis tucked his hands into the front pockets of his slacks and rocked onto the balls of his bare feet. "So, food's en route. Wanna watch a little TV while we wait? Or did you have something else in mind? I'm down for whatever you wanna do, boss."

Landon glanced at the two double beds facing the old-school tube television. "Yeah, no, ah, that sounds good. TV, I mean."

Nodding, the man wandered to the closest bed, snatching the remote off the nightstand with the flickering lamp before stretching out with his back propped against the cracked pleather headboard. He patted the bed beside him and cocked his lips into a lopsided grin. "Hop on board. Let's see what gems local television has to offer on a Saturday night."

Following the quiet directive, Landon slipped onto the bed. A scrumptious combination of sandalwood and leather drifted his direction, and Landon's cock twitched unhelpfully in his pants. He shifted, placing his folded hands over his lap and praying to achieve the level of nonchalance he aimed for.

As they skimmed through the slim selection of channels, Landon cleared his throat. "So… are you allowed to tell me your name?"

The guy lifted a careless shoulder. "Not something my clients usually wanna know, but I'm not against a first name exchange if you aren't." He offered a hand, and Landon took it with a tentative squeeze. "Name's Toby."

Toby. The name suited his Adonis perfectly. A punch of fuck-yeah-that's-hot with a hint of cute to soften the blow. Landon pulled his hand back and recrossed his arms. He was hesitant to share his own name, but since he'd been the one to ask in the first place, it was only fair to offer his in return. "I'm Landon."

Toby's brow arched, and a crooked grin lifted one corner of his lips. "Landon, eh? Doesn't quite fit your adorable awkwardness. You sure you're not making that up?" When Landon's eyes widened and he opened his mouth to say god knows what in response, Toby winked. "Just kidding. It actually fits you quite well."

Adorable awkwardness. Jesus. He really had made an ass of himself, hadn't he?

They landed on a local horror movie host who wore a theatrical vampire costume and spoke with exaggerated mouth movements and elongated vowels. Before the first scene of the B-movie flashed onto the screen, they'd shared several chuckles. When their food arrived a half hour later, Landon had to wipe tears of laughter from his eyes as he answered the door.

They ate their Chinese on the bed, sitting cross-legged, while they finished the ridiculous movie. By the time it was over, their food was gone, and Toby had mastered the host's outlandish overdone speech pattern, drawing deep belly laughter from Landon each time he spoke.

He turned to Landon, and in that almost indiscernible, ridiculous cadence, he asked, "Wood eet bee oh-kay eef I kees-ed yew?"

Landon clutched his stomach as he came down off a

rolling wave of laughter and swiped at his eyes. "I'm sorry, say what?"

This time, Toby spoke in his normal honeyed-whiskey voice. A surprising intensity filled his eyes when their gazes met. "I said, would it be okay if I kissed you?"

The question threw a wrench into Landon's inner gears, and his brain stuttered to a halt. They'd agreed to take it slow, and if Landon was being honest with himself, *this*—the innocent companionship he and Toby had shared over Chinese takeout and a movie so bad it had circled right back around to good—had done more to ease the ache of loneliness than any physical act with a stranger ever could. In fact, he'd almost—*almost*—forgotten the reason he was here in the first place.

Clearly, Toby hadn't. As if he could read minds, Toby traced a knuckle down the thick beard covering Landon's jaw. "I can practically hear your brain overthinking right now. Would it help if I told you I *want* to kiss you? Not because you paid me to, but because I'm dying to know what your lips taste like. On a personal level, not professional."

"Oh." Landon cursed the heat scorching his flesh, bringing a cold sweat to his brow.

"Does 'oh' mean yes or no?"

"Oh, ah…" A cackle rose up Landon's throat. He squeezed his eyes closed in horror. "God, I swear I'm not usually this awkward."

Toby's warm palm pressed against Landon's cheek. "Look at me."

Landon obeyed the gentle command, lifting his lids until his gaze fell on those soft golden-green eyes. Toby's countenance was no longer amused, but filled instead with kindness and a sense of understanding Landon had never expected to find in a situation like this.

"All the stigma of being with a whore aside, is there any part of you that wants to see what might happen if I kiss you? Not because you paid me to, but because I want to. Because, maybe, you want to as well."

Deep-seated insecurities clawed for freedom in Landon's subconsciousness, screaming into the abyss of his conscious thoughts that no one like Toby could possibly want him. Not unless Toby had recognized him. And if he had, it wouldn't be Landon he'd want, would it? It'd be the man Landon had needed so badly *not* to be tonight.

That would be almost worse than not being wanted at all.

He'd paid for the illusion of being wanted. Of being needed. This show Toby put on was part of the pricy package Landon had purchased to not only assure his anonymity, but to guarantee the happy ending he couldn't seem to find anywhere else.

Whatever possessed him to believe this was a good idea? Why was he treating another human being like nothing more than a body to be used? Simply to slake his own needs and hide from his own failures?

He was such a piece of shit.

"Listen, I really should go. I, ah, I'll still pay you, of course. I just—"

Toby raised his other hand and cradled Landon's face with both palms, forcing Landon to make eye contact. "You came here tonight for a reason. I'm not judging you, so stop judging yourself." The soft pads of Toby's thumbs brushed over Landon's lips. "Now, I'll ask you again... What's 'oh' mean?"

Chapter Two

What the fuck was he doing? Since when had Toby ever tried to talk a skittish client—one willing to pay without services rendered—into not only staying and collecting his payout, but also into *kissing* him?

Toby never willingly kissed a client. But damn, there was something about Landon. Sure, he was really fuckin' adorable, and those silky, smooth lips—surrounded by a dark, well-groomed beard that was soft to the touch— begged to be kissed. But there was something else Toby couldn't quite put his finger on. Something under those stuttering nerves and contradictory bad-boy looks that had Toby yearning to just hold him.

What the hell?

How long had it been since he'd last voluntarily kissed a man, anyway? Was it sadder he didn't know or that he didn't really care?

"Don't worry, I don't bite." Toby cocked his head, a grin kicking up the corners of his mouth as he switched to the goofy host's fake-vampire speech for the second part of his statement. "Unless you want me to."

Those expressive eyes widened as Mr. Contradictory worked his delicious mouth open and closed, phantom words weaving into the silence of the room. He speared both hands into his hair and slipped off the bed.

What was Toby's problem? Why couldn't he drop the damn arrogant act? Clearly that particular selling point of his wasn't a winner here.

Landon's snug gray T-shirt—nearly the same shade as his eyes—hugged a slender, fit torso, showing off well-toned arms bearing intricate full-sleeved tattoos that stretched over both wrists. A pair of dark-wash jeans were plastered to his thighs as if painted on, the well-defined muscle of a runner's build evident beneath the fabric.

Nothing about Landon screamed adorable on the surface. If anything, his appearance should set off warning bells in Toby's brain, but it didn't. It was nothing short of paradoxical when compared to his sweet, stumbling words and shy, hesitant smiles.

Landon's long on the top, shorn close at the sides black hair was messy and playfully youthful, while the mass of tattoos and dark, skintight clothing spoke of a long rebellious streak going nowhere fast. Yet a light smattering of silver-gray hair at his temples and shallow laugh lines at the corners of his eyes indicated his age likely fell a decade or so above Toby's own twenty-six years.

He was a walking contradiction. Mr. Contradictory, indeed.

Toby itched to run his thumbs over those luscious lips another time, but this client was jumpy and nervous. Landon needed to make the next move, not Toby.

"You're the boss here, my man." Toby slid off the bed and held his hands up to prove his intentions were innocent. "You paid for this, so you take from it what you want. I won't force anything on you." Those last words nearly caught in Toby's throat, but he coughed them free.

Before Toby could take the step necessary to place more distance between him and his delightfully nonplused client, a shaky hand snaked out and latched on to Toby's wrist. "Yes."

One whispered word. *Yes*. It meant so much, and yet

so very little. Toby stifled a sigh and pushed those murky thoughts into the back of his mind. He twisted his wrist free of Landon's slack grip and hiked his lips into a well-rehearsed grin, skirting the line between wicked and sexy. "So, 'oh' means yes. Noted." He closed the distance between them and wound his arms around Landon's waist, pulling until their bodies were flush. Landon was maybe half an inch taller than Toby, making him an even six foot, and every delectable inch of his leanly muscled height trembled as it pressed into Toby.

Their noses were a mere hairsbreadth apart, and soft, panting breaths fanned over Toby's cheek. To ease his john's trepidation, Toby ran a gentle hand up and down Landon's back, maintaining a chaste distance above the belt.

Landon threw Toby off-balance, but that was hardly a reason to complain. Why couldn't he drop the act and enjoy a client every now and again? Who said he had to resent them all?

With that thought spurring him on, Toby pressed into the flat of Landon's back, forcing their bodies closer. He marveled over his cock's interest in the goings-on—something he usually had to work really fuckin' hard to achieve, if he achieved it at all—but as the hard body of the man in his arms rubbed against Toby's dick, it leapt to attention rather than trying to crawl away. A zing of honest-to-goodness lust shot up his spine, then sank hot and heavy into his groin.

An involuntary moan slipped past Toby's throat. He swiveled his hips forward, thrilled to find proof of their shared arousal pressed against the fly of those painted-on jeans. Good, he wasn't in this alone. That "yes" had sounded genuine enough, but the unmistakable physical response offered the confirmation Toby needed. His tongue darted out and traced over the seam of Landon's mouth, eliciting a delicious little groan that hung in the air between them like a promise.

Toby gave that full bottom lip a light nip before diving into the warm cavern of Landon's mouth, not even bothering to seek permission first with a careful dip and retreat. The initially tentative response shifted almost immediately to a battle for control that lit a fire deep inside Toby's chest. Their tongues lashed back and forth, their lips moving together as if they'd always known this dance. As if they'd been partners for eternity.

He slipped both hands beneath Landon's form-fitted T-shirt and gave a yank, tearing his lips away to pull the fabric free and toss it to the floor. He paused a beat to draw air into his starved lungs as he drank in every inch of newly exposed flesh. The same elaborate tattooing that rained down Landon's arms covered the firm, lean muscles of his torso. The decorative designs stretched over his abs and disappeared into a pair of designer briefs poking out of the top of his jeans.

Designer, eh? Mr. Contradictory didn't look the type to spend money on fancy clothes. Not that Toby much cared about the details of his wardrobe in that moment. He just wanted access to what hid beneath. "I need you naked. Now."

Landon bit his lower lip but kept his eyes focused on Toby as he obliged. His deft fingers popped the button of his pants and dragged the zipper down. Without a whisper of the hesitation that had strangled him before, he shimmied out of his skin-tight jeans. The boxer briefs closely followed.

"*Fuck.*" Toby made quick work of removing his own clothes. Once free of the restricting fabric, he latched on to his aching dick and gave it a firm squeeze as his gaze wandered the length of Landon's beautiful body. No doubt he was a runner. Long, lean, and gorgeous. His fully erect cock nestled in a thatch of trimmed black hair, glistening at the tip with precum.

And Toby wanted to lap it up so bad he could already taste it.

What? No. He didn't suck clients off unless they wore condoms. He *wanted* it that way, both for safety and for dignity's sake. No one wanted some stranger's cum shooting down the back of their throat.

Then why did he want *this* stranger's dick—in all its bare, beautiful glory—so fuckin' bad? It didn't make sense, but it also didn't matter, because that wasn't happening. *Safety.* He couldn't forget the importance of safety.

Toby released his cock and stalked forward, thrusting both hands into that artfully mussed black hair and pulling them together for another ravenous kiss. He lurched his hips forward when Landon's arms wrapped around his waist. That first touch of bare skin drew moans from them both that mingled in the shared space between their lips. Their dicks slid together in agonizing torment. Enough to make Toby crave more, but nowhere near enough to satiate his desperate longing.

Toby broke the kiss again and grabbed Landon by the shoulders, whirling him around and throwing him onto the bed. He joined him and their hungry kissing resumed, frantic hands touching and searching and stroking as their wanton bodies writhed together, finding friction wherever they could.

"You a top or bottom?" The husky timbre to Toby's voice should've surprised him, but it didn't. Landon groaned when Toby latched on to one of his nipples, nibbling on the sensitive flesh as he suckled.

"B-bottom."

Now *that* surprised Toby. He released Landon's nipple and levered onto an elbow, considering Landon's flushed face in the dim light. The men who bought Toby's time usually preferred to do the fucking. "You sure about that?"

Was he trying to talk a client out of letting *him* top for a change? What was his problem tonight?

Landon's head bobbed, his strong hands clamping

onto Toby's biceps. "One hundred percent. I want you inside me, like, yesterday. Can we make that happen, sooner than later?"

Toby arched a brow. "I'd say there's a distinct possibility I could make that an immediate reality." He chuckled and shook his head as Landon's face split into an endearing grin. "Give me a sec."

When he pushed off the warm, lithe body and cool air blew over his flushed skin, Toby's stomach clenched with an unmistakable and not wholly sexual-based yearning. He ignored the out-of-place feeling as he snatched the bottle of lube and a condom off the nightstand and settled between Landon's eagerly spread legs.

Toby rolled on the condom, then squeezed lube into his palm. He coated two fingers and used the remainder to cover the rubber sheathing his dick. Landon tucked his elbows behind his knees, lifting them higher.

Swallowing to wet a parched throat, Toby nearly laughed aloud. Was he *nervous*? He gave a mental shake of his head before placing his lubed index finger at Landon's opening. When Landon groaned at the contact and his eyelids fluttered closed, a genuine smile crept over Toby's face.

Nothing about this encounter fit with his typical client experience. It was far too... authentic. Both his reactions, and those of the john beneath him.

He rubbed a few smooth, gentle circles over the puckered flesh before breaching the surface. Landon's dick bounced on his abdomen and his muscles tightened around Toby's finger.

"Hey." Toby frowned. "You okay?"

Landon opened his eyes and sought out Toby's. He nodded, and that adorable grin returned. "I'm no virgin. You won't hurt me. Do it. I'm ready. I'm *so fucking ready*." He wiggled his ass, drawing an unexpected laugh from Toby. "I *want* to feel it tomorrow, you get me?"

Yeah, Toby got him. He remembered, once upon a

time, that delicious idea of holding on to the feel of a lover, long after the deed had finished. Now the frequent reminders of what had been were unwelcome at best. Still, he appreciated the sentiment. Something from a distant past he'd long since let go of but could still catch a glimpse of if he tried.

Like now, when this stranger stared into his eyes with an unexpected trust glimmering from those smoky gray depths that made Toby want to give him so much more than his body. He wanted to offer a mutual pleasure they could cherish together, rather than a one-sided fuck they'd both forget in the morning.

With his absurd new goal in mind, Toby worked his finger the rest of the way inside, rocking in and out to assure the lube coated deep within. He pulled free and pressed both digits in, stretching the tight muscles with meticulous care. Landon tensed again, so Toby wrapped his free hand around the firm, heated girth of Landon's cock, moving in a languid tandem rhythm with the fingers he shifted inside.

Fuck. The wanton moan that escaped Landon nearly sent Toby over the edge without physical stimulation. He clenched his jaw and focused on the task at hand rather than allowing the scene to ratchet up his aberrant desires.

Once satisfied he'd prepped Landon enough to avoid any unnecessary pain, he removed his fingers and wiped both hands on the scratchy, pilled-up fabric of the hideous floral bedspread.

"Fuck me. Please." Landon's frantic plea was nothing more than a breathy whine, followed by a growled "*Hard.*"

Toby's control snapped like a frayed wire. He positioned his cock and shoved forward with enough force to breach the outer and inner muscles with a single thrust. They both cried out at the brutal connection, and Toby fell forward, their lips meeting in yet another lust-fueled collision.

That slick, tight heat gripping Toby's cock was like

heaven and hell all rolled into one. He nearly lost control when Landon's body first welcomed him inside. Not only would that have embarrassed him beyond words, but worse, it would've left his client unsatisfied—something he could *not* allow.

Sweat dripped down Toby's brow as he fought his body's desires. It'd been far too long since he'd been engulfed in a pleasure quite this sweet, and the urge to ride that wave of euphoria to its ultimate completion was so intense it all but blinded him. But then Landon's desperate arms clutched at his torso, and his strong, toned legs wrapped around Toby's hips, forcing their connection deeper.

Toby closed his eyes, and with little effort, allowed reality to take a back seat to the guise of true fervor and mutual desire. He focused on those strong limbs holding him close, the soft urgency of Landon's tongue, and the sweetness of his lips. He imagined the body writhing beneath him did so not because he'd paid for Toby's services but because they'd met at random—maybe at a bar, or a party, or on a lazy Sunday morning at their local coffee shop—and passion had sparked between them. Their shared need had drawn them together in a carnal blur of limbs and lips and lust.

"Please, I need you." Landon peppered insistent kisses against Toby's mouth between each breathless word. "Fuck me. Please, god, *please.*"

A guttural growl stole up Toby's throat. He found the will to move, spurred on as much by the pleas spoken against his lips as by the fantasy playing through his desire-hazed brain. He pulled out almost all the way, then pressed inside with slow, torturous precision. The tip of his cock grazed over that bundle of nerves, and Landon groaned as lasciviously as Toby.

Fuck, that felt good.

"Oh god, yes." Landon gripped Toby even tighter, the muscles of his ass following suit. Toby grinned against his gasping mouth, nibbling his plump lower lip as he thrust again. "Fuck. Yes. Just like that. *Jesus*, please don't stop."

Toby set a leisurely pace, careful to angle his hips so each movement brought Landon an extra little jolt of gratification. His reward was some of the sexiest noises he'd ever heard. With each stroke, his dick wept for release. He fought the need by focusing instead on the twisting and squirming of the man beneath him, paired with those glorious sounds of pleasure and the unexpected delight of his first real physical connection in years.

Those already tight muscles went delectably taut around Toby's cock, and a loud, keening cry paired with a flood of wet, molten heat that pooled between their joined bodies. Toby's own release slammed through him moments later. He shuddered and shook as he rode the wave of sheer bliss, and then he collapsed.

They lay there together, twitching through aftershocks, breaths intertwining in hot, labored gasps. The cool air evaporated the sweat glistening on their bodies, and Toby shivered at the shift in temperature. He pried himself free, pinching the condom to his deflated cock to hold it in place before pulling away.

Landon remained motionless on the bed, his arms and legs splayed like a starfish as little puffs of air escaped his kiss-swollen lips. He turned his flushed face until their gazes met, and dread settled over Toby's heart. Something stretching well beyond the guileless trust he'd displayed earlier glowed in the depths of Landon's pleasure-glazed eyes. Something Toby had no right to seek from another. Something he didn't deserve. Not now. Not ever again.

Shit. What had he done?

Chapter Three

With what little strength he had left in his well-fucked, fully sated body, Landon levered onto his elbows, cocking his head at the look on Toby's face. In a matter of seconds, it had shifted from one of languid, tranced-out bliss to a shuttered mask. "Ah, you okay?"

"Yep. I'm good." The closed-off façade fell away, and Toby offered an only half-convincing grin. He bounced off the bed and strode across the room without an ounce of shyness, his delectable body on well-deserved display. That jarring clank rang out as the archaic pipes chugged water to the faucet, and when Toby resurfaced a few moments later, he'd rinsed off and held a damp washcloth. "Need a little cleanup on aisle one?"

Landon accepted the warm towel and wiped the cooling puddle off his chest and abdomen. *Jesus.* When was the last time he'd come that much and that hard? He made a quick pass between his legs to remove the leftover lube, then tossed the washcloth to the floor. "So..."

Toby tilted his head, his megawatt smile kicking up a few degrees. "So, what?"

Landon shrugged. "Hell, I dunno, what's supposed to happen now?"

Pursing his lips, Toby lowered a hip onto the edge of

the bed. "That's kind of up to you, boss. You paid for the whole night. I'm yours until morning."

A strange pang that made absolutely no sense in the context of the situation arrowed through Landon's heart. He'd just had mind-blowing sex, sure, but it was with an escort. A man paid to pretend.

So why had it felt so... real? The reminder that it wasn't stung.

Landon pushed the rest of the way into a sitting position, suddenly all too aware of his lanky thirty-five-year-old frame sharing space with the stacked muscles of his youthful companion. The vivid reminder of all he lacked, and all the ways he'd never be enough, dragged his ass back to reality. He folded his arms and hunched his shoulders, doing his best to hide in plain sight.

He couldn't let himself forget Toby was an escort. That this was all fake. None of it was real. Even the humiliation currently eating at his floundering self-worth would fade with time.

Landon ran his tongue along the back of his teeth as he studied a line of frayed stitching in the floral print bedspread. "What do you usually do now? I mean, you know, after?"

Lifting off the bed, Toby padded over to their pile of clothing. He snatched their briefs and dangled Landon's from the tips of his outstretched fingers. "Mind if we knock the awkward down a peg if we're gonna chat?"

Heat bloomed up Landon's chest, stealing over his already flushed face. He nodded and accepted his underwear with a restrained whimper when Toby offered another one of those knee-weakening wink-grin combos as he passed off the garment. Landon slipped them over his hips, wishing Toby had grabbed his T-shirt too.

After a lifetime of hiding behind an ever-evolving series of physical and proverbial masks, Landon relied on the fortification only true concealment offered during his most vulnerable moments. Although he loved the ink camouflaging his body, and each design spoke to something far deeper than its outward beauty, it did little to disguise the flaws beneath.

To make up for the lack of clothing, Landon yanked back the covers and slipped beneath their protection.

Pulling his own briefs over an ass so perfect it should be criminal, Toby cast a sidelong glance at Landon as he settled under the blankets. "Thinking about catching some Z's?"

Landon raked his teeth across his still plumped lower lip, and the memory of Toby's fierce kisses drew a shudder up his spine. "No, just a little cold."

"Want me to turn down the air?" Toby jerked his chin toward the prehistoric window unit humming with a disjointed rattle at the front of the room.

Landon shrugged. "Nah, I'll be fine. Unless you want to… then, yeah, I mean, please, go right ahead."

Toby chuckled and moved to sit beside Landon on the bed, propping his back against the cracked pleather headboard but remaining outside the covers. He crossed his ankles and ran an absent hand through his short, disheveled hair. "When you chose the all-night package, what did you have in mind?"

"Oh, ah…" Landon cursed the incessant blush that barely faded before reemerging with no purpose beyond heightening his embarrassment. Why had he paid to keep the escort overnight instead of the one-and-done offer that would've knocked the bill down by a hefty percentage? That was easy. His fractured psyche couldn't handle getting fucked and forgotten again, even if Toby *was* only staying because he'd been paid to. Watching another man walk out the door, leaving him used up and alone… Yeah. That would've sucked. "I guess I thought that's how it was supposed to go."

It was the illusion he'd wanted. Plain and simple.

The *illusion* of normalcy was all Landon had ever known. His folks were part of the upper crust of Chicago's elite. His dad was in politics—a long-standing and highly respected incumbent Republican senator with far-right views—and his mother was the heir of old blue-blood money. Landon had never been good enough in their eyes, more a disgrace than anything they'd proudly claim. Yet they couldn't have any other children. He was it. The epitome of parental shame and failure all rolled into an inconsequential C-average, gauche waste of space.

And the icing on his layered cake of dysfunctional irrelevance? He'd had the audacity to be born gay. Something his parents had done everything in their power to correct.

Landon had picked this seedy rat-trap motel to avoid being seen, and had chosen to pay for the whole night because he'd wanted make-believe. He'd wanted to forget his real life, feign normalcy, and use whatever unsuspecting man had shown up to support that fantasy.

Yet somehow, Toby's quiet confidence and gentle understanding had managed to turn Landon's idea of a simple "fantasy" on its ass. Because whatever the hell was happening between them now, it wasn't simple, and he sure as hell didn't want it to be make-believe.

Toby offered a dialed-down, lopsided version of his gorgeous grin. "This is 'supposed to go' however you want it to. There's no standard. You forked over the cash, so you get to decide how this plays out."

Landon hated the reminder that this was nothing more than a business deal. Money in exchange for services rendered. No emotion, no room for interpretation. Cut and dry and painfully heartless.

He sighed. "I guess I hadn't considered the logistics of what 'all night' really meant."

"Fair enough." Toby scratched a thumb down his stubbled chin. "I don't get asked for overnights very often. Usually when I do, the clients have a preplanned purpose in mind. So… I'm afraid I'm not much help here. This is new territory for me too."

A heavy queasiness settled into Landon's gut at Toby's casual discussion of his other "clients." He had no right to feel jealous, but for whatever fucked-up reason, he did.

Heaving a mental sigh, he sat up a little straighter. His lean shoulders lined up with Toby's broad ones against the headboard. "I guess getting a little sleep wouldn't be such a bad idea."

"Whatever you say, boss." Toby leaned forward, massaging his neck before angling a glance at Landon. "You want me here or over there?" His chin tilted toward the second bed.

Landon frowned and let his gaze fall. Nothing about this felt right. No one should be allowed to pay for the things he'd paid for. No one should hold the level of carte blanche over another that their agreement allowed. Toby should be able to choose which bed he wanted to sleep in. Hell, Toby should be able to choose whether he wanted to sleep here at all.

And he damn well should've had a choice whether to have sex with Landon or not.

"You know what, I think I'd rather sleep at my place. My bed's way nicer—not to mention way cleaner—than this piece of shit."

When the silence stretched thin between them and Landon chanced a glance up, Toby watched him with hooded eyes.

"Don't you have a wife or someone else you're hiding this from?"

Landon drew back at the unexpected direction of Toby's question. Although for most of his life it had been, his sexuality was no longer a secret. The few people he cared about had either accepted that part of him or made damn sure he knew it was why they no longer spoke.

If it got out Landon had hired an escort, the press

wouldn't be fun, but it wasn't anything he couldn't deal with. Would it go against his contract with those bastard producers? Yep. Did he care? Right now, with an unexpected hurt glistening in the depths of Toby's golden-green eyes, that answer was easy. Not one fuckin' bit. "I'm openly gay and currently single. Not hiding anything."

"Okay." Toby pursed his lips. "Mind if I ask where you live? I'll have to check in with my handler if we're making a location switch."

Landon dropped his head and scrubbed at his face with both hands. "I'm sorry, I wasn't intending to drag you across town. I was just trying to give you an out."

Toby's warm hand fell on Landon's shoulder and offered a gentle squeeze. "Landon?" Toby gave a little shake when Landon didn't look up right away. When their eyes met, Toby smiled. "I appreciate that. More than you know. But I don't want an out. Not from you. Hell, if I could, I'd give you your money back. I feel like I'm the one who should've paid for tonight. It's been... unusual, but in the most unexpectedly positive ways."

Landon nearly swallowed his own tongue. That had to be a scripted answer Toby gave all his clients. There was no way the evening had the same effect on him it'd had on Landon. He cleared his throat and returned Toby's kind smile with a weak one of his own. "Is there any fine print against sharing a bed, and I dunno... cuddling or whatever?"

The molten claws of mortification threatened to suffocate Landon. Had he really just asked a man he'd never met before to *cuddle* with him? What was his major malfunction tonight?

Toby's whole countenance relaxed as his grin amped up to the megawatt version that lit the room with its radiance. "Even if there were, I'd make an exception for you."

Chapter Four

Toby's heart beat into the relative silence of the room. The only other sound was the rattling hum of the archaic window air-conditioning unit, and even that wasn't enough to mask the thrumming in his ears. This beautiful man—who had thus far given him nothing but respect, kindness, and a sense of belonging he hadn't believed still existed—wanted to *cuddle* him?

Landon reached over to snap off the flickering lamp, the muscles of his back and shoulders bunching and stretching beneath his inked flesh. Despite the mind-blowing, hella-intense orgasm Toby just had, his dick twitched at the sight.

When the harsh fluorescent glare of the motel's signage visible around the edges of the poorly hung curtains cast the room into stark shadows, Toby's pulse quickened even further. Landon's silhouette shifted, a hesitant expectation hanging between them as Toby pulled back the covers on his side of the bed and slipped between them. Once he'd stretched out flat on his back, Landon turned onto his side and scooted the short distance necessary for his warm skin to meet Toby's.

A small sigh slipped past Landon's lips as he settled in, nestling into the crook of Toby's shoulder and neck, placing a tentative hand over Toby's left pec.

Could Landon feel the wild, erratic rhythm of Toby's heart? Did he know it beat so fast because of him?

Toby curled his arm around Landon's shoulders and allowed himself a moment to marvel at the sweet warmth of their foreign connection.

He'd been a twenty-one-year-old frat boy jerkoff when he fell into this life. While he'd come out as gay in high school, his first boyfriend hadn't been until college, and it had been more of a fuck-buddy situation than anything resembling a real relationship. Then, when that finally ended, he'd been too focused on partying to care about anything beyond the occasional random hookup.

Which meant this moment—this powerful, poignant moment—was the first time Toby had ever held a man this way. And it was with a john who'd paid to fuck him. Nothing about that screamed pathetic or anything.

Toby closed his eyes and suppressed a sigh, tightening his grip on Landon's shoulders when he shifted as if to pull away. "Don't. Please." *Don't*? Don't what, exactly? What did he want Landon to do? Stay with him? Hold him? Make him feel something other than used?

It wasn't his place to make such demands. Landon had paid for his services, not the other way around.

Landon moved again, but this time he draped a leg over Toby's, further melding their bodies into one. "You sure this is okay? I don't want to make you uncomfortable."

"You're not." Toby resisted the urge to brush a kiss over Landon's forehead. "This is nice." *Nice*? Try the best fucking night of his life. At least the best night he'd had in the past five years. No question there.

"Yeah, it is, isn't it?" Landon's voice was soft, barely audible over the thundering pulse in Toby's ears. "A far cry from what you signed up for, but I appreciate the indulgence. It's been a long time since anyone shared my bed beyond the time it takes to bang out a not-always-mutual orgasm."

Toby nearly barked out a laugh but managed to swallow it down and maintain some semblance of dignity. That made two of them, didn't it? But Landon hadn't paid good money to listen to his whore complain. This was about his needs, not Toby's. "Been a while since your last serious relationship?"

"You could say that."

Landon traced haphazard designs over Toby's chest, leaving a trail of goose bumps in the wake of his feather-light touch. Toby let his lids slip closed and relished the joy brought on by that unsolicited but welcome physical connection.

"The last asshole I dated didn't want me; he wanted what being with me represented. Tends to be a trend. I don't really inspire the whole lovesick romance thing from the men I'm with."

Toby's eyes drifted open. He squinted at the ceiling as he tried to make sense of Landon's cryptic words. How could Landon *not* inspire heartfelt devotion from every man who'd been lucky enough to claim him as their own? And what did he mean by them wanting what being with him *represented*?

"Sounds like you're going for the wrong kinda guys, boss."

Landon snorted. "Yeah, well, I'm not the chasing-after-men type. I get stuck with whoever comes after me, which is usually the fame-hungry sort."

"Fame-hungry?" Toby hadn't meant for those words to slip out, but they fell past his lips before he could stop them. It wasn't his place to question a client.

With a heavy exhale, Landon halted the tender tracing over Toby's skin and flattened his palm over Toby's heart instead. "My dad's an Illinois senator. A far-right Republican asshat, to be exact. He's been in politics my whole life, which means I've been under the public microscope just as long." Landon's thumb picked up the movement his

27

fingers had paused, brushing gently over the spot beneath Toby's clavicle. "I told my mom I was gay in middle school, and my dad freaked out. He was petrified his constituents would discover he'd raised an abomination and kick him out of office."

"Fuck." Toby's chest squeezed, his throat tightening as horror stole through him. "I'm sorry. That sounds awful."

Landon lifted an absent shoulder. "He was so afraid of me turning into an 'effeminate nancy' that he tried to 'toughen' me up with his fists and forced me into every masculine activity he could think of. I was never a coordinated child, but I was in a fall, winter, and spring sport every year, without fail."

Toby frowned, his brows knitting together. "What a fuckin' dick bag."

This time Landon laughed, and it was a beautiful sound. Rich and deep and genuine. "That he is. Hilariously, all those high-testosterone activities he was so sure would flip me back to 'normal' just fueled my certainty it was the male form—in all its sweaty, muscly, jock-strapped glory—I wanted. Plus, I ended up falling in love with baseball." He sucked a small breath through his teeth. "Kinda made a career out of it."

No one needed to force Toby into sports as a kid. They were his bread and butter, and the locker room was where he'd solidified his own sexuality as well. "A career, eh? How so?"

Silence met Toby's question at first, and he kicked himself. He couldn't forget, despite the apparent intimacy they shared, he was still a hired fuck and nothing more. He opened his mouth to withdraw the question, but Landon answered before he could.

"I'm actually retired. From the Chicago Cubs. I kinda figured a World Series win was a good capstone to a fruitful career. And, well, I'm getting old."

"You played for the Cubs?" Toby's brows shot up, his brain spinning as he tried to place the name Landon... and then it hit him. Like a falling brick wall. "Holy shit, dude, you're Landon Jenks."

Toby thanked his lucky stars when Landon chuckled and didn't appear upset by his continued verbal diarrhea. "Yeah, I suppose I am."

Mind reeling, Toby shook his head into the dark. Why had Landon Jenks—*the* Landon Jenks, the four-time Golden Glove winning shortstop of the Chicago fuckin' Cubs—paid for sex with a whore? He could get any guy he wanted... If guys knew he wanted them. Realization struck, and Toby, once again, spoke without thinking. "I thought you were straight."

Landon sighed, and Toby gave himself a swift mental kick straight to the nuts. *Jackass.*

"Yeah, well, what can I say? I'm weak. I let my dad control me even after I'd made a name and a life for myself outside his sphere of influence." Landon shifted but snuggled in closer rather than pulling away. "Anyway, it's out there now. For better or worse, my dirty little secret's been revealed. And with quite the dramatic flair too."

"Uh-oh. Did an asshole ex sell you out or something?"

A self-deprecating chuckle rumbled up Landon's throat. "Not entirely. Kind of my fault there too. I thought I could take control over the endless media storm by agreeing to do some stupid reality show touted as a foray into the struggles to transition from professional ballplayer to business owner. It ended up being more of a shit show focused on my personal life—and relationships—than anything to do with its original intention."

Toby winced. "Ouch."

Landon resumed the tracing with his fingertips, only this time, they trailed lower, following the contours of Toby's abdominal muscles with whispered strokes that sent chills racing up his spine.

"It's okay. Lesson learned and all that." Landon huffed out a breath, its warmth wafting over Toby's chest. "Really pissed off my dad, though. Not sure he plans on ever talking to me again, but... no real loss there, either."

Toby's heart ached. Landon's false bravado failed to glaze over the pain evident in the broken tone of his voice, and Toby longed to steal it away. "No loss on your end, maybe, but certainly a glaring one on his. He's just too blind to see it."

Landon's wandering fingers made their way back to Toby's heart, his heated palm settling over it once more. His jaw stretched on a yawn, and he offered a careless shrug. "Sorry to get all serious on you there. Let's pretend that didn't happen and catch some sleep, yeah?"

"Yeah," Toby murmured, once again fending off the urge to kiss Landon's soft black waves. Instead, he risked a less intimate form of affection by pulling him closer and intertwining the fingers of his free hand with Landon's.

Humming in quiet appreciation, Landon wiggled his fingers into place and snuggled further into Toby's side. Another squeak of a yawn escaped his throat—easily one of the most adorable sounds on the face of the planet—and the soft fan of his breath over Toby's chest slowed into a steady, even rhythm as sleep overtook them both.

When Toby awoke the next morning, he was face-down, his body sprawled over something deliciously hard and sinfully hot. It took him only a moment to remember the gorgeous man he'd fallen asleep beside, and he emitted a happy little purr. It was met with a delightful chuckle that vibrated against Toby's cheek.

"Morning." Landon carded his fingers through Toby's hair. "I can't tell you how much I hate saying this, but

I need to use the bathroom."

It was Toby's turn to laugh as he rolled off Landon and rubbed a hand over his face. "Sorry, I'm not usually so clingy in my sleep." Not that he could accurately make such a statement, considering he'd never really slept beside anyone before, but it felt like the right thing to say since he'd woken up pinning the poor guy down like a sack of cement.

Landon sat up and knuckled the sleep from his eyes. "I'm the last person you should ever apologize to when it comes to being clingy. I wrote the book on that disorder." His lips curled into a shy grin. "It was nice to share a bed and not wake up every hour to someone shoving me away. I slept like a rock."

Toby tried to ignore the longing twisting in his chest when Landon slipped out of bed and padded to the bathroom. Some early riser's headlights beamed over the top of the curtains and played across the ceiling as his mind sifted through the memories of the previous night. A smile pulled at his lips when he remembered how quickly he'd passed out. For him, insomnia and restless snippets of nightmare-fueled sleep were the norm, not a contented drift into unconsciousness followed by waking up however many hours later feeling refreshed and oddly giddy.

But his gaiety had nothing to do with the rest he'd gotten. As Landon emerged from the bathroom, his sleep-mussed hair finger-combed into submission and a sweet smile on his face, Toby couldn't deny the light-headed, belly-twisting sensation had far more to do with the man he'd shared his slumber with than the actual act itself.

Toby's own bladder screamed for relief, so he kicked off the covers and darted a glance at the bedside clock with a groan. "Shit, is that the right time?"

Landon peeked at the digital numbers himself before crawling under the blankets. "I think so."

Toby slammed his palm against his forehead. How had he slept past six? He was so screwed. "I gotta go, man."

He hurried to the bathroom, grabbing his clothes off the desk chair en route. He emptied his bladder, swished tepid water to get rid of the dead animal taste in his mouth, and got dressed. When he stepped back into the room, Landon hadn't moved. He hunkered under the sheets, a dejected look pinching his face as he stared at the clock.

Regret slithered into Toby's stomach, twisting his insides into knots. "I'm sorry to tear outta here like this, but I overslept."

Landon shook his head. "No, no, don't apologize. I understand." He swallowed, a soft sigh slipping free before he angled his gaze to meet Toby's. "Do you think... I mean, ah, could I see you again sometime?"

Those words hit Toby like a punch to the gut. Did he want to see Landon again? To have another night like the one they'd just shared? Hell fuckin' yeah, he did. But to what end? How many times could he survive a night like that without getting hurt? The one time had already left its mark.

No matter how intimate the evening had felt, it was anything but. All it had been was exactly what Landon wanted it to be. He'd paid for sex because he'd had his heart broken and needed a rebound. A quiet, discreet rebound who wouldn't go to the press and further the media circus his private life had become.

But it meant more than that to Toby. Even if it hadn't been real, it sure as hell felt that way, and he wouldn't risk the hope it instilled. Because there was no hope. Not anymore and certainly not with someone like Landon.

Still... who was he to say what his john was or wasn't allowed to do? If Landon wanted to buy his time again, Toby couldn't stop him. His heart heavy and aching, Toby forced a grin as he closed his palm over the doorknob. "You know the number. For the right price, you can see me whenever you want." With that, he yanked on the handle and left.

Easing the front door closed, Toby snicked the lock into place as quietly as possible. He paused a beat, then hitched out a breath when no sound met his ears. The opulent two-story entryway made stealthy entrances nearly impossible, as every noise was amplified tenfold by the marble flooring and vaulted ceiling. He slipped out of the soft, shiny black Italian leather shoes—a staple of his work uniform—and padded toward the back hall in his socks.

He almost made it. Only a few more steps and he could've tucked himself inside the sanctuary of his room. The one place he didn't have to hide the puddle of hot mess he really was with a façade of cool, calm, collected confidence.

"You're late, Tobias."

The arctic chill that always followed Joseph's arrival settled over Toby like a blanket of ice as he turned to meet his handler's hard glare. "I'm sorry, sir. The location wasn't on the bus route. I had to walk to—"

Joseph sighed and held up a hand. "I don't want your excuses. I'm aware of the location. I sent you there, after all. But the client paid for an overnight, not a half-day event. You should've left with plenty of time to catch the early train."

"Yes, sir." Toby clenched his jaw but kept his expression passive. "I won't let it happen again."

"Let's be sure it doesn't." Joseph cracked his knuckles. "Get cleaned up. Close shave, fresh trim. Wear your charcoal Brioni, a white shirt, and neutral tie. I expect you ready and waiting within the hour. You've got a full-service brunch date with a diplomat who emphasized the importance of punctuality."

Irritation vibrated under the surface, straining the last remnants of Toby's control. "Sir, it's Sunday—"

"I know what day it is, you fuckin' whore." Joseph stalked forward and boxed Toby against the wall with his significantly larger frame. Wintergreen and the scent of a freshly smoked cigar wafted into Toby's face, turning his stomach sour. "I give you Sundays off as a courtesy, not a rule. If you think talking back to me is going to win you any favors, you're wrong. Do as I say. *Now.*"

With that, Joseph pushed away and left. Cheerful sunlight filtered through the skylights above, ill-fitting with the darkness consuming Toby from the inside out.

He staggered the short distance to his room, grateful for the blackness awaiting him on the other side of the door. At least in the dark he could pretend—however briefly—his life was still his own.

Chapter Five

Landon slammed his keys on the foyer table and stripped out of his bike jacket, then tossed it over the sleek cherrywood banister. He stalked through the open-concept main floor of his penthouse condo to the three-season sunroom off the back with its gorgeous panoramic view of the Lincoln Park Zoo, and beyond that, Lake Michigan.

He flopped into his favorite chair, positioned to soak up the early-morning sun as it rose from the bay and turned the water into mirrored glass, reflecting the first rays of light with a kaleidoscopic pop of color. Through the afternoon and evenings, it provided a cool, shaded spot where he could get lost in his own world and forget the one outside this private oasis. Much as he fully intended to do now.

"I was worried about you. Where've you been, sweet cheeks?"

Landon groaned at the concerned drawl of his part-time live-in assistant and full-time couldn't-live-without best friend. Steffon sank into the chair beside Landon's and draped his legs over the side, kicking bright pink painted toes up to rest in Landon's lap. Angling a glance Steffon's way, Landon attempted a carefree smile. Based on the arched brow he got in response, it hadn't worked.

The question was, did he tell Steffon the truth or cover his humiliation with a lie? He slumped further into the chair and frowned. "I was getting laid."

Steffon sucked in a breath and choked on what Landon could only guess was his own tongue since nothing foreign occupied his mouth. He smacked Landon's shoulder as he struggled to compose himself, then dropped his jaw in dramatic fashion. "Landon Alexander Jenks. You cannot release a bomb like that on an unsuspecting party without fair warning." He swatted at Landon's shoulder again for good measure before settling into his draped sprawl and cocking his head. "Garret?"

It was Landon's turn to choke on his tongue. "Hell no."

"Oh, come on, babe, would it be so bad if it were? Garret's such a tasty morsel. I still don't understand—"

"Do I question why you end things with the litany of costars who share your bed?" Landon raised a brow, and Steffon harrumphed into a pout. "I told you, things with Garret are over. So very, very over. We can't make it public until the season finale airs or we break contract. But just because he shows up and we play nice at all the media events doesn't mean either of us has interest in getting back together."

Steffon sighed and shook his foot against Landon's thigh, twitching his lips in thought. "I dunno. He makes googly eyes at you, even when the cameras aren't watching. Maybe if you talked to him—"

"No." Landon blew out an exasperated breath. "I told you all I'm going to tell you about Garret. I'm sorry 'it's over' isn't enough to satisfy your curiosity, but that's all you're getting."

"I'm your best friend. You've never hidden stuff from me before. Why start now?" Steffon whined, his foot bouncing faster with his growing agitation. "If this has something to do with the stupid contract and not being able to talk about what happened on the show until after the episodes air... I mean, come on, you know I won't tell anyone. These lips are zipped, babe."

Landon let his head fall back with a groan. "You already know more than anyone else who wasn't directly involved in filming or production. Can't that be enough?"

Silence met his words, but Landon didn't have the energy to apologize. He was being a dick, but he didn't want to think about Garret Ramsey or the TV show that was quickly and succinctly ruining his life. All he wanted to think about were those gorgeous hazel eyes, that brilliant smile, and the full, unexpected spectrum of feelings the man they belonged to had managed to elicit in the span of a single night.

"Lan?" Steffon's voice was soft, and a gentle hand snaked out to rest on Landon's forearm. "You know I'm razzing you, right? My 'I fucked-up' meter is telling me I might've picked the wrong time to do it. Is something wrong? I can be a real pain in the pleasure hole, but you know I'm always here. I can simmer down and wear my serious face for you, babe. Anytime you need me."

Landon's throat tightened, and he slammed his eyes shut, warding off the ridiculous sting of tears with a slew of mental curses.

Steffon pulled his feet from Landon's lap, then plopped his butt in their place. He tossed his arms around Landon's neck and pressed their foreheads together. "Look at me, sweetie. Talk to me. What happened last night? Whose ass do I need to beat?"

A chuckle slipped past the knot in Landon's throat, and he let his lids drift open. He met Steffon's intense chocolate gaze and sighed. "I... hired an escort."

Steffon drew back in surprise, his eyes blinking in slow motion. "Well, I wasn't expecting that. Wanna start at the beginning there, champ?"

"Only if you get your bony ass off my lap first."

Steffon narrowed his gaze. "I'm not going anywhere

until you talk. I know the ways of the wily Landon Jenks. If I let you go, you'll squirm out of this conversation and disappear on some long, introspective bike ride. Then you'll claim you don't need to talk anymore because nature's beauty or the open air solved all your problems... or some such shit like that."

Landon shook his head, but a wry grin twisted his lips. "Already had that ride this morning. Didn't help."

"Well, hell." Steffon wriggled off Landon's lap and returned to his chair, crossing his legs at the knees. "So, spit it out. Let's unpack this mess and find the solution."

Landon shrugged and let his focus wander to the tiny specks meandering around the Lincoln Park Zoo, wondering briefly at the story behind a cluster of dots huddled near an opening in the trees. Was it a family out for a Sunday afternoon trip for the kids? Or was it a group of pre-teens avoiding the parents who waited around the corner to hustle them home to finish homework before their Sunday evening meal? Or maybe it was two couples, on a double date, trying to decide whether they should get ice cream or cotton candy.

What would it feel like to be in one of those normal, everyday situations? What did normal even feel like? Would he ever know?

"Earth to Jenks, Earth to Jenks, come in, Jenks." Steffon snapped his fingers in front of Landon's face until he blinked to attention. "Jeez, something's definitely got you wigged. Either start talking, or I'm going to ply you with whiskey until you do."

Spearing both hands into his hair, Landon gave a tug before letting his arms fall to his lap. "I know you think Garret's a real 'winner' and I'm a jackass for letting him go, but have you ever stopped to think maybe it was a little too convenient that he appeared in my life at the same time the reality show people started sniffing around?"

Steffon furrowed his brow and crossed his arms.

He might be a slender man, but his personality was big enough—and bright enough—no one dared to overlook him. Ever. "You think Garret came sniffing around for some airtime on a reality show?"

"I don't think, Steff, I know." Landon cracked his neck a few times before dropping his head against the back of the chair. "Let's just say I played right into their plans. I fell for Garret's act, and the network got to not only film the dramatic coming out of Senator Jenks's son, they also got to humiliate him in the process."

"Aww, sweetie, that episode was so well received. Everyone supported you. I mean, not everyone, but this is a country willing to elect a sweet potato waving a tiny little Nazi flag as president, so clearly there are some questionable humans roaming the land. If you discount their reactions, it really was positive."

"I know." Landon rubbed absently at his forearm, startling when Steffon laid a tender hand on top of his to halt the nervous habit. Brushing a thumb over one of the scars hidden beneath the ink covering his flesh, Landon frowned.

"Don't let what your waste-of-space father thinks matter to you, Lan. He could drive his my-shit-don't-stink mobile right off the highest cliff and few would mourn the loss."

Landon pulled away, crossing his arms over his chest to stop his fingers from seeking out those disturbing reminders of the years he'd spent drawing his own blood with the sharpest blades he could find. Only during those brief moments of exquisite pain had the endless echoes of his father's cruelty left him in peace. "It's not about that."

"No?" Steffon propped his chin on a fist and pinched his face in concern. "So, what *is* it about?"

Landon worked his jaw side to side before shifting his gaze to meet Steffon's. "After the finale was filmed, Garret told me the truth."

Steffon sucked in his bottom lip but remained silent, allowing Landon to work out the story in his own time, in his own way. Just one of the many reasons he loved Steffon. He understood Landon's needs better than he did.

Blowing out a heavy breath, Landon turned to the gorgeous summer day visible beyond the floor-to-ceiling windows. He couldn't handle the look that would undoubtedly cloud Steffon's face when he confessed his ultimate humiliation. "Garret proposed to me. During the last day of filming, he whipped out this beautiful speech and asked me to be his. Being the lovesick fool I was, I said yes. Made for quite the dramatic finale."

"Oh shit," Steffon hissed, his hand lifting to cover his mouth.

"Yeah." Landon shook his head at his own stupidity. "We came back here and made love. Or, you know, so I thought. But after he finished, he jumped out of bed, got dressed, and thanked me for the ride of a lifetime. He said he was leaving in the morning to start filming that movie he'd gotten the supporting role in, and he wouldn't have been able to do it without me. Then he left."

Steffon licked his lips and sat forward. "Wait, what the actual fuck? He... he broke up with you? Immediately after *proposing*?"

Landon chuckled. "No, he didn't even bother to end it. Not really. He let the producers do that. They'd hired him to seduce me to add a little 'zest' to the show. Turns out the only reason they even approached me in the first place is because they'd heard rumors I was gay and knew it would mean big ratings if they could get me to come out on their show."

"Oh god, Lan." Steffon shook his head in disbelief. "It was Garret who convinced you to say fuck the man and stop hiding. To be proud of who you are. He's the reason... Oh, sweetie."

"Yeah, well." Landon hugged himself tighter and

continued to avoid Steffon's gaze. "I don't regret coming out. You're right, fuck what my dad thinks. I'm not going to hide behind his intolerance anymore. I'm thirty-five years old. I deserve to be who I am without fear of what my asshole father's going to think or do."

Steffon placed a hand on Landon's thigh and offered a supportive squeeze. "I wish you'd talked to me, babe. I wish you'd told me this sooner. I've been such a little bitch about Garret. I didn't know."

Because Steffon needed reassurance, Landon shifted his eyes to meet his and forced a small smile. He untucked one of his arms and threaded his fingers with his best friend's. "You haven't been a bitch. And I... I couldn't. I was too embarrassed. To think I fell in love with a man who'd been paid to..." He barked out a laugh. "Jesus. I'm a dumbass."

"No, you aren't. How were you supposed to know? The guy had me convinced too. Hell, based on the ratings and crowd response, he has the TV audiences convinced as well. As much as I hate to admit it, he must be a pretty damn good actor."

Landon scrubbed his free hand over his face. "It's not just that. I mean, fool me once, shame on you, fool me twice..."

Steffon drew his brows together. "Wait, what?"

Sighing, Landon pinched the bridge of his nose. "I hired an escort, remember?"

"Okay, what does that have to do with Garret?"

"It has everything to do with him. I hired Toby because I wanted to make believe for a night that someone could want *me*, you know? Not the professional ballplayer. Not the idiotic reality TV star. But *me*. And how stupid is that? I turned around and did the same thing the producers did. I paid someone to pretend to want me."

Steffon blew out an exasperated breath. "That's hardly stupid. It makes sense to me. You might have hired this Toby fella, but you both understood the arrangement. There was no deceit involved. What those bungholes did? That was some serious shade, babe."

Lowering his chin, Landon picked at a loose thread hanging from the hem of his T-shirt. "Maybe it would've made sense if I hadn't managed to totally fuck the whole thing up." His heart twisted as memories of spending the night tucked into Toby's strong arms washed over him. "I know this is going to sound completely moronic—mostly because it is—but I think... I think I kinda fell for him."

Steffon's brows lifted, and a corner of his mouth twitched into a smile. "Who, the escort?"

"He has a name, Steff... but yeah. Him. Toby."

With a squeal, Steffon clapped his hands and bounced in his chair. "When do I get to meet him?"

Landon refolded his arms and shot a grumpy frown in Steffon's direction. "Have you heard anything I've been saying?"

Rolling his eyes, Steffon shoved at Landon's shoulder. "Of course I have. You said you think you fell for a guy. So I repeat the question, when do I get to meet him?"

Landon blinked and narrowed his eyes at Steffon's show of ill-fitting exuberance. "I'm having feelings for an escort. For yet another guy paid to like me, paid to *fuck* me, even. Jesus." He dropped his head into his hands and moaned. "I'm pathetic."

Steffon jumped out of his chair and faced Landon, fisting his hands at his hips. "No one calls my best friend pathetic, including you. Especially since you're anything but. Who cares if he's an escort? All you paid for was the sex, right? I guarantee anything that happened beyond that—whatever it was about him and about what happened between you two—was real. Why not, I dunno, ask to see him again? You know, minus the paying-for-it aspect?"

Landon groaned and slid into a dejected slouch. "I did."

Steffon squeaked and clapped his hands again. "And? When's your date?"

Lolling his head to the side, Landon caught Steffon's wide, excited stare. "There is no date. He told me I knew the number if I wanted to see him again. Then said for the right price, I could see him whenever I wanted."

"Oh, sweetie." Steffon sank onto his chair with a heavy sigh.

"Whatever I thought was happening between us was clearly one-sided." The tears Landon had fought since the moment that motel door closed behind Toby's retreating form finally broke past his defenses. His vision wavered, and his throat squeezed shut, making the next words that fell from his lips high-pitched and raspy. "He was only there for the money. He's no different than Garret."

Chapter Six

Narrowing his eyes, Toby studied the chipped blue paint on the door before him. Room 103. Again.

It wasn't unusual for Joseph to send him to the same location for different clients, but this motel was well off the beaten path and not one Toby had ever been to before. He'd assumed Landon requested the location—likely to avoid running into any press or fans—because it wasn't one of Joseph's regular spots. To be sent here again, and to find himself in the exact same room? What were the odds?

But he knew better than to hope Landon would be on the other side of the door. No, Toby's dickheaded final remark had landed with the sharp, painful blow he'd intended at the time. Of that, he was sure. If Landon had planned to follow through with that timid, stuttering request to see Toby again, he would've done so by now.

It'd been nearly a month since Toby's encounter with the man who'd fucked with his head so hard. The man who happened to be a famous and successful baseball player with the sleek, toned body to prove it. The man who, now that he was out and proud, could get any guy he wanted, so why would he even consider a second night with a used-up whore like Toby? Landon had gotten what he needed, and rightfully so, had moved on.

Toby's heart stuttered when he remembered pressing against, and deep inside, that beautiful man. But it wasn't Landon's physique that prevented Toby from shoving him into the darkest corner of his mind, locking him into the same box he put the rest of his johns, and forgetting he existed. It was his aberrantly awkward, genuine, unassuming persona that had Toby fixated on their night together.

Landon had been so caring, open, and honest. He hadn't talked down to Toby or gone out of his way to make him feel like the hired fuck he was. He hadn't stepped over the agreed-upon boundaries, nor had he made Toby do things that stretched far beyond them, as so many of his clients were wont to do.

No, if anything, Landon had done the exact opposite. He'd treated Toby like more than a body to be used. He'd made him feel included. Wanted. Hell, even *needed*.

It was a miracle Landon had made him feel anything at all, to be honest. Toby rarely remained mentally present during a client meeting, and he hardly ever got turned on. The few instances where he did, it had nothing to do with lust or desire. It was biology and body mechanics. Nothing more.

But not with Landon. With him, the craving was real. Toby wanted him more than he'd wanted any man before, including the few he'd slept with prior to his introduction to prostitution.

Landon about destroyed Toby when he'd snuggled close and fallen asleep. He'd meant it when he said he only wanted to cuddle and talk. He hadn't asked for anything more than that initial hot-as-hell fuck that left Toby reeling. The talking had been new too. Toby's clients didn't typically converse with him beyond the necessary exchanges to get the job done.

But damn, had it ever felt good. So good, in fact, Toby didn't even care about oversleeping and landing himself in hot water with Joseph. He hadn't had a Sunday off since, but it'd been worth it.

Heaving a weighted sigh, Toby curled his fingers around the key in his hand and shoved it into the lock.

The room looked as it had the last time, right down to the damn flickering lightbulb. It was a wonder the thing hadn't burnt out by now. Toby tossed the key onto the cheap wood veneer of the desk near the door and ran a thumb over one of the worn holes revealing particle board beneath.

If it weren't for Joseph, he'd own things like this. Economical yet functional, not overpriced and fragile. God forbid he were to break or damage anything under Joseph's pristine roof, even within his own room. He'd have to pay for it with his ass, and it wouldn't come cheap.

Toby closed his eyes to center himself. He needed to get his head on straight before the client arrived. They expected cocky confidence they could control with their wallet, not a preoccupied mess.

A key jostled in the lock, and Toby cursed under his breath. It was showtime.

He ran a hand through his hair and another down the front of his navy fleece vest. The client had requested casual attire, so despite the summer heat, Toby wore worn and comfortable jeans paired with an undershirt he'd spruced up with the vest. They were hardly the designer level Joseph preferred him in, but it was the best he could do with what he had to work with. The "casual attire" request required digging into his limited personal collection.

Toby plastered on his practiced "sexy" grin and cocked a hip on the corner of the desk. When the client turned the knob and the door swung inward, he prepared himself for the worst.

But instead of another of the litany of horrors he'd grown to expect, Toby locked eyes with those beautiful gray pools that had haunted his thoughts for so many weeks.

Toby's smile fell as his jaw dropped. At the same

time, Landon's face lit up with the brightest grin to ever cross those stunning features in Toby's presence. He hip-bumped the door closed and strolled into the room with a confidence that hadn't been there during their last meeting. He walked right up to Toby, cupped his jaw with both hands, and crushed their mouths together with a ferocity that drew a whimper up the back of Toby's throat.

Without hesitation, Toby levered off the desk, wrapped his arms around Landon's torso, and pulled their bodies flush. When their dicks collided through a dual layer of denim, Toby's already thickening cock strained toward the hard heat of Landon's. He rolled his hips, grinding into Landon with a wanton need he hadn't felt since the last time he'd been in his arms.

When the demand for air forced them apart, Landon clutched at Toby's shoulders as he tried to pull away. "Don't, please. God, I know this is crazy, but I... just don't. Not yet."

Toby nodded against Landon's neck, sucking ragged breaths into his lungs. He didn't want to let go any more than Landon did. It *was* crazy, but he felt it too. Whatever it was.

Eventually, Landon threaded his fingers through the hair at Toby's nape and brushed a gentle kiss over his temple. "I'm sorry. I shouldn't have done this. I... *fuck*... I wanted to see you again, and I..."

Toby pulled away enough to match his gaze with Landon's without losing the connection between their bodies. "Don't apologize." He smiled and shook his head. "This was one hell of a nice surprise."

The truth of it was, if Toby could have, he would've reached out to Landon himself. But Joseph would never permit him to contact a client directly, and certainly not for a personal reason.

"I thought maybe we could do something. You know, go out." Landon's face crimsoned, and his eyes fell away.

"I mean, I'll obviously still pay for your time, but it doesn't have to be about that. About, ah, about *sex*. I... I wanted to see you. Not, you know, I mean..." He cringed away from his own words. "I guess I was hoping we could spend some time together. Like, you know... kind of like a date."

Toby's chest squeezed. He couldn't remember the last time anyone had wanted to spend time with *him*, not his ass. He planted a kiss on the tip of Landon's nose. "I'm not allowed to leave the agreed-upon location unless I clear it first, and that gets complicated sometimes. Do you mind if we stay here?"

Landon's stare shifted to Toby's, and his brows drew together. "Not allowed?"

"It's a safety thing." Toby cleared his throat and forced an easy smile. "My handler keeps tabs on where I'm at, at all times, in case anything gets out of hand. Makes it easier to get away if I need to."

"Oh. Yeah. Makes sense." Landon toyed with Toby's hair for a moment. "Well, it still doesn't have to be about... that. Um, maybe we could rent a movie this time or... or something? Order a pizza maybe? Or Chinese again? Or I could get takeout if there's something else you'd rather have. Ah, maybe grab some beers or something too while I'm out?"

A grin pulled at Toby's lips. A movie, some beers, and greasy cheat food with a hot guy who demanded nothing more from him than his company? That sounded like the best Thursday night plans he'd had since... well, since long before Joseph came into his life. "Pizza sounds amazing, but I wouldn't turn my nose up at a beer or two, either. There's a carryout next door. Why don't we order some pizza, and I'll come with you to pick up the beer while we wait for it to be delivered?"

Landon nodded and licked his lips, his gaze drifting to rest on Toby's mouth. "I know I said it wasn't about, you know, anything like that, but... Can I kiss you again? One more time? Then I promise, hands off the entire—"

Without a moment's hesitation, Toby slanted his lips over Landon's, dipping into the warmth of his mouth and moaning when their tongues collided. Landon's grip on the back of Toby's hair tightened, and a whimper of his own drifted into the air.

Landon might be offering a pressure-free night—one where Toby could make believe he was a normal guy, on a normal date—but that didn't mean nothing would happen. It meant whatever *did* happen would be by Toby's choice, because he wanted it to, and because *Landon* wanted it to.

And didn't that sound like one hell of a perfect date?

When Toby snagged the last piece of pizza and shoved half the slice into his mouth with one bite, Landon groaned and rubbed his belly, casting a half-assed glare his way. "Dude, where do you put it all? You've had three more pieces than me, and there isn't an ounce of fat on you. Meanwhile, I'm about to explode over here and look nine months pregnant."

Toby shot Landon an overflowing-with-pizza grin before tearing off another exaggerated bite, filling his already stuffed mouth to the brim on principle. He never got to eat pizza, so he damn well wasn't going to waste the opportunity to enjoy every morsel his admittedly overfull stomach could handle.

"Must be your damn twenty-something metabolism." Landon stretched his legs out on the bed and crossed them at the ankle. "Us old guys gotta watch what we eat."

Toby washed down his slice with a long chug of beer, then wiped his mouth with the back of his hand. "You're not old, dude. You're in your prime." He waggled his eyebrows and clinked the butt of his bottle with Landon's. "Plus, you're retired. I'm still on active duty. Gotta fuel the twice-daily gym visits somehow."

"Twice-daily?" Landon's arm froze midair, his beer poised to tip into his mouth. "Seriously? I didn't even do two-a-days during spring training. Don't you give your body a chance to rest, like, ever?"

Toby laughed and tossed back the rest of the lukewarm fluid at the bottom of the bottle. Like Joseph would ever let him skip a workout. "It's part of the job. I don't really have a choice." He bounced off the bed and strode over to the twelve-pack they'd left on the desk. "Up for another?"

Landon eyed his half-full beer and groaned again. "Yes, but my stomach is at capacity. Unless you want me ralphing all over you—which, if I do say so myself, would be decidedly unwelcome—I might have to take a breather. You go ahead, though."

A frown touched Toby's lips as his hand froze over the half-empty twelve-pack of beer. "I should probably slow down too. I don't get to drink very often, and I can't afford a hangover tomorrow."

"Big Friday plans?"

Toby massaged the back of his neck and averted his gaze. "Yeah, life's been keeping me pretty busy lately."

"I guess that means my grand idea of asking you to spend the day with me tomorrow is going to fall flat, huh?"

Toby's shoulders slumped on an exhale, and he wandered to the bed and tossed the empty pizza box on the floor before climbing in next to Landon. He sat in silence for a moment, studying his fingers as he picked at the zipper on his fleece vest. There was nothing he'd rather do than spend his day with Landon, but that wasn't his choice. His time was already spoken for.

Heart aching, he licked the lingering taste of beer and pizza from his lips. "I like you, Landon."

The admission had Landon's head drawing back in surprise, and he beamed in response. "I like you too, Toby."

A half-hearted smile lifted Toby's lips, but he resumed staring at his own fidgeting hands rather than meeting Landon's eager gaze. "This has been nice. It's not something I really get to do, you know? But..."

Landon leaned forward. "But...?"

Toby swallowed. It would hurt, but it needed to be said. He couldn't lead Landon on. "But it can't go anywhere. After tonight? We can't do this again." He finally lifted his eyes and latched on to Landon's, their smoky depths glistening in the flickering light from the TV neither had paid an ounce of attention to all night. "You can't keep paying to see me, Landon."

"Okay, then give me your number. I'll stop setting up backdoor meetings, and we can do this the legitimate way."

Toby rubbed at his temple. "I'm a prostitute. This is the only way I *can* do things. There is no 'legitimate' way for a whore."

"I don't care what you do for a living. It doesn't bother me."

A flash of irrational anger lanced through Toby's gut, and his jaw clenched. "That's bullshit, and you know it as well as I do."

Landon blew out a long breath and let his head fall against the headboard with a soft thud. "Okay, sure, looking into the future I could see it becoming an issue, but not because I think any less of you for it. We all do what we must to survive in the world. But if this goes where I want it to go? I'd like to think you might consider letting me help you find something else to focus your passions on."

A dark chuckle simmered in Toby's throat. "You think I'm *passionate* about giving my body to any man willing to fork over the selling price? You think I *want* to do this?"

Landon sucked in a sharp breath. "I wasn't trying to imply—"

"Fuck, Landon." Toby dropped his head into his hands. The nausea coiling in his overstuffed belly had little to do with the pizza and beer that filled it. "What's it matter? Why're we even having this conversation?" He cast a sidelong glance Landon's way. "I'm a whore, and you're a client who shelled out an obscene amount of money to fuck me. That's all we'll ever be to each other. The rest of this is a fantasy. Just part of the illusion you bought and paid for."

"You don't really mean that." Landon's voice was small, nearly inaudible.

With a cruelty Toby never would've believed he could possess, he flashed an icy glare Landon's way. "Don't I? You so sure about that?"

Chapter Seven

The callousness of those words slammed into Landon like a runaway train, crashing into his chest with a raw physical ache that had him clutching a fist over the site to ward off the pain. Toby couldn't believe there was nothing between them but the money that had switched hands. He *couldn't*.

Landon might've believed it for a while. He might've agonized over it, lost sleep over it, beat himself into the ground over it. But all that changed the minute he'd opened the door and seen Toby waiting for him. He hadn't been sure what he'd find, but after nearly a month of doing little else but wondering what could've been, he'd decided enough was enough and reached out to Toby the only way he knew how.

Not that he'd been thrilled to make that connection a second time. The male escort service run by the slimy Joseph Coulier had been recommended to him by one of the body techs at the custom motorcycle shop Landon started up after retirement. A lifelong dream only mildly tainted by the clusterfuck that was Garret and that damn reality show.

The look of happy surprise on Toby's face when Landon had stepped into the room, followed by his immediate and genuine response to Landon's kiss, told Landon all he needed to know. Toby hadn't forgotten about him, either. And there was more between them than for-hire sex.

"I *am* sure." Landon firmed his jaw and forced himself to meet Toby's cold stare. "Because this is about more than the damn money."

Toby startled Landon by surging forward, his lips crashing over Landon's with a ferocity that spoke more of desperation than anger. Their tongues warred for control as their hands tore frantically at the other's clothing, pulling and tugging as they rolled across the bed. Their mouths only separated long enough for a shirt to be yanked over a head or a pair of jeans to be kicked free.

When their boxer briefs joined the rest of their clothing, flung blindly across the room, a feral growl rumbled up Toby's throat, and he planted his full weight over Landon's willing body. "This is what you want, isn't it? This is what you paid for, after all. You want the well-trained whore to fuck you rough and hard into the mattress." Toby thrust his hips into Landon, his cock pressing hot and heavy against Landon's own. "Well, guess what? I'm not only well trained, I'm also a professional. I make sure my clients *never* leave dissatisfied."

Those words hit like a bucket of ice that all but drowned Landon's libido in a wave of numbing shock. He pushed against Toby's chest, angling his chin away when Toby tried to kiss him again. "Stop." He shoved harder, mortified when a tear slipped down his temple. "Fucking *stop.*"

A keening wail pierced the air, and Landon threw a hand over his mouth to halt the sound. Only it wasn't coming from him. A flood of cool air washed over his naked body, and he levered onto his elbows. He sucked oxygen into his heaving lungs as his eyes sought out Toby.

Toby stood in the middle of the room, staring in wide-eyed horror at the bed where Landon still lay sprawled atop the covers. "Oh my god... What did...? Fuck, Landon, fuck. I'm... I'm so fucking sorry."

"It's okay—"

"No, it's not. No, it's fucking not." Toby shook his head and took a step back. "I don't know what... I can't... Fuck. I'll have your money refunded. All of it. For both times. I... I'll leave. I'll go. I'm so sorry."

Landon sat bolt upright, panic squeezing his throat. "No, please, don't go. *Please.*"

Toby kept shaking his head, his eyes darting around the room. When they landed on his underwear, he lunged forward and scooped them off the desk chair where they'd landed during their frenzied stripping. Landon launched off the bed and grabbed both of Toby's wrists before he could step into the briefs. "It's okay, Toby. I was totally on board with what happened... until I wasn't. You stopped as soon as I asked you to. You didn't do anything wrong, okay?"

When Landon released Toby's wrists, Toby remained frozen in place, staring blankly through Landon.

"Toby?" He placed his palms against Toby's stubbled cheeks. "Come back to me."

Toby's eyes drifted shut. He let the underwear fall to the floor and covered Landon's hands with his own, taking a small step forward until their bodies touched. "I'm a mess. You deserve so much better than anything I could ever offer."

A bubble of laughter jumped free of Landon's slack jaw. "I'll meet your 'mess' and raise you about ten thousand pounds of fucked-up." His thumbs brushed the tired bruises under Toby's eyes. "I'm sorry if I hit a nerve about your work. I meant it when I said I understand. I'd never ask you to quit for me. I was only saying I'd be here if you *wanted* to and needed a little help getting there. That's all. I'll take whatever I can get. I don't care if it doesn't include sexual exclusivity. I just want to spend time with you. You have this insane ability to make me feel things I didn't think I'd ever feel again. Call me selfish, but I want more of that. I want more of *you.*"

Toby touched his forehead to Landon's. "I wish it were that easy."

"It doesn't have to be complicated. I'm not looking for a commitment, only a bit of your time now and then. I get your job keeps you busy, but there's a connection here. A real one, not some fabricated farce. I know you feel it too. You wouldn't have greeted me the way you did if you didn't."

Toby dropped his hands and wrapped his arms around Landon's waist. He brushed a gentle, innocent kiss over Landon's lips and held it there. A sweet, hopeful pressure that had nothing to do with sex and everything to do with a promise of the future Landon longed for.

It wasn't until it ended that he realized his mistake. Toby wasn't making a promise for the future; he was putting an end to their present. When Toby pulled away and gathered his clothes—handing Landon bits of his own without meeting his eyes—Landon's heart twisted.

"Please, can't we at least try? I'll take whatever you can give me."

Toby tugged on his pants and shirt with stilted movements. "I don't have anything left to give."

A shiver snaked up Landon's spine, but he slipped into his clothes before risking a glance at Toby. He stood adrift in the center of the room, his eyes glued to the floor. He zipped up his vest and ran a hand through his sandy-brown hair in an attempt at smoothing the kinks from their brief but heated encounter.

"I'll make sure you get a refund for tonight at least. I don't know if I'll be able to swing the first payment too, seeing as how services were rendered, but me bailing tonight is justifiable cause to earn full reimbursement without question."

Landon's gut cramped at the wrongness of those words. He hated that money had ever changed hands as part of their "relationship." It didn't feel that way to him—

it hadn't from the first moment he'd locked gazes with To-by's. For wrong or for right, he'd allowed himself to forget their reality yet again. He'd believed his own fantasy rather than facing the truth.

He sighed and averted his eyes. "I don't want a re-fund. I just want *you*."

Stillness met his words, then a lock clicked, and Landon's head flew up. Toby stood by the door, his palm resting on the knob, his chin tucked against his chest. "You can't have me, Landon; I'm already owned." He turned the handle and pulled the door free. "Please don't ask for me again."

"Toby, please…" Landon drew his arms around his shoulders in a self-hug to stave off the ache radiating through his chest. When Toby continued wordlessly out the door, Landon took a step forward, reaching toward his re-treating form. He couldn't be sure if Toby would hear his final plea, but as the door swung closed, he called out, "If you change your mind, come back to our room… You can always find me here."

"Hey, good-lookin', this seat taken?"

Landon gritted his teeth but allowed his lips to tug into a socially acceptable smile. "Doesn't appear to be at the moment."

Garret flopped onto the empty stretch of couch be-side Landon in the VIP area of Sukho, one of Chicago's most elite nightclubs. It was Friday night and the place was hop-ping. Thick resonating beats vibrated the very air around them, muffled only slightly by the dense glass and heavy curtains acting as a privacy barrier. A rainbow of pulsing lights cut through the carefully constructed darkness, fash-ioning a dreamlike ethereal glow that paired flawlessly with the deco-modern décor to create a sense of surrealism and mystique.

Crossing his ankle over the opposite knee, Garret leaned into the couch, draping a casual arm over the back before taking a sip of his customary bourbon sour. His fingers weaved into the short hair at Landon's nape and massaged his scalp. "I was surprised to hear you were out tonight. You should've called me to join. Didn't you get my text letting you know I'd be in town this weekend?"

Landon leaned forward to retrieve his whiskey highball from the glossy misshapen square that served as a coffee table and shifted out of Garret's reach. To the casual observer, it would look like he simply changed to a more comfortable position, but anyone who understood the underlying tension between the two would easily see it for the act of irritated exasperation it was.

"I got your text." Landon took a sip of his drink, then balanced it atop his crossed knees and traced the rim with his thumb. "Who told you where I was?"

Garret let out a hiss of frustration, but that charming grin stayed glued in place. He ran a hand through his beach-blond waves, the only outward sign of his less-than-collected state. "Aw, come on, honey, don't be this way. I've tried to apologize, but it's hard when you refuse to take my calls. This is the first time I've managed to get you alone since—"

"Garret, what a *pleasure* to see you." Steffon's arrival couldn't have been timed any better. His chocolate eyes iced over as he smiled with forced politeness. Without seeking permission, he settled himself in the narrow space separating Landon and Garret with uncanny grace.

"Steffon." Garret nodded his greeting, but his mask slipped a little, and his disappointment showed briefly through. He repositioned to allow for a bit more breathing room between them, then stuck a finger into the knot of his tie and loosened it a few inches. With renewed fervor, he picked up the act again, his pearly whites flashing in the variegated light. "How's my favorite blond doing this evening?"

Steffon tossed his head, adding a flick of his hand to mime a hair flip, had his platinum locks been long enough to do so. "Oh, he's peachy." He fluttered his lashes at Garret. "How'd you find out Lan and I were out tonight? I thought we'd managed to avoid the paparazzi circus."

Landon nearly choked on his drink at the blatant accusation behind Steffon's words. It was true, Garret had a habit of showing up uninvited whenever the press leaked Landon's location, even when they'd still been dating. Steffon used to think it was sweet he went to so much effort to find and spend time with Landon, but the chilly bite to his words did little to hide the truth of his feelings now.

Garret pursed his lips into an exaggerated duckface and gave a knowing nod. "A little birdie told me I might be able to find my man and his trusty companion enjoying a leisurely evening at one of our favorite spots. I assumed you two wouldn't mind the added company."

"Oh, well, you certainly assumed wrong, didn't you?" Steffon's smile stretched tight and thin. Landon couldn't stop the laughter that rose in his chest as Steffon crossed his arms and cocked a single perfectly painted-on brow. "Landon has a new man now, Mr. Ramsey, one far more deserving of him than you'll ever be. It's sweet of you to try and keep up the act, but considering the season finale airs next week, why don't we cut the bullshit?"

Garret drew back in surprise, his ankle falling from his knee as he straightened with indignant outrage. "What goes on between Landon and me is our own personal, private, *contracted* business, so perhaps you should—"

"You're a lecherous prick, Garret." Steffon wrinkled his nose as if he'd been treated to a whiff of yesterday's garbage. "Why I ever thought you were even remotely worthy of Landon is beyond me."

Landon bit his bottom lip to suppress the endless rumbling laughter threatening to overtake him. Steffon never ceased to amaze. Still, there was a week before his contractual obligations were fulfilled, so maintaining an outward appearance of friendship, at the very least, was imperative. He placed a gentle hand at Steffon's elbow and tossed him a reassuring smile when he angled a sharp gaze in his direction.

"Garret, I appreciate you stopping by. Have a pleasant rest of your evening." Landon offered Garret a nod of farewell before guiding Steffon back against the couch and giving his shoulder a grateful squeeze.

Shaking his head, Garret pushed to a standing position. "I'll call you later. I really think we should talk. Alone." He shot Steffon a pointed glare, and Steffon returned it with a smirk.

"Toodles, Gar-Gar. Be off with you now. We have no more need of your oh-so-very-lovely company." Steffon wiggled his fingers in a dismissive gesture, and to Landon's utter delight, Garret narrowed his eyes but left without further response.

Once their private bubble was once again that, Landon fell against the couch with a hoot of laughter, clutching at his stomach to fend off the ache in his gut from stifling his reaction for so long. "That was totally Steff-maz-ing."

Steffon grinned and retrieved the Manhattan he'd left behind before going to the restroom. Clinking his glass with Landon's, he tossed out a wink, then downed what remained of the drink. "That felt damn fine. Not gonna lie."

Landon polished off his own beverage and set the empty glass on the large cube table. "That was a smooth move, telling Garret I have another man. I could tell that got under his skin. His jaw did that twitchy thing that used to freak me out. It always meant I'd pissed him off somehow." He chuckled at himself, then frowned as he remembered the fear that little tick had instilled in him. Old habits die hard, and even though Garret had never raised an unwelcome hand to Landon, all men wore the mask of his father when their anger came out. He couldn't help it.

"That wasn't a smooth move, babe." Steffon caught the attention of the VIP server as the young woman peeked in to check on her charges. She pointed at their glasses, and Steffon nodded, raised two fingers to indicate they wanted another round, then refocused his attention on Landon. "You *do* have another man."

Landon scoffed and folded his arms over his snug navy-blue graphic tee. "Is that what you call being left, yet again, with my dick in my hand? Toby doesn't want me. He's made that abundantly clear."

Steffon snorted and patted his immaculately styled bouffant. "I can read between the lines as easily as you can, big guy. He wants you. He's just ashamed of what he does for a living. Give him time. He'll come around."

"Yeah? How, exactly? He has no way of getting in touch with me, and the only way I can get ahold of him is through his skeezeball 'handler,' who Toby made clear was off-limits. No more paying to see him."

Steffon rolled his eyes but didn't respond immediately as the server had returned with their drinks. After she'd scurried off again, he extracted one of his maraschino cherries and popped it into his mouth, stem and all, then spoke around the obstruction. "He can get in touch with you. Mr. Gallant that you are made sure of that, now didn't you?" Steffon worked the cherry stem around his mouth—one of his favorite party tricks—then stuck out his tongue to reveal the bright red, perfectly tied knot.

Landon grinned. Steffon was right. Stupid as it might be, he *had* made sure Toby could find him if he ever changed his mind. All he had to do was heed Landon's final words.

If Toby could find his way back to the room they'd shared during those far-too-brief encounters that had rocked the very foundation of Landon's world, he'd find Landon. And if Toby ever did? Landon wasn't letting him go again.

At least, not without one hell of a fight.

Chapter Eight

Toby heaved a sigh when the pounding started at his door. Joseph never came into his room without permission. It was the one space Toby could call his own, but tonight it was doubtful Joseph would heed that rule.

"Open the fucking door, you worthless piece of shit."

Toby's stomach sank to his knees. Joseph had been angry plenty of times before, but Toby fucked up big this time. Not only had he left Landon high and dry in the middle of a prepaid overnight, he'd also no-showed the VIP scheduled for this evening. Joseph would have to refund them both and play kiss ass to avoid losing their proven repeat business.

Not that one fuckup would cause the sadistic fuck Toby stood up tonight to stop calling. The skeezy old man was a regular who refused any of Joseph's other offerings. He'd soak up Joseph's misguided fawning, accept his payment returned in full, and probably manage to weasel a free chance at Toby's ass out of the bargain. Scarcely a hardship on the client's part. Barely an inconvenience.

As for Landon? If he had an ounce of intelligence— which wasn't even a question—he'd consider himself lucky to get half his money back for the time he'd wasted trying to play at wannabe-boyfriends with the likes of someone like Toby.

Another loud knock rattled the door on its hinges. "If I have to fucking break down this door, you aren't getting a replacement."

Equal parts frustration and bone-deep exhaustion stole through Toby as he peeled himself off the bed and tugged the door open. He attempted to parry out of Joseph's warpath, but that meaty grip wrapped around his throat and mimicked the choking dread closing off his airway.

"What the fuck is wrong with you? First you come home in the middle of the goddamn night, telling me I have to fork over cab fare *and* pay back a high-dollar client in full because you fucking *walked out*, then you stand up your best meal ticket? Do you have any idea what I had to promise that man to make up for your insolence? I can promise *you*, you ain't gonna like it."

Toby's vision wavered when Joseph squeezed tighter. He clawed at the constricting vise until Joseph gave him a firm shake and threw him to the floor. The pointed toe of an expensive Italian shoe slammed into Toby's ribs as he struggled to suck oxygen into his lungs, rendering his efforts wasted. All the air he'd managed to recover was stolen again when the sharp pain jolted through his chest.

"Cover that pretty face, Tobias. You have quite a busy week ahead of you. Don't want to scare any more clients off with a damaged mug, now do you?"

Instinct took over and Toby shielded his head with his arms only moments before another well-aimed kick landed against his hipbone. He should retaliate. Or at the very least attempt to get away. But he had nowhere to go even if he could, so why try?

Toby winced at the flash of white-hot pain stealing through his body when he climbed the handful of steps leading into the smoke-filled, mildew-scented office. The little old white-haired man who had manned the front desk of the run-down motel the night before cast a pinched look Toby's way. "Can I help you, son?"

It hadn't been his brightest move to venture all the way to the outskirts of the city in the middle of the night, using the last of his meager funds to pay the Uber driver who'd deposited him outside the motel. But after his run-in with Joseph, Toby couldn't stop thinking about Landon. It made no sense, but those circling thoughts had driven him when he skipped out on his VIP client earlier that evening. How could he let another man touch him when he saw nothing but Landon every time he closed his eyes?

Still, it made no sense to traipse out here with no money and no plan beyond a hope and a prayer. Toby straightened and held a hand over his smarting ribs. What was he doing here?

But that was easy enough to answer, wasn't it? Because Landon had told him to come, and Toby was just stupid enough to believe his parting words had somehow held an impossible truth.

Come back to our room... you can always find me here.

It was ridiculous to blindly seek a man he'd walked out on the previous night. Even more ridiculous to do so knowing the consequences when he returned to Joseph's after this blatant breach of trust.

He didn't deserve Landon, but Toby needed to see him. They could never share a life, despite both wanting it, but they could have one more night. It wasn't asking too much. Just one more night to paint the perfect memory, one he'd hold close during the sleepless nights ahead.

Not that Landon would be here, in this derelict roadside motel, twiddling his thumbs and waiting on Toby to return. It was asinine to consider such a thing might be possible. And yet, he had to try. He'd never forgive himself if he didn't.

If nothing else, Landon deserved an apology and a proper goodbye. And Toby needed closure. A definitive end to the spark of longing for *more* their time together had brought to the surface, and a sturdy patch to mend the crack in his armor so he could continue down his path of the damned.

"You wouldn't be Toby, would ya?" The desk clerk narrowed his eyes when Toby snapped to attention and their gazes locked. "Yeah, yeah, you are, aren't you? I never forget a face. Got a steel trap memory, I do."

"I…" Toby didn't know what to say. How did the man know his name? Better yet, *why* did he know his name?

Old White-Hair chuckled and fumbled under the desk a moment before producing a sealed envelope and slapping it on the scratched wooden surface. "That fella you shared a room with last night left this for you. Said to make sure you got it if you ever came back this way asking after him."

Toby swallowed and licked his lips. He stepped up to the desk and took the envelope, offering a nod of thanks before turning away to open the package in private. When he ripped open the top, something slipped from within and fell with a clatter to the floor.

A key. But not just any key. It was worn at the edges and attached to a cracked red plastic key chain with the remnants of a gold inlay trapped in the corners of the recessed numbers.

The key to room 103. To *their* room. Toby's heart kicked to sudden life, beating strong and fast against his bruised ribs. He bent to retrieve the fallen treasure, angling a glance at the little old man as he did. A mostly toothless grin spread the man's wilted cheeks.

"Your friend prepaid that room for the next six months. Said he'd be back then if you hadn't shown, and put down another six. Only thing I had to do was keep it clean and give you that envelope if you ever showed." His eyes twinkled. "He gives tattooed hellions a good name, that one. Seems like a fine fella."

Toby could only blink and nod his agreement. He clutched the key like a lifeline as he peered into the envelope, praying Landon had left some way for Toby to reach out. But void of the key, it now sat empty in his palm. "Did he leave anything else? Say anything else?"

"All's I got is what's in that envelope, son."

Toby nodded again. "Thank you, sir."

"Not a problem. Have yourself a fine evening and thank your friend again, for us both, yeah? That money did this old man and his loving wife a far stretch of much needed good."

"I will." Toby offered a small smile before pushing out the door. He jogged the dozen or so yards it took to reach room 103 and jammed the key into the lock. When he threw the door open, he laughed at his own disappointment. Had he really believed Landon would be waiting for him?

No, but damn, wouldn't that be the icing on the cake?

Toby eased the door shut and chuckled when he flipped the light switch and that damn flickering bulb kicked to life. The sound caught in his throat when he saw a note propped against the fake tiki wood of the lamp's base.

He darted across the room and snatched up the envelope, then shredded it open as he fell onto the edge of the bed. His body revolted against the rough treatment, but he couldn't care less. Right then, whatever was inside that envelope held his full attention.

A folded-up piece of yellowed stationary with the motel's name stenciled across the top gave him everything he wanted and more.

Toby,

I don't know if you'll ever read this, but I'll pray every night that fate finds a way to bring you back to me. I know it doesn't make any sense—we barely know each other—but I've never felt as alive as I do in your presence. I refuse to believe it's possible to feel so connected to someone and not have them feel it too. At least a little.

I'm going to hold on to my hope that someday we might cross paths again.

XOXO, Landon

P.S. I'm leaving my cell number below. Please, call me. I don't care what time it is, night or day. I'll be waiting and wishing, no matter the hour.

Without hesitation, and without glancing at the clock as perhaps he should have, Toby dragged the phone off the nightstand and into his lap. He scooted up on the bed and leaned into the headboard, taking a moment to breathe through the lance of pain before shaking out the letter again.

The phone was of the clunky, old-fashioned variety in a puke-green color. He wrinkled his nose at a crusted orange substance near the mouthpiece but snatched up the heavy receiver anyway, tucking it between his shoulder and ear as he dialed the ten-digit number scrolled in Landon's careful script at the bottom of the page.

On the second ring, Landon's first-thing-in-the-morning drawl met Toby's ear. "'Ello?"

Toby grinned. "Hi."

Rustling created static between them, followed by a quiet thud and a distant curse not fully picked up by the phone's microphone. More fumbling followed, then an almost frantic Landon came back on the line, the sleep gone from his voice. "Toby? Is that you?"

"I'm so fucking sorry."

Landon released a shaky exhale. "Don't be, please, don't be. You didn't do anything wrong."

"Yes, I did." Toby clenched his fists, the knuckles wrapped around the receiver cracking in protest. "Then I ran away. Like a coward."

More quiet swooshing noises indicated Landon had shifted again. "You're not a coward. This is all big. Really fucking big. And scary. At least, for me it is, but I don't care. You're worth it."

Toby's chest constricted, and his throat slammed closed. "I'm in our room."

Landon sucked in a sharp breath; then a pregnant pause filled the air between them. "Don't go anywhere. I'll be there in fifteen minutes. Twelve if I don't obey traffic laws."

"How much time will it shave off if you don't bother getting dressed?"

A slew of creative curses tumbled from Landon's lips, bringing an aberrant laugh bubbling up Toby's throat.

"I'll be there in ten. Time me."

Chapter Nine

Landon slammed the kickstand down on his custom, built-for-speed street bike and cranked off the engine. He hopped free of the seat and yanked his helmet off as he bolted toward the welcoming sight of the crooked, rusted signage denoting his arrival at room 103.

He didn't bother knocking or fishing the key out of his pocket, giving the handle a vicious shove instead. When it propelled the door inward without resistance, he marched into the room. He slammed the door with an inexcusable bang, especially for the hour, and tossed his helmet to the floor.

Toby waited for him on the bed, his back against the headboard, his legs stretched out and crossed at the ankles. He wore a pair of soft gray sweatpants and a skintight black T-shirt. A grin pulled at the corners of his mouth.

"Damn, Turbo, did you teleport here?" Toby glanced at the nightstand clock and let loose a low whistle. "Nine minutes, but barely. Probably closer to eight if we're being honest."

"I even had time to get dressed." Landon's grin shifted into a cocky smirk. "Do I get bonus points for that?"

Toby's plump lower lip popped into an exaggerated pout. "You're saying I could've had you here sooner—and naked? I fail to see the benefit to your decision. No points awarded. In fact, I'm adding a five-minute penalty for coming clothed. That means it took you *fourteen* minutes. That's no longer impressive. I rescind the nickname Turbo and dub thee Slowpoke instead."

Landon broke character on a laugh, his heart too full to carry on the ruse. He needed Toby in his arms. He needed proof this wasn't a dream. "Could I earn a penalty forgiveness if I got naked now?"

Toby drummed his fingers over his still-protruding lip. "Depends."

Landon cocked a brow. "On?"

"How good a show you put on."

His single raised brow turned into two, and Landon exhaled with a chuckle. "You want to see this"—he motioned up and down his body—"do a striptease? Are you on drugs?"

Toby spread his lips into a shit-eating grin. "The answer to the first question is easy. It's less about 'want' and more about 'desperately fucking need.' I *desperately fucking need* to see your fine ass do a striptease. As for the second? Brace yourself. Corny cliché in three… two… one… No, I'm not on drugs, but the thought of getting my hands on you makes me high." He stretched his arms up, threaded his fingers together, and rested them behind his head, getting comfortable against the headboard. "So, what do you say? You gonna make a go at shedding the Slowpoke title?"

Landon never would've considered doing something like that for any of the other men he'd been with. But then, none of them had been interested enough to ask, nor had any of them looked at him with the same level of raw, naked hunger.

The guys in Landon's past—Garret included—hadn't really wanted *him* at all, which made Toby's laser-focused stare even more powerful.

"I don't know." Landon unzipped his lightweight nylon riding jacket with a slow, deliberate tug down the front of his body, allowing his fingers to graze his erect cock through his jeans. "I dressed for safety purposes. I was riding my bike at least twice the speed limit. Had I skipped clothes, I would've had to decrease my speed. I think my decision was a wise one. It got me here faster than even I'd predicted, after all."

Toby licked his lips and let his arms fall to his lap. He adjusted on the bed, the evidence of his own arousal tenting the soft cotton of his sweats. "You're right. Safety is a top priority. Taking this new information into consideration, I'll withdraw the penalty." He dipped his right hand and took ahold of his cock through the fabric of his pants, giving it a firm squeeze and a long, exaggerated tug. "I believe a reward for good behavior should replace the aforementioned punishment, although I'd like my own loss and suffering due to this change in plans to be taken into consideration moving forward."

A laugh barked up Landon's throat, paired with a tingle at the base of his spine spurred on by the combined idea of rewards for good behavior and punishments for... He cleared his throat and put the mental kibosh on that train of particularly dirty thoughts. "Duly noted."

Toby sucked his full lower lip into his mouth and moved his hand in slow, sensual strokes over his still-clothed dick. "So, about this reward... Why don't you get naked, and I'll show you what I've got in mind?"

Landon moaned, biting the tip of his tongue to prevent the sound from escaping his throat at full volume. He tugged off his jacket, keeping his eyes glued to Toby's crotch as he worked himself over, his hips rolling in tandem with the movement of his hand.

Toeing out of his boots, Landon popped the button on his jeans and tore down the zipper, yanking his briefs and pants off in one fell swoop before kicking them free of his feet. He was still pulling the T-shirt over his head when he fell into bed beside Toby, plastering their bodies together and sealing his lips over Toby's with a desperate groan.

The warmth of Toby's palms met Landon's bare flesh and roamed his body with open, greedy, reverent motions. His soft lips molded with Landon's as their tongues played chase, but when Landon rocked his hips forward with a hard thrust, Toby broke their connection on a gasp.

"Shit, you okay?" Landon's brows pulled together at the pinched look on Toby's face. "Did I hurt you? Fuck, I'm sorry—"

Toby shook his head and pressed the heel of his palm between his eyes. "You're fine. Seriously. I got a little banged up at the gym earlier. A few bruises that twinge a bit, but nothing I can't ignore now that I've got you to distract me." He waggled his brows and returned his hands to their exploration. "This ink is gorgeous, by the way. It's unfair to have a body this delicious paired with such stunning art. One person shouldn't be allowed to have so much beauty on their person. It's an imbalance in the universe that's sure to cause all kinds of paradoxes and shit. Or so I assume."

Landon snorted. "Speak for yourself, Mr. Impeccably-Ripped with those suck-out-my-soul eyes and that damn megawatt smile. You couldn't be more perfect if you tried."

Toby's wandering hands came to a stop, his head tilting to the side. He studied Landon with a furrowed brow. "I'm far from perfect."

"Yeah, well, that makes two of us, then."

With a slow nod, Toby resumed the delectable tracing over Landon's heated skin. "Perfection's boring anyway." His thumb brushed Landon's nipple, sending a shiver down his spine. Toby's lips quirked at the involuntary response. He performed the action again, grinning when a shudder rocked Landon a second time.

"I thought I was getting a reward, yet you're still fully clothed. Something's wrong with this picture."

Toby narrowed his gaze and gave Landon's hip a squeeze. "I also remember there being mention of my loss and suffering and how it should be taken into consideration. I'm processing through my denied striptease with a little much-needed groping and fondling. *Then* you get your reward."

When Toby's meandering hand finally found its way to Landon's cock and wrapped around the aching flesh, Landon dropped his head back and groaned. "Please, *please*, get naked."

Toby chuckled but released Landon's dick and obliged his request. He tugged the form-fitted T-shirt over his head, then shimmied out of his sweats and boxer briefs, tossing it all onto the floor before pressing his now gloriously naked body flush with Landon's. "That better?"

"Oh *fuck* yes." Landon wiggled his hips until their cocks grazed and they both sucked in a breath. "I need you inside me. Please. Fast. And hard. I need to feel you. *All* of you."

Toby rolled on top of Landon, crushing him beneath his solid mass. Their hands, bodies, and lips tangled and collided in a frantic rhythm that sent sparks shooting over Landon's skin and arrowing straight into his groin.

Tearing his lips free of Landon's, Toby moved to devour his neck, kissing and sucking and licking as he traveled lower. He nibbled at Landon's collarbone before soothing it with a gentle swipe of his tongue, then worked his way down to trap Landon's nipple between his teeth. At the sharp punch of pleasurable pain, Landon cried out and clawed into Toby's shoulders.

A pinch and twist met Landon's other nipple before Toby continued working his mouth farther south. The warmth of his breath trailed over Landon's abs, sending a shiver over his skin that raised goose bumps in its wake. When the soft heat of Toby's tongue skated up the seam of Landon's balls, Landon fisted his hands into the bedspread. He glanced down his own trembling body and whimpered when Toby's gaze caught his moments before that magical mouth lowered over his cock.

"Oh fuck." Landon white-knuckled the sheets, his head tipping back. "Oh Jesus fuckin' Christ."

Toby hummed as he relaxed his jaw. He lowered all the way onto Landon's dick, enveloping it in the warm cavern of his mouth. His tongue stroked the underside of Landon's shaft as he lifted his head so *sweetly* slow, swirling around the tip before sinking down and repeating the process. Over and over, gentle and caring, in a blissful rhythm unlike any Landon had experienced before.

He wasn't just trying to get Landon off or fulfilling an obligation. The attention Toby paid to the task, and the tender way his hands massaged Landon's thighs as he did, were reverential, not some arbitrary means to an end.

Landon squeezed his eyes closed and clamped down on his lip. A wellspring of unexpected emotion slammed into his gut to war with the coiling arousal Toby's skilled mouth and loving hands kept simmering beneath the surface. When it all became too much to bear, an imminent orgasm tightening at his core, Landon begged for reprieve from the exquisite torture.

Rather than obliging his mewled requests, Toby released Landon's cock, leaving him writhing and desperate for a final breath of stimulation that would send him toppling. Toby wasn't ready to give him that yet, and Landon thrilled at the idea of handing over control.

"Shh, it's okay." Toby pressed a kiss to the inside of Landon's thigh. "I'm gonna take care of you. I promise. I'm gonna make you feel so, so good."

Landon gave a jerky nod, his trust in Toby endless and complete. He focused on breathing through the torment of need until, finally, it subsided. Toby must have sensed the downshift in his desperation because he chose that moment to run the flat of his tongue up the underside of Landon's cock, pulling the tip into his mouth and applying gentle suction. The maddening sweetness of the sensation wasn't enough to tilt Landon over that edge, but it held him there, firmly in the grip of agonizing desire.

When he thought he couldn't possibly take another moment of the delightful anguish, Toby released him once more. Toby's mouth explored its way up Landon's body, eventually landing on his mouth. Their lips connected, and they drank from each other like men starved.

And maybe they were starved. Each of them, in their own way, ravenous for a genuine connection. For a bond that could only be built on trust. For passion. Real, bright, blistering passion like the kind pumping through every vein and sparking through every nerve of Landon's oversensitized flesh.

"Shit. I didn't bring anything." Toby's voice broke on a growl as he leveraged himself over Landon's body. "Any chance you pack protection in your wallet?"

Landon shook his head as he gasped for air, then jerked his chin to the side. "Nightstand drawer. You left it last night."

Toby's face split into a grin before he planted a smacking kiss on Landon's parted lips. "Good lookin' out." He leaned over, slid the drawer open, snatched his prizes, and angled onto his knees between Landon's splayed legs. He readied his flushed cock with a condom and lube, then pressed two coated fingers to Landon's opening. "Fast and hard, you say?"

Landon groaned and thrust his hips forward, attempting to spear himself on Toby's teasing digits. "Lube me up and put it in. I don't need prep."

Toby bowed forward and drew Landon's cock into his mouth again, sucking gently as he ran his tongue in circles over the sweet spot beneath the head. In the swirling chaos of his pleasure-hazed mind, Landon was so lost to the heated desire pounding through his veins he didn't even notice Toby had inserted his fingers until they brushed his prostate with delicate finesse.

Frenzied need crawled into Landon's gut, and he nearly begged for Toby to stop, afraid he'd come before he got what he wanted. But Toby popped his mouth free in time, leaving Landon clinging to the precipice of release yet again.

After positioning himself, Toby breached Landon's slickened opening. The stretching sensation consumed him as Toby's thick girth worked its way inside, but when he thrust his hips, the burn died away to an aching, needy sensation that had Landon craving more, not less. "Fuck me. Hard. Please. *Now.*"

Seemingly satisfied that Landon had adjusted to the invasion, Toby scooped his arms behind Landon's knees for leverage and did exactly as Landon asked.

He fucked him.

Hard.

Chapter Ten

Toby tied off the condom and tossed it into the bathroom trash. He twisted the tap to get the warm water flowing but splashed the cool liquid over his flushed face before it had a chance to heat up. He snatched a towel off the back of the toilet and patted dry before shifting his gaze to the floor-to-ceiling mirror attached to the wall beside the sink.

He cringed at the black-and-blue blooming over his torso and hips, then thanked his lucky stars the lighting in the bedroom was shitty.

Not so shitty, however, that he hadn't thoroughly enjoyed unraveling Landon at the proverbial seams. Having that exquisite man all to himself, free to touch and taste and tease to his heart's content, had been better than anything Toby could've ever imagined.

Landon had opened to Toby fully and completely, allowing himself to feel every stroke of Toby's tongue and every trace of his hands over that smooth, overheated skin. His reactions had been sinful—honest and sincere, vast and unchecked, poignant and intense.

Like a fighter who'd taken one too many hits to the head but didn't know when to stay down, Toby's cock twitched ineffectually as he closed his eyes and played back the moment Landon finally found his release.

So focused on making Landon feel good, Toby hadn't worked himself to that edge yet. But as soon as Landon had thrown back his head, locked those strong runner's legs around Toby's waist, and cried out in devastated glory, Toby followed him down that splendid path to completion. It had been, beyond a doubt, the most intense orgasm of his life.

And they'd barely begun. It lasted only long enough to locate Landon's sweet spot, not nearly long enough to sink into a rhythm. But even in its brevity, it had been perfect. Mind-bendingly, excruciatingly perfect.

With a sigh, he tossed the towel over his shoulder and soaked a couple of washcloths in the warm tap water. He used one to make a quick pass over his groin to remove what remained of the lube, then tossed it into the corner and strode to the bedroom.

Landon hadn't moved a muscle. He sprawled across the bed in a boneless heap, his chest rising and falling in slow, exaggerated motions as he tried to regulate his breathing.

"Mind if I clean up the mess I made?"

Landon turned his head and blinked at Toby with a dazed, dreamy smile pulling at his swollen lips. "This is my mess. Yours was contained. Mine's in my damn beard. No fuckin' clue how that happened, but there ya go. You fucked me so well I jizzed in my own face."

Toby couldn't stop the laughter that rippled up his chest. "I'll do a full wipe down. No spots left unchecked. You've got my word."

Landon grinned, a spark of life cutting through the sleepy, smoky gray of his eyes. He spread his limbs to allow Toby easy access. "I'll be sure to hold you to that."

Returning Landon's grin with one of his own, Toby set to work. Once satisfied he'd checked every possible location for stray sticky substances—enjoying the discovery of several unexpected ticklish spots along the way—Toby threw the towel and washcloth onto the floor. He gave the bedspread a yank, sending Landon's lax limbs flying. Landon barked out a laugh but rolled over and shimmied under the covers when Toby held them up.

Settling on his back, Toby welcomed Landon's warmth against his side, pulling him close enough to tangle their legs. He brushed a kiss over his brow and traced lazy fingers over the intricate designs gracing Landon's leanly defined shoulder.

Landon's own hand wandered, skating over Toby's chest to rest over the worst of the bruising visible above the line of covers. "What the hell happened at the gym that caused this, anyway?"

Toby stifled a sigh and forced out a lie. "Boxing." He offered a thin smile when Landon glanced up and quirked a brow in question. "You should see the other guy. Brutal stuff, man. I'm talking blood and guts in the ring." He mock shuddered for effect, then grinned.

Landon traced his knuckles over Toby's cheek. "At least you seem to have a handle on blocking. It doesn't look like your face caught any blows."

Heat crept up Toby's throat. What would Landon think if he knew the truth? Would he still look at him with those adoring, smiling eyes if he knew Toby had sustained his injuries while huddled on the floor like a spineless child?

A yawn stretched Landon's jaw, causing his beard to tickle the sensitive skin of Toby's inner arm. Toby huffed out a laugh and jerked away, cursing when his ribs raged at the injustice of the quick movement.

Landon lifted off Toby and stared down at him with a pinched brow. "Do you make a habit of getting the ever-loving shit beat out of you like this? It doesn't really do a body good. There are better, safer, less damaging forms of exercise, you know."

Toby shrugged and stared over Landon's shoulder. "Gotta toss things up."

Another yawn tugged at Landon's lips, and he fought to stifle it. He blinked against the effort and rubbed at his eyes with the knuckles of his thumbs.

"Why don't we get some sleep? I know I woke you when I called."

Landon tilted his head. "Why did you? Call, that is. I mean, come. I mean, not *come*, I didn't..." He sighed and pinched the bridge of his nose, pink tinging his cheeks. "Let's try that again. What made you change your mind? Not that I'm complaining—*at all*—but just... wondering."

Toby threaded his fingers through Landon's thick black hair, massaging them into his scalp. How could he be honest without giving away his secret? Even more important, how could he say what needed said without hurting them both? "Nothing's changed, Landon. Not where it matters. Not really."

Visible hurt tweaked Landon's brow. "So this was a one-time thing? Like, what, a goodbye or something?"

A mixture of longing and regret slithered through Toby's gut, turning his stomach sour. If it were up to him, he'd never leave this bed again. He'd wrap his arms around Landon, pull him close, and never let go.

But it wasn't up to him.

He released an exhale and dropped his hand from Landon's hair. "I had to see you again. I couldn't leave things the way they were. I had to apologize for what I did, how I acted, the way I bolted."

Plus, he'd fuckin' needed *this*. He'd needed one more shot at that connection, that *real* connection he hadn't felt in far too many years. It was weak of him, and exceedingly selfish, but he'd needed one more night with Landon in his arms. One more night to forget the life he hated but couldn't escape.

Landon shifted so their bodies no longer touched. The distance was minimal, but in that moment, it was an endless chasm Toby might never be able to bridge.

"No need to apologize." Landon flattened his lips into a thin smile. "I understand."

"No, you don't. It's not what you think." Toby sucked in a shaky breath and rolled his head away. He'd give Landon as much of the truth as he could offer. He deserved that much. "I meant what I said that I'm not free to be with you. If it were my choice, I would. Please believe me, I would."

The heat of Landon's body returned to Toby's side and a warm palm cupped his cheek, guiding his face to meet Landon's smoky gaze.

"Are you dating someone?" Landon's forehead creased. "Married?"

Toby shook his head. "No, it's not like that."

"Then how *is* it? If you aren't with someone else, why can't you be with me? I also meant it when I said I'd take whatever you could give. I won't be needy. I-I mean, I guess I *am* being needy right now, but I won't be if you agree to see me again. I'll be happy with any time you can find to spend with me. Anything is better than goodbye. Anything is better than *nothing*."

Toby's heart clenched beneath his bruised ribs, drawing a pain deeper and more visceral than any physical wound. In another place, at another time, this man could've stolen his heart. And Toby would've gladly let him have it. "Landon, I'm a prostitute—"

"No, that isn't a valid excuse. I told you I don't care about that." Landon's palm pressed more firmly against Toby's cheek. "I accept you for who you are."

Why was Landon so infuriatingly kind, compassionate, and understanding? How could he look at a whore like Toby and see anything other than the countless other men he'd been with? Why would he want Toby for anything beyond that same purpose?

"I work every day of the week." It was a lame excuse, but it was all Toby had.

"You told me 'overnights' weren't common. So that means I could have you during the night, right? When you aren't working? And my job is super flexible. I can be available at any hour of the day you have free. Part of the charm of being the boss." He ran his thumb over Toby's cheekbone. "And I'm not suggesting these times as hookups and nothing else. It's obvious I'm attracted to you, and you've given me two of the most mind-blowing orgasms of my life, but I want more than sex. I want *you*. All of you. Heart, body, and soul. The total Toby package."

Why didn't Landon care about the myriad of strangers he serviced every day of the week? Was Landon seriously still trying to be his *boyfriend*, even with that thought fresh in his mind?

How was he supposed to respond to that?

Toby closed his eyes for the briefest of moments, then locked his gaze on Landon's waiting stare. "I have a contract. It doesn't expire for three more years."

"So... when your contract's up, you could quit? That's not that long. We can make it work for a few years. No problem."

Except there was no way in hell Joseph would let them see each other unless Landon forked over an hourly rate for every minute they were together. And that sure as fuck wasn't happening.

The only way Toby had managed a getaway that night was because Joseph forgot to set the alarm. Or maybe he never armed it anymore and Toby was too conditioned to test that boundary.

Either way, after tonight? There was no doubt it would be armed. Joseph wasn't one to let his sellable goods roam the night, free of charge.

Toby ran his tongue over the back of his teeth and snaked his arm around Landon's torso, keeping him close. "Until my contract's up, my time isn't my own. I'm only here tonight because my handler doesn't know I am. If he did, you'd be footing the bill."

Landon's chin shrunk back, and his nose wrinkled. "Someone can't *own* your time. When you're off the clock, you're off the clock."

A mirthless laugh escaped Toby's lips. "I'm never off the clock. I haven't been for over five years now, and I won't be again until my eight-year contract is up."

Landon shook his head. "I don't understand. There's no way that's legally binding."

Toby tried to ignore the twinge crawling under his skin like a thousand ants marching to the tune of humiliation and regret. "It's not the kind of contract that needs a judge, jury, or courtroom to uphold."

Landon froze, his face draining of color as the truth of Toby's words sank in. "Are you in some kind of trouble?"

Toby offered a weak smile. "As long as I abide by my contract, I'm not."

"Fuck. That." Landon shoved away, his eyes flashing like darkened clouds during a summer storm and filled with simmering bolts of electricity waiting to slice through the raging tempest around him. "If you're doing this against your will, it stops now."

Just because he didn't want any of this now didn't mean he hadn't agreed. Once. In a different lifetime. Before he'd understood what it really meant to be a whore.

He'd signed the contract with a free hand, although there hadn't been any other choice. Not really. And no one held him down. No one physically forced him to offer his body to the endless supply of johns he serviced. At least not since the beginning. He shuddered and shoved those thoughts into the black hole where they belonged, then pressed the heel of his palm to his temple, wincing when the movement triggered his damaged ribs.

Landon's face darkened even further. "Did that really happen in the boxing ring?"

Cold fingers of dread snaked down Toby's spine, settling into his gut with a nauseating chill that flashed over his skin. He angled a glance at Landon, whose gaze rested on the ever-darkening discolorations bleeding over Toby's torso. Maybe if he told Landon the truth about their origin, he'd realize Toby wasn't worth his efforts and walk away. "No."

The muscles in Landon's jaw jumped, but he showed no other visible response. "Did your handler do it to you? Or one of your clients?"

Toby sighed. It was time to face the music. "My handler."

Landon nodded. "Okay." He sat up and threw off the covers, scooted to the edge of the bed, stood, and walked to the bathroom. He slammed the door closed, and a moment later, the now familiar bang followed the sound of water running.

Toby waited in silence, his breath coming in short, quick gasps that had him light-headed and dizzy. When the water finally turned off and the bathroom door opened, he sat upright. Anxiety clawed at his throat.

Landon leaned against the doorframe, crossed his tattooed arms over his beautifully inked chest, and angled a pained stare Toby's direction. "I wanna know everything. Don't keep anything back. We'll figure this out. Together, we'll figure this out."

Chapter Eleven

The look on Toby's face said it all. Pain, remorse, humiliation... The emotions washed over his gorgeous features in torrid waves that had Landon's gut clenching. He wanted nothing more than to crawl into bed and pull him into his arms. He wanted to hold Toby close and take on every ounce of heartbreak as his own.

And what stopped him from doing it? Who said he couldn't offer Toby comfort and support?

Landon shoved away from the doorframe with a silent curse. They might not know each other well, but in the short time he *had* known Toby, his feelings and their connection had grown at an alarming rate. Hell, he'd almost— *almost*—landed a bomb on Toby when his innocent flirting struck a chord at the very heart of Landon's desires.

His yearning to be dominated was something he'd only admitted to once before. In his blind desperation to believe in the beauty of the narrative Garret had woven into their farce of a relationship, Landon had confessed his deepest, darkest secret. The ultimate result was catastrophic, but for a brief period, he'd found his happy place.

Offering total and complete submission required a level of trust he'd never truly had with Garret. But after that first night with Toby, a tentative seed was planted. One lonely month, two staggering orgasms, and three blissful nights in Toby's company, and the seed had sprouted into something undeniable. Something tenfold more genuine than anything he'd ever felt with Garret. Something Landon wasn't ready to give up, and something he would protect to the bitter end.

Toby sat stiff against the headboard, his eyes glassy and glued to the floor. Landon closed the distance between them and slipped beneath the covers, drawing Toby down with him as he stretched out against the pillows. Toby buried his face into Landon's neck but otherwise remained distant and still.

"I can't imagine it's easy to talk about this, but I can't help if I don't know how." Landon rested his cheek on Toby's soft sandy-brown locks. "I'm not going to judge you. Not for what led up to signing the contract, and not for what's happened since you did. Talk to me. Let me help you."

Toby shifted into a more comfortable position, draping one of his firm, muscular legs over Landon's lower body and snaking an arm around his waist. The blankets moved with him, dipping to reveal the top curve of his delicious ass, along with those sexy dimples above it. Landon trailed his fingertips over Toby's damaged ribs to trace the twin indents on his back. Toby shivered at the touch but offered a hum of appreciation.

After a few minutes, Toby spoke. "I did it for my sister."

Landon's brows drew together. He'd signed a prostitution contract for his sister? How? *Why?*

Toby exhaled, his warm breath fanning over Landon's chest. "Khloe's two years younger than me. She's strong-headed, rebellious, and was always looking for trouble, even when we were kids. She dropped out of high school not long after I graduated and disappeared for a few years. She'd pop up every now and then, so we knew she was alive and *mostly* well, but it was painfully obvious she'd fallen into a dangerous lifestyle."

Landon continued his gentle stroking over the small of Toby's back but otherwise remained silent and immobile. He wanted Toby's story to flow at its own pace, without interruption.

"I was a senior at Arizona State when she showed up at my apartment one night. She was frantic. She'd gotten mixed up in some really fucked-up shit, with some really fucked-up people." Toby sucked in a hissing breath. "I didn't know what to do. I didn't know how to help her. Life back then was all about the next party, about finding the next black-out drunk. I put myself through school working as a barback, then eventually a bartender, but that meant I drank on the job too. I worked at a gay bar and got bigger tips if I let guys buy me shots. Management turned a blind eye as long as the booze I drank was paid for and the customers were happy. Even when I was underage."

Nibbling on the inside of his lip, Landon pictured Toby as a bartender at one of his own college-aged drinking holes. He hadn't gone to college, but he'd partied with his buddies who'd stayed local at the University of Chicago.

It was easier to dredge up a mental image of Toby as a grinning, scantily-clad bartender with glitter stuck to his sweaty, sculpted abs than to focus on the words that had a solid fist of dread squeezing his throat closed. *She'd gotten mixed up in some really fucked-up shit, with some really fucked-up people.* He could connect the dots that hadn't been drawn. Whoever those fucked-up people were, they had something to do with the contract Toby was under now.

"Anyway, I was a cocky bastard who thought I could help her set things straight with the assholes she was indebted to without getting outside help. She didn't want our folks involved, and she was convinced bringing the police into the mix would make things worse, not better." Toby's breath hitched on a shaky sigh. "I was so fuckin' stupid."

Landon pressed his lips to the crown of Toby's head.

"Whatever happened, you did it for your sister. You did it for a good reason."

Toby gave Landon's ribs a gentle squeeze. "Khloe took me to see her dealer. She'd started running drugs for him over the border to pay for her habit, and one of those runs had gone awry. Two of the girls she was with got snatched by the border patrol, another ran off and never came back, and Khloe freaked out and ditched the supply before bolting herself."

Landon's heart kicked against his chest. He could guess where this was going, and he didn't like it.

"Khloe isn't always the brightest bulb. She didn't run away and keep going like the one girl. She returned to her dealer, empty-handed, thinking a blubbering apology would fix things." Toby shook his head against Landon's throat. "They'd been doing more than packing balloons. The car the girls drove was stashed to the brim with high-grade heroin. The asshole decided to lay the blame—and the sizeable loss—square on her shoulders."

Landon's stomach pitched, and he squeezed his eyes closed. He forced himself to take several long, slow steadying breaths.

Toby let out his own deep exhale. "I honestly don't know how it happened." His shoulders trembled, so Landon snatched the edge of the blankets and covered them both. "She told me her story, begged for my help. She kept telling me they'd listen to me, that she was a dumb junkie, but they'd listen to me. I was on a bender that had lasted almost four years straight and woefully convinced of my own invincibility. So I believed her."

When Toby stopped talking for a long stretch, Landon planted another kiss on his brow. "Did she know what they wanted from you?"

Toby shook his head. "I think she genuinely believed, in her drug-addled brain, I'd be able to swoop in and talk her out of the mess. Just like I had countless times during our childhood when her impulsive mule-headedness got her into trouble."

Jesus. Landon's heart quickened and his stomach lurched, a clammy sweat clinging to his brow as he waited for the anvil to drop.

"They offered me a chance to save my baby sister. To wipe her slate clean. All I had to do was agree to work for them. For eight years. Eight years of my life to free her of her debt and keep her safe."

Toby swallowed and huffed out a puff of air. "I agreed. I had no clue what I was really agreeing to when I did, but I agreed. I was young and dumb and had this... Shit. I had this idea in my head it might be fun. I pictured having all this hot, crazy sex with all these hot, crazy boys. As a horny twenty-one-year-old, that didn't sound half bad, you know? And they sold it that way too. Like it would be some sort of exotic sexual adventure."

Fuck. Landon carded his fingers through Toby's soft hair and sent a frigid mental blast to freeze the tidal wave of emotions swelling in his heart before they could over-take his senses. He could unpack his feelings later. When he was alone. When Toby wasn't relying on him to keep his shit together. Clearing his throat to fight the knot of tension compromising his air supply, Landon whispered hoarsely, "How'd you end up in Chicago?"

A mirthless laugh escaped Toby's lips. "My contract was sold about three years ago, and I got moved up here."

Landon's stomach plummeted to his knees. How the fuck was this shit real? "What are the... terms? Of the con-tract?"

Toby shrugged. "I live under my handler's roof. I'm only allowed out of the house with his permission, and that's only for jobs. Like I said, he doesn't know I'm here or you'd be paying for the privilege." He coughed out a chuck-le. "Anyway, I used to be heavily monitored when I left the house, but Joseph trusts me now. Or, he did. He won't anymore, not once he realizes I gave him the slip tonight."

Landon clung helplessly to Toby as the ice around his heart cracked under the pressure, threatening to shatter with the slightest provocation. "You aren't seriously thinking of going back there, are you?"

"I have to. I have three years left."

Shoring up his defenses, Landon scoffed and shook his head. "Fuck that. You can come stay with me. Hell, we can move somewhere far the fuck away from here where they can't find you. No way in hell are you going back there. Never again. No way."

Toby sighed and pushed out of Landon's arms. "It's not that easy. They know where Khloe is. They know where my parents are. I haven't had direct contact with my family since that night, but Joseph shows me pictures." He ran a hand through his hair, giving it a shake to even out the disheveled strands. "Khloe's got a kid now. She got back on track. Or as back on track as Khloe will ever get. But she's safe. Her kid's safe. My folks are safe. If I fuck up, they'll go after her. They'll go after *them*. No fucking way am I gonna let that happen."

Shit. Landon clenched his jaw. That fuckin' complicated things, but did it change the fact that there was no way in hell Landon was going to let Toby go back to that asshole's house? Not one bit. They'd figure something out that would free Toby *and* keep his family safe.

They had to. There was no other option.

Toby threw off the covers and climbed out of bed. When he bent to collect his clothes, Landon shot upright. "What are you doing?"

"I should try to catch the early train and be back at a decent hour. I'm already in enough trouble as it is. If I miss a job because I'm out of the house without permission, it'll make shit worse." Toby slipped into his boxer briefs, then tugged the sweats over his narrow hips. He cast a glance over his shoulder at Landon, who sat in frozen horror.

"Don't. Please. I know it's fucked up, but it's my life. For now. There's nothing I can do about it."

Landon's heart ached for Toby. To be trapped in such an existence… "Yes, there is. Let me help you."

"You can't help me. No one can. I have to bide my time. Three more years isn't that long. Then I'll be free to pick up my life where it left off." Toby pulled on his T-shirt and turned to face Landon. "Maybe I'll look you up. If you're still single—which I highly doubt—and still willing to overlook everything I am, everything I've done, then…" He shrugged and offered a tired smile. "Maybe."

Landon scooted out of bed and tugged his jeans on commando before stalking over to Toby and wrapping him in a gentle embrace, careful not to put too much pressure on his wounded torso. "I'm not giving up that easy. This isn't over."

"Landon—"

"No." Landon squeezed a little harder, trying to convey the magnitude of every emotion he couldn't put into words with that simple physical connection. "I'm going to let you go today because I don't fucking know what else to do, and I don't want to make things worse for you. But *this isn't over*. I'm going to fix this. You can bet your ass on that."

Toby weaved his arms around Landon's middle and pressed him closer. "You can't fix this, but it means more than you'll ever know that you want to. Thank you." He sealed their lips in a soft, innocent kiss that sent an arrow of longing straight through Landon's frozen core. "I need you to promise you'll forget about me, okay? Nothing you could do would help; it would only put you and my family at risk. I can't have that. I'm fine. I promise. There's a light at the end of the tunnel, and when I reach it, I'll be more than fine. I'll be free. I won't take that for granted ever again."

Landon blew out a shaky breath when Toby stepped out of his arms. This all felt too real. Too final. But how could he argue when Toby's family was at risk? Toby would never put their lives in danger, and Landon didn't blame him for that resolve.

But that wouldn't stop Landon from finding an answer that removed risk to their safety from the equation. Landon didn't give a shit about his own.

He gathered up the rest of his clothes, yanked on his shirt, and stuffed his boxers into the back pocket of his jeans. "Can I at least drive you home? No sense in taking a train when I've got a perfectly good bike outside."

Toby cocked his head, and that megawatt smile lit up the room. "I've never ridden on a motorcycle before."

"No?" Landon tried to return the grin, but it fell flat. "Well, I'm the perfect guy to introduce you to 'em. I build custom bikes for a living, after all."

If it were possible, that grin spread wider. Like Toby hadn't admitted only moments before to being trapped inside a literal nightmare. "You make motorcycles? Like, from scratch?"

Landon nodded and scooped up his jacket from the floor, then shoved his arms inside as he met Toby's sparkling gaze. If Toby wanted to change the subject and pretend he hadn't dropped an atomic bomb in the room, Landon would play along. For now. "I opened a shop after I retired from ball. It had always been my dream to own one. I worked as a body tech in high school and through my farm team days. That was supposed to be the premise of that damn reality show before my relationship with Garret took center stage and the whole thing derailed."

Toby shoved his hands into the front pockets of his jeans and rocked on his heels. "It'd probably be best if I took the train. I wouldn't want anyone to see us together and risk screwing with your show or reputation."

Landon curled his lip. "Fuck that noise. Nothing about being seen with you would screw up my reputation, and I couldn't care less about that damn show. The finale is next week; then it's over and done. There will be no season two, I can promise you that. Please, let me drive you. I'm not ready to say goodbye."

The air-conditioning kicked on, and the loud click preceding the droning hum made Toby jump, which jarred his battered body. He winced and placed a hand over the largest area of bruising, now hidden beneath his T-shirt. "Okay, I guess if you really don't mind, I'd appreciate it. I may have missed the first train already, anyway."

"I really, really don't mind."

Toby returned Landon's half-hearted smile, then dipped his head to avoid Landon's gaze as he strode past him toward the door. When his hand landed on the handle, Landon's heart squeezed. How many times was he going to watch this man he cared so much for walk out the door, unsure of when or if he'd ever come back? "Toby?"

He turned at the sound of his name, his brows drawn into a frown.

Closing the distance between them in three large strides, Landon crushed his lips over Toby's. He returned Landon's desperate kiss, spearing his hands into Landon's hair to hold him in place so he could plunder his mouth.

When they finally came up for air, Landon pressed his forehead to Toby's and cradled his jaw with both hands. "I'm not going anywhere. You can't get rid of me that easily, do you hear me?"

To Landon's surprise, Toby gripped Landon's wrists with trembling, clammy palms. When he spoke, his voice was barely a whisper. "Promise?"

The tears won out, and Landon didn't bother holding them back as he pulled Toby into a crushing hug. "I promise, baby. I promise."

Chapter Twelve

Toby rubbed his thumb over the indented numbers on the hard-plastic key chain for the hundred-thousandth time since Landon had pressed it into his palm that morning. As he did, Landon had stolen one last kiss—a tender, soft caress Toby could still feel like a whispered promise over his lips if he closed his eyes—and murmured into Toby's ear, "No matter what, our room is always there if you need an escape."

Our room.

Who would've thought a sketchy, run-down motel off I-55 on the outskirts of Chicago would become a shining beacon of safety, happiness, and hope?

Not that Toby could ever take Landon up on that offer. The very idea was beyond laughable at this point. Joseph had not only made sure to set the alarm when Toby returned, he'd also latched the deadbolt on his bedroom door—the one on the *outside*—and reminded Toby how happy and healthy his family had remained over the past five years while he'd followed the rules. And how quickly that could change.

Toby sighed and rolled onto his stomach, staring into the darkness of his room. He folded his hands under his cheek and cupped the key between them. He didn't know what time it was but didn't care enough to check his watch. His bedroom and attached bath were located on the interior of the house and were windowless by design. When he'd first arrived at Joseph's—and now again, thanks to his breakout last night—the space served more as a prison cell than a comfort zone.

Over time he'd proven his fear of Joseph complete enough to warrant a sense of trustworthiness, and the external deadbolt had been left unlatched. An internal one had even been added, allowing him a space where he had at least the illusion of privacy and control.

But all that was gone now, taken away as surely as the internal deadbolt had been, and replaced by the reinstatement of the external one and the promise of a "very busy schedule" to make up for the money he'd lost and the irritation he'd caused.

The deadbolt slid open with a bang, and Toby sat up, his heart slamming against his still-aching ribs. He shoved the key under his mattress and threw an arm over his eyes to shield against the bright midday sun slanting into the pitch-blackness as Joseph stalked into the room.

"It's your day of reckoning, whore. Time for your ass to answer for your defiance." Joseph wheeled a black garment bag behind him and propped it against the wall. "Get yourself cleaned up and presentable, then pack some clothes. Enough for a week."

Toby let his arm drop and blinked incredulously up at Joseph. "A week?"

"I promised a busy schedule, didn't I?" Joseph flashed a cruel grin. "Can't get much busier than full-time live-in service, now can you?"

"Sir, I—"

"Think long and hard before you let another word slip past those cock-sucking lips. Do you really want to make this any worse for yourself than it already is?"

Despite Joseph's admonition, Toby had to work to swallow the futile plea for reprieve that threatened to spill from his lips. How could he possibly be expected to spend that much time under the thumb of a client?

His stomach cinched into a knot of molten dread. Only one man would pay the kind of money necessary to garner an entire week of Toby's services—the VIP regular Howard Mayson, who happened to be sitting on an ace.

After all, he was the one Toby no-showed on Friday. Joseph had made him obscene promises to compensate for Toby's "insolence," and considering Mayson's tastes, those promises—with a week of continual control over Toby's body—could turn ugly. And fast.

Toby clutched the handle of the wheeled suitcase until his knuckles blanched beneath the strain. A tremble rocked through his body as he stood at the designated pick-up location on the corner of Clark Street and Lincoln Avenue. On such a clear, sunny Saturday afternoon, the Lincoln Park Farmers Market was in full swing across the street.

The cheerful brightness served as a sharp contrast to the demons stirring in Toby's mind.

Not only was he to spend an entire week under the rule of one of his worst nightmares, but Joseph had informed him on his way out the door that the typical security measures would be suspended during that time. There would be no reporting of his whereabouts, which meant no impending rescue were he to need it.

"Hey there, handsome, need a ride?"

Toby froze. A prickle spread over his skin when he turned infinitely slowly to find a glossy-black ground-hugging sports car idling at the curb. But it wasn't the sexy sleekness of the car that had his heart hammering at his pulse points—it was its owner.

Behind the wheel, wearing a crisp white dress shirt with two buttons popped at the collar, the sleeves rolled to the elbows to display gorgeously inked arms, sat Landon. A grin stretched his lips from ear to ear. He leaned across the console and tugged the handle on the passenger door until it swung outward in greeting.

"I said you weren't going to get rid of me that easily, didn't I?"

Toby darted his gaze around the busy intersection, searching for some telltale sign that this could be believed. He sought Joseph's hulking form, or the corpulent bulk of Howard Mayson's aging frame. But no familiar faces roamed the crowd, and on the street before him, Landon had exited his vehicle. He skirted around its hood and stopped in front of him, cradling Toby's clenched jaw in his gentle hands.

"Hey. Look at me." Landon ran both thumbs in soft, soothing strokes over Toby's freshly shaven cheeks. "I know it's only a week, but that'll give us time to figure something else out. For now, at least, you're safe."

Toby pinched his brow and shook his head. "I don't understand... *You* bought me? For the whole week?"

Landon sighed and dropped his hands, shoving them into the front pockets of the charcoal dress slacks sinfully hugging his narrow hips. "I didn't buy *you*, Toby. I... I bought *us* time. That's all. Time to figure this out. I don't... I mean, it isn't like that. If you don't want to come back to my place with me, I totally understand. I'll gladly get you a hotel. Whatever you want, whatever you need. Just ask."

A car horn blared, and Toby startled, his dazed eyes drifting out to the road. Landon cursed under his breath. "I'm illegally parked. I should really move my car. Ah... I can call you a cab if you'd prefer—"

"No." Toby drew in an unsteady breath and gripped the handle of his suitcase even tighter. "I want to come with you."

A timid but stunning smile lifted Landon's cheeks. "Yeah? Oh, um, yeah... Ah, let me pop the trunk." He hurried to the rear of the car and raised the lid, then waited patiently as Toby's sluggish brain churned to awareness and he followed with stilted movements.

He settled his bag into the tiny trunk space, then collected himself enough to climb into the passenger side and close the door behind him. When Landon slid into the driver's seat a moment later, Toby had even succeeded in buckling himself in.

Landon shifted into Drive and eased into traffic before slanting a glance Toby's way. "So, ah, I thought we could get you settled at my place and then, I dunno, grab some lunch or something? Have you eaten already?"

Toby's stomach chose that moment to growl. He groaned and slapped a palm over his noisy—and decidedly empty—belly. When *was* the last time he'd eaten? As part of his punishment when he'd returned home that morning, Joseph hadn't given him breakfast. He'd missed dinner the night before because that was supposed to be part of his evening with Mayson, which he'd skipped out on. And Joseph had already been upset with Toby after he'd bailed on Landon in the middle of the night, so while he'd given him his protein shake after his morning workout the previous day, there hadn't been any lunch offered.

Another rumble vibrated through Toby's palm to fill the silence. "I could definitely eat."

"Okay, I live close. That's my building right there." Landon pointed through the windshield to a tall modern structure with angular architecture and an excessive amount of glass and chrome. "We can drop off your bag and head right back out."

Within a minute, Landon stopped at a gate leading to an underground parking garage, then wound his way down a few levels and parked in a reserved spot near what appeared to be a private elevator. He turned to Toby and offered a shy smile. "Ready?"

Toby nodded, his brain processors still numb but his unease and disbelief fading. Maybe this was actually happening. Maybe he really was going to spend a week, not hurting under the cruel hands of Howard Mayson, but in the presence of the one man who'd somehow breached the protective barricade he'd built around his heart.

In its own way, that was almost scarier than anything Toby had imagined happening in the quiet solitude of Mayson's suburban fortress. Toby had relied on that frozen barrier to keep the real Toby—the weak, terrified, broken Toby—from coming to any more harm. If he let those walls crumble, could he build them up again?

And if he couldn't? If he couldn't hide his true self beneath a mask of cocky confidence and false consent? How in the hell would he ever find the strength to give his body over to so many men he didn't want?

He'd surely break. And if he did, what would happen then? He only lived the cushy existence he led now because he played by Joseph's rules. Or, he *had* played by Joseph's rules. Right up until Landon entered his life and ripped down his walls.

Landon hopped out of the car and retrieved Toby's bag before he had a chance to unbuckle his belt. By the time Toby joined Landon in the elevator—which was definitely private, as Landon had to type in a code before it would move—Toby's heart raced beneath his tender ribs.

A week with Landon. The very idea should send sparks of excitement over Toby's flesh, but instead a weighted stone of dread plunged into the very pit of his food-starved belly. He dragged his feet as he trailed after Landon into a private foyer directly off the elevator. Landon typed in another code on a keypad beside the only door, and when it clicked open, Toby followed him into a large, sweeping, handsomely decorated living space.

It was all whites and creams and dark, dark cherry-wood. A pillow here, a vase there, or a slash of bold color in an otherwise muted or gray-cast work of art provided a few smatterings of accent hues. It was classy yet welcoming.

"Let's leave your bag here." Landon leaned Toby's suitcase against a cherrywood banister attached to a half-curved staircase leading to the upper level. He stepped around the stairs and into the kitchen, where he snatched an envelope off the island. When he returned to Toby, he proffered the thick packet with an outstretched hand. "This is for you. It's, ah, the security codes for the elevator and front door, plus a keycard for the main lobby, gym, and pool area. There's also some cash, and one of those prepaid debit cards. Oh, and the spare key to my car. I'll take one of my bikes if I go anywhere, so it'll be at your disposal whenever you—"

"Landon." Toby held up a hand, his head spinning in a million directions. He pinched the bridge of his nose and squeezed his eyes shut. "Jesus, dude."

"I-I'm sorry. I wasn't trying to overwhelm you. I... I wanted you to have freedom while you were here. I didn't, you know, want you to feel like you had to... like you had to wait around for me or anything. If you wanted to do something. Or needed something. Or... or whatever." Landon huffed out a frazzled breath, and Toby opened his eyes, his heart squeezing at the flush of embarrassment coloring Landon's cheeks. "I don't want you to feel obligated to me in any way. This week can be whatever you want it to be. I don't have to be involved... I mean, it's never too late to get a hotel if you'd prefer—"

"Landon, stop." Toby blew out a heavy exhale. "Just... stop."

Dipping his chin, Landon nodded and repeated on a hoarse whisper, "I'm sorry."

Toby tested the weight of the envelope in his hand before tossing it in the general direction of his suitcase. The muted thud as it hit the hardwood floor had Landon wincing away, and Toby gritted his teeth. He stalked across the short distance separating them before placing both hands on either side of Landon's face, forcing his head up, then

101

crushing their mouths together in a vicious display of desperate need mixed with agonizing regret.

How could anything about the time he spent with Landon—and the time he had to look forward to with him over the next week—be anything other than a gift? Fuck his walls. Fuck his life with Joseph. Fuck the clients who would come later. He'd deal with the repercussions when they came. For now, he'd enjoy every fucking minute he had with this beautiful, wonderful angel of a man.

Something warm and wet spilled over the back of Toby's left hand and he pulled away, horrified to see tears streaming down Landon's flushed cheeks. "Fuck, I'm so sorry. I'm not handling this situation well. At all. The last thing I meant to do was hurt you." Toby tugged Landon into his arms, cradling his head against his shoulder. "This—all of this—is so much more than I could've ever expected. I'm having a hard time processing it all because... Well, Joseph didn't tell me who'd bought me. I didn't know it was you. I... I'd prepared myself for something else entirely."

Landon wrapped his arms around Toby's waist, squeezing until Toby's cracked ribs could take no more and a whimper drew past his lips. Almost immediately, Landon's arms fell, and he stepped away from Toby with a horror-stricken gasp. "Oh my god, I'm so sorry... Jesus, I'm so sorry."

Toby shook his head and once again invaded Landon's space. "Don't apologize. I want you to hold me. I want your hands on my body." He snaked his arms around Landon's middle and yanked him close, pressing their foreheads together. "I need to feel you, to touch you, to taste you, because I need to believe this is real. Right now, it feels like a fantasy. Make me believe, Landon. Please, make me believe."

Chapter Thirteen

A wave of indescribable emotions crashed over Landon. He clung to Toby—careful this time not to crush his bruised torso—and buried his face into the crook of his neck, allowing the soft cotton of Toby's white T-shirt to dry the tears still clinging to his lashes. A warm, solid hand rubbed his back, and soft, soothing words tumbled into his ear.

Landon cursed himself. He should be the one comforting Toby, not the other way around. He angled his face away to wipe the last remnants of his meltdown on the rolled-up sleeve of his collared shirt. "I'm so sorry."

"Shh." Toby kept Landon close with a firm hand at his lower back, but the other continued the slow, steady strokes that brought far more solace than Landon deserved. "You apologize too much. I'm the one who made you cry. I'm the one who should be groveling for *your* forgiveness."

Landon snuffled in a wobbly breath. "You didn't make me cry. I did. I mean, I... I want to fix this, and I don't know how. I feel so helpless. I want... I want you to be happy. And safe. And free. But I don't know how to make that happen, and I'm so afraid... I mean, I don't want you to feel like I... like I'm trying to *use* you. Because I'm not, I swear I'm not. I hate that I had to *buy* this time. I hate what it means, how it makes you feel. Because I don't—"

"Landon." Toby offered a half smile that warmed his eyes far more than it raised his lips. "I know. I promise you, I do. I know your intentions aren't to use me, but I need some time to wrap my head around this whole thing. This is a very different situation than I thought I was walking into. I'm just... shocked." He chuckled and combed his fingers through Landon's hair, brushing the loose strands from his eyes. "In a good way, but still shocked."

Make me believe. Toby's breathy plea rang in Landon's ears, and a new resolve settled over him, one that had him biting his lower lip to stop the wicked little grin pulling at the corners of his mouth. If Toby needed proof this was real, Landon would be more than happy to oblige.

"I know you said you were ready to eat, but do you think you could hang tough for a little while longer?"

Toby beamed a big, bright Toby-grin for the first time that day, and something tight and twisted inside Landon's chest loosened and unfurled.

"As long as you aren't asking me to 'hang tough' by myself." Toby winked. "If I have you to distract me, I could last all week."

"Good." Landon gave a toothy smile. "And you're not too hungry and weak to stay on your feet if, say, you got... very, very distracted?"

Toby arched a brow, his lips pursing to hide the smile clearly tugging at his lips. He marched in place several times, as if to prove his stability. "Yep, I think I'd be okay."

Satisfied, Landon nodded and made to pull away. When Toby's iron grip closed around Landon's torso to keep him from moving, a flood of warmth coursed through his system. "Don't worry, I'm not going anywhere. But I do need a little, ah, wiggle room."

Toby relaxed his arms, then sucked in a sharp breath when his hands slid off Landon's hips as Landon sank to his knees. "What are you—"

"Focus on staying upright, big guy. I've got everything else under control."

Toby stiffened. "Landon, you can't—"

"Shh. Yes, I can." Landon gripped Toby's thighs and glanced up until their eyes met, Toby's a raging tempest of desire warring with uncertainty and a tinge of fear. For Landon, no doubt. "You're tested regularly, right?"

Toby released a strangled note of assent when Landon slipped his hands up to cup his ass.

"And you always use condoms? Take PrEP?"

Narrowing his gaze, Toby nodded. "Yes."

Satisfied, Landon nuzzled into one of Toby's slackened palms, placing gentle kisses over its soft warmth. "And you *want* me to touch you, right? You're not stopping me because you're uncomfortable, are you? Because that's the only reason I'm stopping. If it's because *you* don't want it, not because you're worried about me when there's no reason to be. I was tested, you were tested, we've both been tested. We're as safe as any two guys with a sexual history can be."

Which was true. Part of the package in booking his original night with Toby included proving he was clean, and a hefty sum of the money he'd paid went toward guaranteeing the same about Toby.

Something he refused to focus on in that moment. There was plenty of time to agonize over their next steps when he wasn't about to blow Toby's mind... among other things.

Huffing out a strained breath, Toby twisted his features into a mix between a grimace and a smirk. "There's no question whether I want this or not. I do. Trust me, I do."

When Landon hummed in agreement and shifted his openmouthed kisses from Toby's palm to his jeans-clad thigh, Toby gasped anew. His cock stirred enticingly beneath his zipper. Landon grinned, working his way over Toby's clenched quads until his lips met the thickening proof of his desire trapped under the stiff designer fabric. He ran his tongue over the unyielding bulge, and Toby groaned.

Encouraged by his response, Landon undid the buckle on Toby's belt. Those intense hazel eyes locked on Landon's like a laser beam, Toby's chest heaving as he licked his lips and swallowed. His Adam's apple bobbed with the movement. "You don't have to do *this*. This isn't what I meant—"

"I know." Landon let the two ends of the belt fall free, his fingers seeking the button on Toby's jeans. "I'm doing something I've desperately wanted to do for a month now." He moved to the zipper, gripping the little metal tab between trembling digits. "You wouldn't deny me something I want"—*zip*—"so"—*zip*—"desperately, would you?"

Toby whimpered, his knees giving out for the briefest of moments before he locked them into place. His hands fell to Landon's shoulders and latched on for support. "Jesus fuck, you're gonna be the death of me."

An uncharacteristically cocky grin stretched Landon's mouth, and his hesitation all but fell away. With far steadier hands, he eased Toby's jeans a few inches down his hips, then slipped his boxer briefs to meet them. As soon as he pulled the constricting fabric away, Toby's cock sprang free, and it was Landon's turn to moan and go weak at the knees.

Thankfully, he was already on them, so there was no fear of falling.

When Landon trailed the flat of his tongue up the seam of Toby's balls and continued up the underside of his shaft, Toby growled and sank his fingers deeper into Landon's shoulders. The second Landon closed his lips over the tip of Toby's dick and traced his tongue in a slow circle around the sensitive head, that growl turned into a groan, and Landon's cock responded by throbbing against the fly of his slacks.

Landon flicked his gaze up and caught Toby's head falling back as that delicious rumble continued to spill from his lips. Toby's lustful, unrestrained response amped

Landon's confidence, and he sucked Toby's cock as far down his throat as it would go. He massaged with his tongue as he drew the length in and out of his mouth, using his hand to cover the surface area that wouldn't fit inside. With his other hand, he kneaded Toby's balls, tugging gently with every downward pass of his mouth.

Eventually, Toby's panting plea broke through the lust-fueled haze of Landon's mind. "Lan-*don*... Y'gotta s-stop." When Landon merely picked up the pace, using his tongue to circle the tip of Toby's dick as he hollowed out his cheeks and worked his hands as purposefully as possible, Toby huffed out a breathless whine. "I'm gonna come... You... You gotta... s-stop... Oh fuck... *Landon*..."

Toby's hands clutched at Landon's shoulders like twin vises as he let loose a feral roar and a flood of warmth hit the back of Landon's throat. Landon hummed with delight as Toby's cock kicked into his mouth, emptying its bittersweet fluid onto his tongue. He greedily swallowed every drop, lapping away any residue before allowing Toby's spent dick to fall from his lips.

When Landon sought Toby's gaze once more, his stomach lurched. Toby stared down at him with wide, unblinking eyes.

Landon pushed to his feet and drew Toby into his arms, pressing their foreheads close. "Hey, what's wrong? You okay?" *Fuck*, had he stepped over a boundary he shouldn't have crossed? Had Toby asked him to stop not because he didn't want to come in Landon's mouth, but because Landon had hurt him somehow? Or worse, had he changed his mind and Landon wound up forcing him into something he didn't want? "Oh god, Toby... I'm sorry. Fuck, I'm so sorry. Did I... I mean, are you... are you okay? Tell me what to do. How can...? What can...? Oh god, I'm so sorry."

An unexpected chuckle filled the air, and Toby shook his forehead against Landon's. "How many times do I have to tell you, you apologize too much?"

Landon furrowed his brow. "I'm sorry, I—"

This time, Toby barked out a deep belly laugh before pulling Landon in for a mind-bending kiss, their tongues mingling with sweet perfection within the cavern of Landon's mouth. When Toby drew away, he peppered Landon's lips and the tip of his nose with kisses before offering a wide, brilliant grin. "I can't believe you gave me the hottest, most insanely fantastic blowjob I've ever had and then tried to *apologize.*"

Landon's brows popped, and his eyes widened to fill the space. "But... but you were looking at me like... I mean, I was afraid I'd..." Heat flooded his cheeks, and he lowered his eyes. "You asked me to stop and I didn't."

"Oh, Landon." Toby moved his hands to cup Landon's jaw. "I was trying to warn you, that's all. I sure as fuck didn't *want* you to stop, but I also didn't want to blow without giving you the chance to run for cover." He huffed out a chuckle. "Incidentally, can I say, literally the best blowjob of. My. Life. Jesus, dude, your mouth is fuckin' magic... and your hands. *Have mercy.*"

Landon's flush intensified, the heat seeping under his skin to crawl up his neck and spread like wildfire over his face. He lifted the corner of his mouth into an awkward half grin. "I, ah, I mean... It wasn't exactly a hardship. I've been wanting to do that since the first time I laid eyes on... Ah, well." Landon cleared his throat, then groaned when more laughter shook Toby's chest.

"You are so fucking adorable." Toby shimmied his pants up his hips. "I swear to god, I can't even with how adorable you are."

Landon rolled his eyes. There was that damn word again. *Adorable.* What grown-ass man—in his midthirties, no less—wanted to be deemed *adorable* by a delectably sexy twentysomething? He blew out a dejected sigh. "Yeah, well... Anyway. What sounds good for lunch?"

The warmth of Toby's palm closed over Landon's still-hard cock, offering an enticing squeeze before stroking slowly up and down its length through the thin fabric of Landon's dress slacks. Landon gulped and clamped both hands on Toby's forearm.

"I can think of something I'd like to get my mouth on." Toby growled into Landon's ear as he continued the languid caress. "Why don't we move this party to the couch? I want to take my time with you. I want to taste every—"

"No," Landon squeaked, shaking his head as he stepped out of Toby's reach. "That was for you. J-just for you."

Toby pinched one eye closed and raised the opposite brow. "No way, dude. I don't do one-sided." He paused a beat, and his eyes darkened. "At least not that direction."

"I may have paid to have you with me this week, but I'm not a client." Landon squared his shoulders, resolve firming his voice. "I care about you. There aren't rules like that for people you care about. There aren't obligations, expectations, or requirements. It's okay if things are a little one-sided sometimes in personal relationships. I wanted to do that for you, and I don't want anything in return. Other than your happiness… and maybe the gift of your company for lunch."

Toby rubbed at his neck, a tinge of pink staining his cheeks. "Jesus, are you trying to break me?"

"Break you?" Landon drew his brows together. "No, of course not, I—"

Toby surged forward and once again sealed his lips over Landon's. But he didn't dip in for a taste, he simply pressed their mouths together and sighed when Landon melted into him. He traced his tongue over Landon's lips, then kissed the corner of his mouth before pulling away.

"I care about you too." Toby nuzzled Landon's nose with his own. "Thank you. Thank you for giving us this time together. Thank you for going above and beyond to make me feel wanted and needed and special. Thank you for taking care of me, in every way possible. But most of all, thank you for being you. I don't know how I got so lucky to find you in my life right now, but I promise you, I'm gonna cherish every fuckin' minute we have together."

Landon blinked to clear his vision when the tears he'd only just staved off threatened to return. "I told you already, I'm not going anywhere. I'm all about cherishing our time together, but it isn't limited. I don't know how I'm going to fix this, but I am. This is going to be your new reality... *Our* new reality. I promise, on all things good in this world, I promise."

Toby's mouth flattened into a thin smile. "Let's not worry about that right now. I'd like at least one day to *live* without Joseph and all the rest of that bullshit stealing the spotlight. Let's talk lunch instead. Because I was hungry before, but now that you nearly sucked the ever-lovin' life outta me, I'm positively ravenous."

Landon donned one of his preferred fedoras in charcoal gray and a pair of opaque aviator sunglasses before tugging Toby down the street to his favorite casual eatery. It had a spacious, private outdoor patio and served quality Chicago-style deep dish pizza, an array of traditional pub foods, and had at least a hundred craft beers on tap.

Once settled into a cozy, cushioned cabana-style eating area—a flight of beers and an all-the-way pizza en route—Landon drew a knee up onto the bench so he could face Toby. He carded his fingers through those soft, windswept locks and they shared a serene smile. "After lunch, what do you want to do? I know you aren't from Chicago... Have you had the chance to do any of the touristy stuff since you, ah, moved up this way?"

"No, I've pretty much only seen the inside of Joseph's

house and the gamut of upscale hotels the city has to offer. Well, those, and one shithole motel off I-55." He threaded his fingers with Landon's. "So far, that's been my favorite."

Ducking his head, Landon ran his tongue over his lower lip. "I'm sorry for dragging you to such a crappy place. It had nothing to do with disrespect; I just—"

"It's okay, seriously, zero worries." Toby winked. "You were trying to maintain your anonymity. Which, by the way, looks supersexy on you." He flicked the brim of Landon's fedora and waggled his brows.

The server showed up then with their beers, and before they'd had a chance to taste all eight, their pizza arrived as well. Toby dove into the greasy pile of deliciousness like a man truly starved, devouring over half the pie—a considerable feat, indeed—before Landon managed to finish his first slice.

They talked about everything and nothing as they ate and sipped at their beers, laughter bubbling between them one moment, serious whispers drawing their heads close the next. By the time Landon paid the bill and they all but waddled their way out to Lincoln Avenue, they decided to take a much-needed walk through the Lincoln Park Zoo to aid in the digestion process.

Landon had never openly dated a man before. Sure, he'd been with Garret during the filming of that blasted reality show, but they'd kept their dating life within the confines of his condo, his business, and a select few establishments that guaranteed discretion and security.

But heedless of the sidelong glances that sent a shiver of conditioned humiliation and ingrained irritation down Landon's spine, Toby intertwined their fingers and held Landon's hand the entire time. He even stole a few kisses and playfully smacked Landon's ass once or twice. It was refreshing to be with a man he could be himself with who didn't fear the inevitable repercussions their public affections triggered.

Although not everyone responded negatively. In fact, to Landon's great surprise, it was a distinct minority who even spared them a passing glance. But those who did held little back.

Still, despite the sprinkling of hatred, Toby's grin never faltered. He ignored those blind to the harmless joy he and Landon shared on their Saturday afternoon walk in the park, and was sure to smile in return whenever a kind stranger offered that effortless human gift.

This—everything this was between him and Toby— kept getting better and better. Being with the man he cared for in a very public way, and not being afraid or ashamed to show how he felt, proved to be a delightful and liberating experience.

When Landon spotted a familiar opening in the trees, he darted his gaze up and grinned at his building in the distance. "So..." Toby turned and cocked his head in question. "This is going to sound insane, but I can see the park from my condo. After our first night together? I was sitting there moping and noticed a group of people in this very spot. In my melodramatic mindset, I wondered what it would feel like to be in some normal everyday situation that would find me standing down here instead of hiding up there."

Toby used their joined hands to pull Landon into a hug, wrapping his strong arms around Landon's waist and brushing one of those uncomplicated kisses over Landon's lips. "So, how's it feel?"

"Perfect." Landon grinned. "Absolutely fuckin' perfect."

Chapter Fourteen

❝ Holy. Fucking. Beefcake.❞

Toby's head snapped up as a drawn-out wolf whistle followed those words. At the foot of the gleaming curved staircase stood a sprite of a man. He had platinum blond hair shaved close at the sides and styled into a pompadour at least three inches tall. Each ear had multiple piercings, including a barbell through the outer shell of his right, and a tiny silver hoop adorned his bottom lip. An impish grin spread foundation-flawless cheeks, and expertly applied guy-liner accentuated sparkling emerald eyes. The unnaturally intense green was far too vivid to be anything other than colored contacts.

But it was his outfit that brought a grin to Toby's lips. He wore a slim-fit black velvet blazer with white silk trim over a skintight shirt covered in a kaleidoscope of sequins. Dark-washed skinny jeans hugged his legs and disappeared into a pair of pristine Converse high-top Chuck Taylors. To top it all off, a feather boa in all the polychromatic colors of the rainbow draped roguishly around his neck.

The walking, talking stereotype planted a fist on his hip and pursed his lips, arching a perfectly sculpted brow as his gaze trailed the length of Toby's body. Then his free hand lifted into the air, the boa threaded through his fingers, and he flicked his wrist. "Twirl, hot stuff. I wanna see the whole package."

Chuckling, Toby spread his arms and obliged, modeling the bespoke charcoal-gray Italian suit he'd paired with a deep purple button-down, sans tie. He brushed an invisible piece of lint from the lapel of his jacket when he'd completed the turn. "Do I measure up?"

The man—who Toby assumed was Landon's friend Steffon—stalked forward and punched Toby square in the arm. Hard. "I totally fuckin' approve. Like, damn, could I get a carbon copy to warm my sheets? I'd never leave my bed. But hey, day jobs are overrated, and Lan would totally pay me simply to exist 'cause he loves me like that." He flashed a minxy grin. "Plus, he'd get it. He knows I'm a thirsty bitch, and he has the original. How aren't y'all a permanent mess of sweat and flailing limbs and lustful moans? Like, does. Not. Compute."

Molten heat flooded Toby's cheeks, and he ducked his head to hide a grin. Before he could work out a response, Landon's disembodied voice floated into the room. "Steffon James, you wouldn't be making my guest uncomfortable out there, would you?"

Toby cast a sidelong glance down the hall leading to Landon's bedroom. The same bedroom they'd ensconced themselves within for a good chunk of the afternoon and early evening, being exactly what Steffon had described—a mess of sweat and flailing limbs and endless lustful moans.

Despite the incredible blowjob Landon had gifted Toby prior to their lunch date, Toby had been more than ready to go for round two... and eventually, three.

Then again, was that such a surprise? Not only did Landon drive Toby crazy with need, he'd also managed something no one else had ever done, even during those quick and dirty hookups prior to his present career.

Landon had wrapped those gorgeous lips around Toby's cock and demanded nothing in return but his pleasure and happiness. He'd put Toby's needs first. Repeatedly.

As those pleasant memories washed over him, Toby's lips quirked, then tugged into a full-on grin when Landon appeared out of the shadows and damn near stole his breath away.

After their joint shower, they'd gone to separate rooms to dress for their evening plans. They'd decided it would be for the best, as they excelled at stripping clothes off each other but doubted they'd be productive in reverse.

Toby's libido was off the hook around Landon. He'd never been so perma-turned-on in his life, even when he was a virile, hormone-riddled adolescent. Then again, he hadn't had a specimen of manly perfection all to himself at the time. That made quite the difference.

Landon returned Toby's wide grin. "Did Mr. James introduce himself, or did he jump right into verbal molestation?" He smoothed a hand down the black satin vest he wore over a freshly pressed white dress shirt. "I apologize; he isn't housebroken yet. I've been trying for over twelve years, but he's a tough cookie to crack."

Steffon wrinkled his nose, stuck out his tongue, and flipped Landon the bird in one smooth, practiced motion that had Toby laughing and Landon rolling his eyes.

"See what I mean? Utterly hopeless." Landon shot a wink Steffon's direction.

"Yeah, yeah, whatever. You love me." Steffon plastered on a sassy grin, then turned his attention to Toby. "So, about those social niceties I so *carelessly* overlooked. Allow me to introduce myself. Steffon James, diva extraordinaire. You can call me Steff, Steffi, or Steffon, just don't call me late to the orgy." To punctuate his statement, he tossed one end of the boa over his shoulder with a theatrical flourish. "Now, let's hear a full name from you, stud."

"Tobias Carmichael, at your service." Toby bowed at the waist. "But my friends—and those who value their lives—call me Toby."

Steffon lifted a hand to his brow and mimicked a

melodramatic Victorian-era faint. "I dare say, Landon old boy, I'm going to need you to fetch my chaise lounge. If your man gets any hotter, I'll be on my ass in two-point-five seconds flat. Best to be prepared."

Landon ignored Steffon, his intent gaze locked on Toby's instead. "Tobias Carmichael, eh?"

Toby narrowed his eyes and fended off a grin. "You might not value your life, but I do. Say it again and you might not like what happens next."

Landon popped his brows, a devilish smirk pulling at the vise grip his teeth had on that plump lower lip. A delicious wordless promise passed between them, sparking through the air like an electric current.

"Okay, ladies, let's focus on the goings-on *outside* the bedsheets, shall we?" Steffon clapped his hands and heaved an exasperated sigh. "You know, I agreed to stay outta Dodge for the week, even though I *live here*, but methinks I made a grave mistake. You're delectable eye candy, Mr. Carmichael. If Lan leaves you bored and alone at any point—which, seriously, he'd be the biggest dumb fuck ever if he did, but that's a whole other ball o' wax—feel free to ring my digits. I'll keep you entertained in return for the occasional blatant ogle."

Toby drew back his chin and chuckled, reluctantly diverting his attention from Landon's heated stare. "I'll keep that rather forward and somewhat offensive offer at the forefront of my mind, I assure you."

Steffon lifted both thumbs in the air and flashed a toothy grin. "Score."

"Jesus, Steff." Landon smacked a palm against his forehead. "Have some couth, man. Just, like, an ounce. Please."

Steffon clicked his tongue. "Where's the fun in that? Come on, kids, the night life is calling and Lan's AmEx is begging for a workout." When Landon only shook his head in response, Steffon blew him a kiss. "Come on, babe, think of the travel points I earn you."

"Yeah, I could fly to China and back again on one night out with you." Landon threaded his fingers with Toby's and stole a deep, delectable kiss. "Come on, let's get this party started."

"You okay, baby?" Landon's question—paired with the term of endearment that twisted Toby's insides into warm, vibrating knots every time he used it—drew Toby's attention from the fawning server who batted her lashes as she set down another round of drinks.

Toby smiled and nodded as convincingly as possible, rubbing his damp palms over the expensive fabric of his suit pants. The truth of it was, despite being three heavily poured drinks into the night and feeling decidedly buzzed— okay, who was he kidding, *drunk*—the nerves had yet to disappear.

When they'd first arrived at the swanky velvet-roped club and Landon led them to the front of the line and through the door with no more than a nod, a horde of screaming fans recognized him and pandemonium ensued. Bright, blinding flashes had cut through the night, and desperate, grappling hands had torn at their clothing, seeking souvenirs to prove they'd been close to *the* Landon Jenks and the posse sharing his Saturday night.

In the process, the suit Joseph had had custom-tailored for Toby ripped at the collar. The bouncers had gotten the crowd subdued and backed off within seconds, but the damage their frenzied pawing had caused clung to Toby as surely as the ringing in his ears following the frantic, blood-curdling shrieks.

Joseph was going to kill him.

But it wasn't only that. Landon had offered a dejected apology and warned some of the pictures would likely get sold and wind up on the internet by morning. That was a lot of *oh-shit* to unpack. For starters, what if someone local recognized Toby and word got out Landon had a prostitute on his arm? It could ruin him.

Furthermore, what if someone from Toby's past recognized him? What if his family saw his photo and got the wrong idea? What if they thought he'd run away to live the highlife in Chicago? Or worse, what if they saw headlines labeling him as the whore he was?

He hadn't decided what to tell his parents when his contract was up, but he didn't want them to know he'd spent his missing years as a human pincushion for endless dicks in the greater Phoenix and Chicago areas.

"Toby?" Landon brushed his knuckles over the stubble on Toby's cheek. "Do you want to go home?"

Toby forced himself to return Landon's concerned frown with a bright "everything is right in the world" grin. "Hell no. Sorry, I'm buzzing pretty hard. I should probably slow down a bit, that's all."

Landon narrowed his gaze, but he gave Toby's knee a supportive squeeze. "Why don't you go splash some cool water on your face? You might feel better."

"Yeah, that's a great idea." Toby popped to his feet, thankful for the distraction. When Landon stood to follow, he held up both hands and shook his head. "No, no, you stay here. Drunky over there needs someone to keep an eye on him. I'll only be a minute." He tilted his chin toward Steffon, who was busy grinding on some rando he'd dragged into their VIP area.

Landon's face pinched, but he nodded his agreement and sank onto the white leather couch with a visible sigh.

There was a VIP bathroom on the top level, but a group of sloppy-drunk party boys occupied the entryway. They reminded Toby so much of his own wasted years of freedom that he breezed past the door and headed for the stairs leading to the main club.

His eyes darted around the near darkness, waiting for the flashes of revolving variegated light to provide him direction in the sea of writhing, sweaty bodies. As he finally spied a sign pointing toward the bathrooms—on the complete opposite side of the club—a hand clamped on to his shoulder with unnecessary force. He turned to shout a protest over the thumping, pulsing beats of the club mix, but his insides turned to ice and rooted him to the spot long before the first word could fall from his lips.

Hot, sticky breath fanned over Toby's neck as Howard Mayson leaned his portly frame into Toby's space. "I suggest you follow me, nice and quiet, unless you want another scene like that one at the entrance earlier."

Toby swallowed over the dry knot at the back of his throat. Mayson took hold of his bicep and tugged him into the blackness beneath the steps. Only a smattering of the club's inadequate lighting breached the darkness of the tiny alcove, the pounding music slightly muted by the architecture surrounding them.

"What are you doing here, Mr. Mayson?" Toby cursed his nerves and gritted his teeth in an attempt at strengthening his crumbling defenses.

Mayson ran a hand through his thinning gray hair and shot a death glare from beneath his bushy salt-and-pepper brows. "First, you have the fucking nerve to stand me up last night. Then I get promised all these goodies to make up for my pain and suffering. But before I can collect, that aging twink Jenks up and buys you out from under me. Well, fuck that, Tobias, *fuck that.*"

Toby clenched his jaw, his hands balling into fists. The alcohol surging through his veins had his emotions swinging from one extreme to the next. The initial jolt of fear melted away, replaced by a scorching rage unlike any Toby could remember experiencing before. "No, fuck *you,* Mayson. I'm not your fucking *toy.* You don't *own me.*"

"No?" Mayson chuckled, the colored lights bouncing off his sweat-drenched brow. "I had a nice little chat with Joseph after discovering you wouldn't be available *for the whole week.*" He pushed closer, his rotund belly pressing into Toby's bruised hip. "Apparently, you're more than an overnight rental."

Toby's emotional pendulum swung to the opposite extreme again and terror lanced through him like a knife, slicing through his flesh, leaving him gutted and trembling.

"That's right, Tobias. I'm going to get my own week of full-time service." Mayson clutched a clammy palm over Toby's nape. "Imagine all the things we can get up to without a set end time to limit our fun."

An involuntary shudder rocked Toby's already trembling frame, and Mayson guffawed, squeezing his neck with renewed vigor. "Handy you chose one of my clubs to patronize this evening, isn't it? I was thrilled to get the security notification when one of our biggest hometown celebrities showed up with none other than *my* personal whore at his side."

Toby's muzzy brain struggled to keep up, but still he fell behind. This hardly seemed the type of place Howard Mayson would frequent.

But of course. Mayson was a big-fish financier. He owned and operated countless establishments in and around the Chicago area. This was likely one of his many investment holdings.

"No worries, my boy. Unlike your owner, who allows his merchandise to run amuck and breach contract with dutifully paying buyers, I'm a businessperson who respects a business deal. I've accepted the terms of your current obligation, but it *is* a pleasure to have the chance to make you aware of what awaits you on the other side. I want you to spend the rest of your time with that pretty-boy twink thinking about me." Mayson's thin lips tugged into an oily grin. "Enjoy your week, because when it's over? You're *mine*, Tobias. All mine."

With that, Mayson slipped away, leaving Toby alone in the darkness, his booze-soaked brain fighting the truth of his new reality.

He didn't know how long it took before he collected himself enough to stumble back to Landon, but based on the panicked flurry that met his arrival, he'd been gone a while. Toby ignored Landon's worried, rapid-fire questions and beelined for the fresh drink he'd left on the table. The ice had melted, and it sat in a sweaty ring on the black bar napkin, but he knocked the whole drink back in one long swallow.

Coughing away the sharp bite clawing its way into his stomach, Toby turned and finally focused his doubling vision on Landon's strained expression. He opened his mouth to toss out a flippant request for another round of drinks, but a dry sob slipped past his lips instead, and he crumpled into Landon's waiting arms.

He only had a few more days of relative freedom left, and then his worst nightmare would come true. His instincts begged for a restructuring of his defenses, but the warmth of Landon's embrace spoke a different tune. Fuck trying to rebuild the walls Landon had crumbled with every gentle touch, tender kiss, and sweet utterance. They wouldn't be enough to save Toby where he was headed anyway.

Chapter Fifteen

Landon set a tray filled with everything he could think of to combat a hangover on the floor beside his bed and cocked a hip on the very edge of the mattress. When it dipped beneath his weight, Toby groaned and threw an arm over his eyes.

It was still quasi early, and Toby deserved to sleep as long as he needed, especially after the night he'd had. But Landon wanted to get some fluids and aspirin into him in hopes they might combat the worst of his symptoms when he awoke later.

There was no telling what had set Toby off the night before, as he'd refused to discuss it, but his emotional turmoil had been palpable. Landon's heart still ached from the powerless pangs of anguish that assailed him as Toby spiraled further and further into the shielding abyss of drunkenness.

"Toby?" He placed a hand on Toby's bare shoulder, wincing at the angry bruises blooming over the visible skin of his torso. "You don't have to get up, baby, but can you try and drink something? Maybe take a couple aspirin?"

Toby grunted but made no move to sit up.

Landon glanced at the tray on the floor, assessing the various fluids he'd brought with him. He didn't know what Toby preferred, let alone what his undoubtedly queasy stomach could handle.

After a silent cab ride home—with Toby pressed into the door, withdrawn into his own little world—he'd bounced back with false exuberance, insisting they have "just one more drink."

That one more had turned into nearly half a bottle for Toby before he eventually passed out facedown and fully clothed on the living room couch.

Landon had opted for water rather than more liquor, which meant he'd mostly sobered by the time Toby's frantic energy finally fizzled. He'd managed to stir Toby enough to get him on his feet—albeit leaning heavily on Landon's shoulders and stumbling—then led him to the master bathroom. He'd stripped Toby to his boxer briefs, helped him empty his bladder, then held a cold washcloth against his neck and rubbed his back when he proceeded to vomit up what Landon could only hope was enough of the excessive alcohol he'd consumed to prevent the poisoning Landon feared.

After a few moments of contemplation, Landon decided on a lemon-and-lime-flavored sports drink. "Baby?" Landon carded a hand through Toby's delightfully spiked-up bedhead. "Can you try a few sips for me?"

Toby whimpered but dropped his arm and cracked a single hazel eye, squinting into the relative darkness of the room. Landon had pulled the curtains tight and had both the bathroom and bedroom doors shut to prevent any excess light from entering the space.

"Hi," Toby croaked, then moaned and closed his eye again. "Am I dead?"

Landon chuckled and twisted the cap off the plastic bottle. "No, I wouldn't let that happen." He fished a pill bottle off the tray. "Do you have a headache?"

A sliver of golden-green reappeared and shifted to meet Landon's gaze. "Uh-huh."

"I have aspirin and a sports drink loaded with electrolytes that'll do a dehydrated body good. Think you can prop up a bit and take a few swigs?"

Toby exhaled on a shaky sigh but pried open his other eye. He creased his brow with a slow blink. "Fuck."

"What's wrong?" Landon's stomach dropped, and he trailed a knuckle down Toby's stubbled cheek. "Feeling sick again? I left a trash can by the bed." He scooped the ridiculous marble monstrosity off the floor—a purchase his decorator, also known as Mr. Impractical himself, Steffon James, had insisted on—and held it out to Toby.

Toby groaned. "*Again*... As in, I've already been 'sick' at least once before?" He huffed out an irritated breath but met Landon's concerned stare. "How big of an ass did I make of myself last night?"

Sensing Toby's issue was less nausea-related and more focused on undue guilt and regret, Landon set the trash can down. "You didn't make an ass of yourself. Not at all."

Toby scoffed out a sardonic laugh and levered onto an elbow. He cringed and placed an absent hand over his ribs. "I don't remember much beyond pounding that first drink when we got back here, but based on the symphony of jackhammers inside my skull and the verification that the sour roadkill taste in my mouth is more than an exceptionally bad case of morning breath... Yeah. It's pretty much guaranteed I made an ass of myself."

"We played video games." Landon grinned and held out the aspirin, relief loosening his shoulders when Toby took them into his palm. "And danced." He offered the sports drink, which Toby also accepted. "It was a total blast. I haven't had a night like that since my early twenties."

To Landon's delight, Toby chugged over half the bottle before setting it on the nightstand and easing onto his back again. "Yeah, but somewhere in there, throwing up was involved. And considering I don't remember undressing myself or tucking all nice and cozy into this big ol' bed, I'm guessing you had to deal with me."

Landon rolled his eyes and crawled carefully over Toby, slinking under the covers beside him, close enough to share Toby's pillow. He pulled Toby into his arms, and Toby came willingly, resting his head on Landon's bare chest and throwing a leg over Landon's thighs. He snuggled in until their bodies fit together like custom-cut puzzle pieces.

Brushing a gentle kiss over Toby's brow, Landon breathed out a sigh of utter contentment. "Nothing about taking care of you is even remotely an inconvenience. In fact, I kinda love it. Feel free to be needy whenever you want... I apparently get off on it."

Toby grunted and poked a lazy finger into Landon's gut. "Shut up. You do not."

"Do too." In truth, the submissive in him positively relished caring for Toby. Landon grinned at the ceiling and planted another kiss on Toby's mussed sandy-brown locks. "Now, how's about we sleep a little longer? I have big plans for the rest of the day. You're going to need your energy."

A telling pause indicated Toby's hungover body revolted against the idea of "big plans," but he valiantly replied, "Sounds fun."

Chuckling, Landon gave Toby's shoulders a squeeze. "I'm kidding. It's Sunday. I fully intend to do nothing but loaf around in front of the TV, eat greasy food, and take lots of naps."

While a Sunday laze hadn't been the original plan for the day, Toby deserved a day of rest, especially after whatever happened the night before to send him reeling. He'd asked Landon for some time to *live* before he had to face the reality of his situation again, and Landon fully intended to give him that. As much of it as he could.

But that didn't mean Landon would kick back beside him and forget his promise. He'd already started the ball rolling when he first woke up that morning, before putting Toby's anti-hangover tray together. Although he still didn't have a clue as to how he could safely free Toby, he'd contacted an elite private investigation firm—one used to working with high-profile clients who required an extra layer of discretion and assured anonymity. Being the son of a politician with a healthy case of paranoia and a conservative constituent base who balked at the slightest hint of scandal meant Landon had access to all the best dirt-digging services.

He just hoped Joseph Coulier and his *associates* had secrets to bare. Or at the very least, left enough of a trail when they'd trafficked Toby—and who knew how many others—into modern-day sexual slavery. With the right ammunition, Toby's freedom and his family's safety might be leveraged in exchange for Landon's silence.

But until he heard from the PI, or a better idea came to mind, his hands were tied. All he could do in the meantime was offer Toby as much uncomplicated enjoyment as he could and make sure everything, no matter how small, was completely under Toby's control.

Including Landon. If he wanted that.

Toby moaned and nuzzled further into Landon's side. "Fuck. Now *that* sounds fantastic."

When they resurfaced from their midmorning slumber, Landon drew them a bath while Toby brushed his teeth and watched with an incredulous stare. Foamy toothpaste dripped over his chin when he spoke around his toothbrush. "Are those bubbles?"

Landon sealed the jar containing his supply of lavender-scented bubble-bath bombs—yet another indulgence Steffon thrust upon him that he'd rather grown to enjoy. "Yep, those are bubbles. I don't mess around when it comes to bath time. Steff would never allow it."

Landon stepped behind Toby as he bent to rinse out his mouth, placing his hands at Toby's hips. To Landon's surprise and delight, Toby pressed into him and wiggled his butt.

"I've never taken a bubble bath before." Toby placed his toothbrush on the counter, then straightened and turned to face Landon, pulling him in for a minty-fresh kiss. "You're gonna spoil me."

"That's kind of the point." Landon smiled and swept Toby's bangs off his forehead. "Go on, hop in. I'll join you in a sec. Just gotta grab something."

Landon flicked on the infrared heater on the ceiling so they wouldn't freeze their asses off when they climbed out of the tub and dimmed the lights before heading to the kitchen. He made quick work of preparing a pitcher of his patented hair-of-the-dog Bloody Mary—with enough alcohol to calm the raging beast, but not enough to spur on another bender—and snagged the basket of cheddar-garlic rolls he'd baked fresh that morning while Toby slept in his bed. He hoped the combo would give Toby's stomach something to churn that wouldn't cause a revolt. Then after their bath, they could figure out what wholly delicious and sinfully greasy meal would finish the job.

When Landon returned to the bathroom, tray balanced in his hands, Toby was neck-deep in the large jetted tub. His eyes were closed, and a serene glow softened his angular features. He peeked open a single lid when Landon clicked on the towel warmer. His gaze caught on the tray, and a sly grin crept up his face. "You do not want to know what obscene things I'd be willing to offer if that's a pitcher of Bloody Marys you've got there."

"Oh, don't I?" Landon tilted his head. "Says who?"

"Says me." Toby growled and sat forward, sloshing water over the edge of the tub. "You have three seconds to get naked and in this bath before I make a groveling fool of myself. It won't be pretty, and you won't like it."

Landon set the tray on the swirled black marble of the double-sink vanity. "So, you want me naked and in the tub, but I can leave the Bloody Marys and cheddar garlic rolls over here for later?"

Toby's eyes widened. "No one said anything about cheddar garlic rolls. Were you trying to hold out on me, Jenks?"

"I wouldn't dare." Landon put on his best posh, scandalized face and placed a weak-wristed hand over his sternum. "So, cheddar garlic rolls and a Bloody Mary take precedence over your demand to get me undressed and in the bath, right? I want to be sure where your priorities lie."

"You wouldn't dare make me pick one or the other, would you?" Toby stuck out his bottom lip on an exaggerated pout. "Because there's no doubt which one I'd pick, but the items in question aren't mutually exclusive. I want both."

The whine in Toby's voice had Landon grinning. "Okay, okay, one naked Landon and one Bloody Mary, with a cheddar garlic roll on the side, coming right up."

He poured the spicy hangover cure into two plastic cups and handed one to Toby, who gulped down a mouthful and emitted a delectable purr from the back of his throat. Landon set his own drink into one of the cupholders at the side of the tub, dropped his pajama pants to the floor, and snatched the basket of rolls before stepping over the lip. He sank into the deliciously warm, bubble-filled water on the opposite side, facing Toby.

"Gimme, gimme." Toby reached for the basket with greedy hands. He dove under the folds of the soft linen napkin and came out with his prize. A grin stretched his lips before he shoved the whole damn thing into his mouth.

"Jesus, please don't choke, I'm so not solid on my Heimlich maneuver. My CPR card expired in high school." Landon snatched the basket of rolls out of Toby's reach when he made to grab for another with his mouth still packed to overflowing with his current bite. "No. Not until you finish that one... very, *very* carefully, please."

Toby rolled his eyes but chewed the bread crowding his mouth with fastidious smacks of his lips that sent crumbs tumbling into the water.

"Were you born in a barn?" Landon gawked at the bits of bread floating on top of the bubbles, then burst out laughing when Toby grinned and more fell from his mouth. "You're hopeless."

Toby shrugged and made a point of swallowing the remaining roll with exaggerated movements, then opened his mouth and spun his tongue around to show he'd done as asked. "Can I have another now?"

"Only if you promise to eat it in at least four separate bites."

"Two."

"*Three*, and that's my final offer or the rolls get thrown out and you starve the rest of the day."

Toby glared out from beneath the still-rumpled locks falling in waves over his brows. "Fine, sheesh. It's a damn good thing I don't have to fight you this hard in the bedroom." He seized a roll as soon as Landon put the basket on the lip of the tub between them. "You might find yourself tied down and at my mercy if I did."

A delicious thrill raced up Landon's spine as Toby's words settled over him like a welcome promise. His cock pulsed to life at the very thought of being restrained and helpless. Of giving Toby complete control over his body. His senses. Both his pleasure... and his pain. The fulfillment or denial of everything from his most basic needs to his darkest desires.

Landon swallowed, his dick twitching further to attention beneath the foamy bubbles.

Toby took a swig of his Bloody Mary after polishing off his second roll and settled into the bath, wrapping his legs around Landon's waist. When his inner thigh brushed Landon's now-raging hard-on, a self-satisfied smirk crept up his lips. "I see my barnyard eating habits won me a few favors down south, even if you were bitching about them."

"First, I was not 'bitching.' I was concerned for your safety and the patency of your airway." Landon allowed Toby to tug him closer as he spoke, then twisted until he could settle between Toby's muscular thighs and lean against his firm chest. He sighed when Toby enveloped him in that solid embrace and placed a gentle kiss over the shell of his ear. "Second, it wasn't your, ah, eating habits that turned me on."

Toby hummed, the noise rising at the end in a questioning lilt. "Is that so?" He enclosed Landon's throbbing cock in the soft pressure of his fist and gave a few cursory tugs that had Landon tipping his head back on a groan. "Do tell. What is it, exactly, that got my sexy man hard for me?"

Landon whimpered when Toby's hot breath fanned over his neck and that tight fist stroked his hungry dick. "Isn't being naked together in a bath enough of a reason?"

"Sure, that's the meat and potatoes of the 'why' behind the wood *I'm* sporting." Toby ground his rock-hard cock into the small of Landon's back to indicate the truth of his words. "But I got the distinct impression you were implying something else—something specific—triggered yours. I'm *dying* to know what that might be. Any insight into this big, beautiful brain of yours is welcome. I'm flying mostly blind right now, and that makes it hard to give you what you need."

Landon snorted. "There's nothing to know. Being in your presence is more of a turn-on than anything I could've ever imagined before." His blasé attitude slipped away when Toby sucked his earlobe into the wet heat of his mouth and nibbled on the sensitive skin while continuing to work his needy cock.

"Tell me."

Toby's whispered command, paired with that incessant stroking, brought images to Landon's mind of being bound to his bed and ordered to take Toby's luscious, swollen length into his willing mouth. A rumbling growl tore up his throat, and he thrust his dick into Toby's fist, desperate to find the orgasm hovering a hairsbreadth away.

"Ah, ah, ah, you don't get to come until you tell me." Toby pulled his hand back, and Landon cried out in a dizzying combo of both abject misery and unrestrained desire.

"Fuck." He gripped Toby's thighs as he struggled to descend off the wrong side of that razor-sharp edge. Did he dare risk sharing this side of himself again? If it were anyone other than Toby, the answer would be a resounding no. "I... It was that, ah, comment you made."

"Which comment?" Toby weaved his legs around Landon's waist, trapping his deprived cock against his belly. It was all he could do not to thrust his hips in search of the stimulation he so needed.

But no, he would wait until Toby chose to give him his release. He wouldn't take it for himself. Toby might not be aware of how much control he already held, but Landon couldn't deny the rush of a submissive under the care of an adoring Dom. Even without the out-and-out knowledge of Landon's subservient proclivities, Toby had fallen into the role with a natural flare Garret had never displayed.

"A-about tying me down and, you know... being at your mercy."

Air hissed into Toby's lungs. He remained there—immobile—for what could've been minutes before blowing out a shaky breath and tightening his hold around Landon's middle. "You like that idea, do you?"

Landon almost denied it. He almost took back what he said and laughed it off as a joke. But the husky drawl of Toby's words against the side of his flushed neck gave him the confidence to own a truth he'd sworn to never speak again. "Yes. Yes, I do."

Chapter Sixteen

Landon Jenks would be the death of Toby. He'd been fairly convinced of that notion before, but now there was no doubt.

His slick, heated body pressed against Toby's, vibrating with the need for release, yet he remained still. Waiting for Toby's response. Waiting for Toby's permission.

Swallowing a groan, Toby clenched his jaw to fend off the urge to grind out his own imminent orgasm against the firm, muscular backside pressed against him. Instead, he focused his attention on Landon. He scooped up one of the washcloths resting at the side of the tub, along with the bar of lavender-scented soap, and dipped both beneath the water. He lathered foamy bubbles into the washcloth, then ran it in slow, meticulous strokes over every inch of Landon's body he could reach.

Faint whimpers and panting moans rewarded Toby as the cloth traced over trembling flesh. Landon sucked in a hitched breath when Toby ran the soapy fabric over his straining cock with a deliberate twist and tug. Nibbling on Landon's ear, Toby moved to his balls. "Spread your legs, sweetheart."

Landon complied without hesitation, his chest heaving as a swell of water broke over the side of the tub. When Toby progressed lower, running the cloth between those glorious cheeks, Landon cursed and dropped his head onto Toby's shoulder.

"I get to return this f-favor, right?" Landon's throaty plea was made all the better when paired with his stuttering awkwardness.

Toby grinned against Landon's neck, then shook his head. "Sorry, but not today. Why don't you start us a shower to rinse off while I scrub down and get the tub drained?"

Landon turned his desire-hazed gaze to meet Toby's amused stare. "That's not fair."

"Life's not always fair, babe." Toby kissed the corner of Landon's pouting lips. "But I promise to make it up to you. Now scoot." He loosened his hold around Landon's waist, biting back a groan when that delicious ass pressed into his eager cock as Landon climbed out of the tub.

Toby pulled the stopper on the tub and ran the washcloth over his body as the water and bubbles disappeared down the drain. He kept his eyes diverted from the elegant mosaic tile walk-in shower. He needed a few minutes to collect himself before he got lost in that beautiful man.

What Landon wanted wasn't something Toby had ever been on the giving end of, but he'd been on the receiving side plenty of times. And not by choice. It wasn't unheard of for clients to use their time with Toby as an outlet to fulfill fetish desires they didn't want leaking into their straitlaced, upstanding lives.

Usually, even though Toby loathed acting out those fantasies more than most, he could endure the encounters well enough. Many of the clients were novices, dipping their toes into the water for the first or second time, so the things they demanded of him weren't past the point of relative tolerance.

Because, of course, he wasn't allowed to say no.

But there were a few... Toby shuddered and closed his eyes. Now was *not* the time to think about the likes of Howard Mayson. Toby still had six days to enjoy with

Landon before all this beauty was torn away so he could spend a week in the clutches of that monster.

Toby finally cast a glance to the shower. Landon waited for him outside the reach of the steaming spray, his leanly muscled form glistening with soap and bubbles. His gaze latched on to Toby's as soon as he lifted his eyes, and Toby's cock stirred with renewed desire.

Landon was gorgeous in every physical sense of the word, but it wasn't the visible, tangible parts of him that pulled at the tightly woven threads of Toby's heart. It was his endless kindness and compassion; his genuinely selfless nature; and that whole-hearted, all-in trust he offered without question or condition.

When Landon's lips lifted into a shy smile, those stunning eyes partially hidden by a sweep of bangs and pinching in puzzled discomfiture, another thread was lost, leaving Toby's heart tender, raw, and utterly exposed.

"You okay?" Landon raked his teeth over his top lip, trapping it briefly between their grasp. "If what I said made you uncomfortable, I-I'm sorry. I didn't mean to. We can—"

"No." Toby stood, cringing at the pain lancing through his ribs. He stepped over the lip of the tub and padded across the tile, heedless of the water sluicing off his body to soak the floor. He knuckled under Landon's chin, forcing his lowered gaze to lift and meet his once more. "You didn't come close to making me uncomfortable."

Toby placed an arm around Landon's waist and guided them both under the spray of the shower. He grabbed a bottle of combo shampoo and conditioner off the shelf, filled his palm, then massaged the cleanser into Landon's scalp.

Landon dipped his head back at Toby's command. Toby rinsed the suds out of his hair, then caressed his toned, inked flesh to whisk away the soap still clinging to his skin. Once Toby was certain all the residue from their bath had rinsed down the drain, he placed a kiss on the tip of Landon's nose.

"Dry off and meet me in the bedroom." Toby gave Landon's backside a playful smack, causing his eyes to fly open in surprise. "Don't get dressed."

With a deliberate swallow, Landon nodded, his lips quirking into an impish grin. He snatched a towel off the heated rack and roughed up his hair as he walked out of the room, the perfect globes of his ass on full display. A pink hue colored the cheek Toby had spanked.

Toby chuckled to himself before washing and rinsing his own hair, then shutting off the shower. He grabbed a towel and wrapped it around his shoulders, relishing its toasty warmth a moment before scrubbing the water from his face, hair, and body.

Once dry, he slung the towel around his hips and leaned both fists on the edge of the double-sink vanity, staring down his own reflection. "Don't fuck this up, Carmichael."

While Toby hadn't enjoyed his previous dalliances into BDSM, that didn't mean his feelings on the subject couldn't change if it were consensual and shared with a man he wanted to be with.

Like it would be now, with Landon.

Domination and submission could be a beautiful thing. He knew enough about kink culture to realize those who participated by choice and within roles that suited their personal needs could find mental, emotional, and physical gratification and boundless pleasure from the lifestyle. He didn't judge those who followed the desires of their heart, even when those cravings took them somewhere he'd never personally found fulfillment.

But the fact remained, even if Toby wanted more than anything to give Landon what he hungered after, he didn't know what he was doing. He only had rookie wannabe dominants and sadistic pricks to emulate. What if he did something horribly wrong? What if he hurt Landon or crossed a boundary that transformed the experience from a pleasurable one into a life-altering mind-fuck?

What if he left Landon feeling the way he always felt after the restraints were removed? Beaten and bruised and a little more broken inside.

That wasn't an option.

Toby scrubbed his hands over his face. He'd take it slow—very, *very* slow—and wait until his head was fully in the game. Hungover Toby wasn't allowed to be in charge of something this big.

Decision made, Toby blew out a steadying breath. He turned from the mirror and headed into the bedroom, fending off a grin when a gloriously bare Landon shot off the bed at his entrance.

"H-hi, I was just—"

Toby closed the distance between them in two long strides, spearing his hands into Landon's damp hair and pulling him in for a kiss. Their tongues danced in a languid, loving rhythm as their lips moved in perfect sync. Landon pressed his pelvis into Toby and groaned as he wrapped his arms around Toby's middle and held him close.

When Toby finally pulled away, they were both breathless. He massaged his fingers into Landon's scalp and nipped at his earlobe. "Do you have any toys?"

Landon froze, his Adam's apple bobbing against Toby's cheek. "Ah, a few. Garret and I bought some together but, ah..."

Toby bit back the unjustified rush of jealousy. Instead, he rolled his hips into Landon's, their hard cocks grazing through the fluffy cotton of his towel. "Where are they?"

"T-top drawer of my nightstand."

Toby grinned against Landon's cheek. Where else? Didn't every man keep his lube and condoms and other such paraphernalia within easy reach? "Lie down on the bed. On your back." When Landon didn't comply instantly, Toby gave his butt another firm smack, the sound cracking through the air in tandem with Landon's sharp inhale. Toby drew Landon's mouth to his, plundering into its warm, welcoming depths with a feral growl. "If you change your mind at any time, tell me immediately."

"Oh god, no." Landon thrust his hips forward with desperate little whimpers. "I want this. I want this so fuckin' bad."

"Good." Toby rested his hands on Landon's backside, giving the cheek he'd spanked a gentle kneading. "So do I."

And the truth of it was, he did. Toby *did* want this. With Landon, *for* Landon, he wanted this. What did that mean? After the experiences he'd had at the hands of merciless men who relished Toby's true inability to say no, could he find the purity and beauty behind consensual domination with a submissive he cared for and had no desire to harm?

At least, not more than he could handle.

Toby gave himself a moment to revel in the stark-naked need dancing in Landon's eyes before arching a brow. "Bed. Now."

This time, Landon obeyed without pause. He pried himself free of Toby's arms and sprawled out on the bed like a starfish, shameless in his eagerness to please. Toby nearly came on the spot when Landon's flushed cock throbbed under his perusing gaze and a drop of precum dripped onto his ink-covered belly.

Toby wandered over to Landon's closet and disappeared inside, grinning when he discovered what he wanted hanging in neat rows from a built-in cherrywood tie rack. He ran his fingers over the soft silk until he found one in pale gray that would perfectly match the swirling tempest of Landon's eyes.

He plucked it from the round wooden rod and returned to the bedroom. Landon watched with hungry, desperate eyes as Toby dropped his towel and climbed onto the bed to straddle Landon's waist, nestling Landon's cock between his own asscheeks. Landon mewled and fisted his hands into the bedspread when Toby rocked his hips.

Holding up the tie, Toby allowed the soft, silken ends to trail over Landon's flushed chest. "Is it okay if I blindfold you?"

Landon's nod of agreement was vehement as he sucked in a shaky breath.

"Say yes or say no. I need to be one-hundred-percent certain we're on the same page, sweetheart."

Landon's throat worked on a swallow. "Yes, you can blindfold me. I trust you."

There it was again. That blind trust. Toby's heart swelled, the tender bits Landon had stripped bare rubbing against his ribs until an ache formed that was both sweet and agonizing all at once. He nodded and cupped Landon's cheek. "Lift your head for me."

Doing as asked, Landon blinked at Toby with every single ounce of that trust shining bright and true in his beautiful eyes. Toby placed a chaste kiss over Landon's lips before thrusting his world into darkness. He secured the tie enough to ensure Landon couldn't see but tested its fit with a finger beneath the cloth to be sure it wasn't too constricting before sitting back to admire the result.

Landon was exquisite. His mouth hung open to facilitate his heavy, panting breaths. His arms strained out to his sides, the lovely inked muscles jumping beneath his skin as he gripped at the silky material of his black bedspread. And those stunning eyes? They were hidden beneath a swath of fabric. A visible reminder this moment was theirs, and that Landon's senses—albeit limited to four now—were all focused on Toby.

"Sweetheart?" Toby placed both palms over Landon's chest, relishing the steadfast beat of his heart.

"Y-yeah?"

Toby laved his tongue over one of Landon's nipples, then nibbled at the sensitive flesh. Landon writhed beneath him.

"I trust you too. Wholly and completely." He moved to the other nipple and awarded it the same attention, garnering a similar response. "Promise me you'll speak up if you want me to stop, or if I get even a little close to crossing any lines, okay?"

Landon nodded, then remembered Toby's previous request and used his words. "Yes, I promise, but don't stop. Fuck, *please* don't stop. This feels so fuckin' good."

Toby chuckled under his breath, not wanting Landon to know how utterly, adorably perfect he was in that moment. He'd sensed Landon's displeasure at being deemed adorable in the past and hardly wanted to kill the mood by bringing it up again. Instead, he did as Landon asked. He returned his attention to Landon's nipples, drawing a hiss and a moan from Landon's lips when he pinched one between his thumb and forefinger while suckling at the other.

Slowly, methodically, Toby worked his way down Landon's body, kissing and nibbling and licking every inch. He traced his tongue over the lines of his tattoos, enjoying their beauty as he paused—for the first time—to investigate the designs up close.

It was a collage of images, more than Toby could wrap his desire-hazed brain around, but one stood out. Or perhaps it was several different ones, but they worked together to tell a story Toby didn't understand.

There was a ferocious, near photo-realistic black-inked tiger stretching the full length of Landon's right side. It pounced down his rib cage, its jaws open wide, revealing vicious teeth a hairsbreadth away from closing over the cowering form of a cub. For the Chicago Cubs, perhaps?

The cub held out one of its front paws as if expecting the adult to latch on to that tiny leg with its fierce killer's teeth. Beside the cub, in the spot where the tiny animal's desperate gaze fell, stood a broken cross. Ribbons dripped from its torn-asunder arms. They possessed the only color to grace the entirety of Landon's torso, and they popped with a rainbow of vibrant gem-toned hues.

Toby made a mental note to ask Landon what that scene meant, then shifted his attention back where it belonged. On Landon's glorious body. He continued south, skipping over Landon's weeping cock, which resulted in a whimpered plea from Landon.

"Lift your leg, sweetheart." Toby tapped Landon's left knee to indicate which one he meant, guiding it into the bent position he desired. He laved attention on Landon's toes—delighting in the little gasps and mewls that resulted—then kissed and nipped his way to his groin.

But instead of taking Landon's dick into his mouth as he so wanted, Toby pressed his hands behind Landon's knees, forcing both legs up and back. "Stay like that. Don't move."

Landon groaned, but stuttered out his intent to obey.

Satisfied, Toby slipped off the bed and dug through the nightstand until he found what he'd been hoping for and more. He grinned, snatched his prizes, and settled on the bed between Landon's spread and waiting legs.

He lowered onto his belly and returned to his kissing and licking, moving lower until his tongue nudged beneath Landon's balls, earning him a whimper and hip-thrust in response.

But it wasn't his balls Toby had in mind. He dipped lower, then lower still, until the flat of his tongue brushed over Landon's puckered opening. Landon gasped, dropped his legs, and levered onto his elbows.

Toby leaned up as well. "You okay?"

Landon hadn't removed the blindfold, but Toby could feel the laser beam of his gaze through the silk. "What... You can't... I mean... Holy fuck."

"You hold all the control here. If you say stop, I'll

stop."

"N-no, that was... I mean..." Landon fell onto the mattress. "No one's ever done that before."

What kind of selfish dickheads had Landon dated? "Did you like it?"

A lovely blush stained Landon's cheeks, disappearing beneath the tie. "Ah, y-yeah. I definitely liked it."

"Good. So did I." Toby guided Landon's legs back into position. "Use your hands behind your knees to make it easier to keep your legs up. It'll be more comfortable."

He waited while Landon did as instructed, then settled at his opening again, stroking his tongue over the sensitive flesh as Landon squirmed above him. He took his time, licking and kissing to ease Landon into the act before spearing his tongue within the tight ring of muscle. Landon cried out, and Toby paused, waiting to see if he'd ask him to stop. But instead, Landon's cry morphed into a groan, and he shifted his hips, the movement shoving Toby's tongue deeper and drawing a moan of satisfaction from both their lips.

Toby worked Landon's ass until he feared any further attention would end things too soon; then he pushed to a sitting position and kneaded Landon's inner thighs. He was strung tight, straining toward that edge of release, the need to come so intense his body quivered and trembled.

But now wasn't the time for that. Toby picked up the object he'd removed from Landon's drawer, his hand shaking thanks to the ledge he teetered just as dangerously upon, and slathered lube over its cool, rounded metal surface.

"Landon?" Toby rubbed one of Landon's inner thighs. "I need you to relax for me, okay? Take a nice, deep breath and relax."

Landon drew in a shuddering breath, and as he did, Toby pressed the tip to his opening and pushed until it hit home. Landon gasped and clenched his muscles, but it was too late. The plug was already inside.

"Good boy." Toby traced his tongue up the underside of Landon's cock as a reward. Considering it was the first attention Toby had paid to his dick since their bath, Landon's shock fell away, replaced by a feral, hungry growl.

"Now, what was it you said about greasy food? I'm starving."

When Toby stood, and the bed rebounded from the freedom of his weight, Landon peeked out from beneath the tie. His eyes narrowed as Toby slipped into a clean pair of boxer briefs.

"Ah... food? But what about...?"

Toby smirked. "Don't worry, babe, I'll take care of you. You're gonna have the best orgasm of your life. Later. Now, it's time for food. Hungover Toby is getting hangry."

Chapter Seventeen

Toby was trying to kill him. That was the only feasible explanation as to why Landon now stood in his kitchen—fully clothed, with a butt plug up his ass—when only ten minutes prior he'd been one touch away from one hell of an epic explosion.

Landon's knife sliced through a jalapeño and thumped against the cutting board with an exaggerated thud. He closed his eyes, trying to focus on the task at hand instead of the heavy metal weight shifting against his prostate with every movement. The sensation hardly cured the incessant, low-grade burn of unfulfilled desire in his groin, but it quenched the need enough to take the edge off. Or make it worse. He couldn't quite tell, and he didn't really care. He fidgeted without shame, fueling his own desperation.

And with every movement, the plug reminded him of who put it there. And why.

Because Toby *wanted* him desperate. He wanted him to feel impossibly achy and unbearably hot. To yearn for touch and to crave sensation—*any* sensation. He wanted Landon laser-focused on his own delectable anguish, so when he found relief, it could only come from one place. *Toby*.

Landon had never suffered such exquisite torture,

and yet it felt so completely fucking *right*. Righter than anything he'd ever experienced before. Something inside him that had lain dormant for far too long rose to the surface, demanding things he never could've imagined wanting before now. Before Toby.

He felt free and cared for and inexplicably *understood* for the first time in his life.

When Toby's strong arms wound around Landon's belly, tugging him against that solid warmth, he ground his plugged ass into Toby's rock-hard cock. The movement sent a zing of white-hot pleasure straight up Landon's spine. He whimpered and rested his head on Toby's shoulder.

Nuzzling into Landon's neck, Toby grazed the sensitive spot behind his ear with a line of whisper-soft kisses. "You okay, babe?"

Landon wanted to bust loose with a loud, crazed cackle at the utter absurdity of that question. Was he okay? Hardly. Did he want Toby to rip the plug out and fuck him until he came all over the kitchen island? Without a doubt. But this was the hottest fucking thing he'd ever experienced. He wouldn't change a single moment of it. Not in a million fuckin' years.

He twisted in Toby's arms, sighing when Toby dropped a kiss on his nose before pressing their foreheads together. "I'm doing great." Landon canted his hips forward to grind their dicks together through the thin fabric of their pajama pants. "How about you?"

Toby groaned. "I didn't think this through very well, did I?"

A genuine laugh bubbled up Landon's throat. "No, I suppose you didn't."

"I think I'm suffering more than you are right now."

There was a whine in Toby's voice that had Landon grinning. "Oh? Are you sure about that? I seem to remember being the one who had a plug shoved up his ass after being edged to the brink of orgasm over and over and over again."

Toby tipped back his head with an exaggerated groan. "That doesn't help, you know." He pinned Landon with his heated golden-green stare. "I was as worked up as you were, and I didn't get off either. Plus, knowing you're wearing that plug is... Fuck. So fuckin' hot. *Have. Mercy.*"

Landon shrugged and gave his most innocent look, complete with batting eyelashes and an overly angelic, toothy grin. "Gee, that's too bad. I guess next time you'll have to make sure you get off before you plug my ass and leave me in this state. Because, quite frankly, I'm having a hard time feeling sorry for you right now." He bumped their cocks again and snickered at the glare he received for his efforts. "Now, you're distracting me from my meal prep, and I *thought* you were hungry."

"I *am* hungry," Toby growled, stealing into Landon's mouth with a ferociousness that spoke to Landon's simmering libido like a promise and a prayer all rolled into one.

When Landon finally tore his lips free of Toby's ravenous kiss so he could suck air into his starved lungs, he squeezed Toby's shoulders and smiled through his heaving breaths. "We're never going to eat if you keep that up. Why don't you head into the living room and watch some TV while I finish lunch?"

Toby narrowed his eyes. "That's assuming I'm hungrier for food than I am for you."

A million butterflies took flight under Landon's ribs, twisting his stomach with the frantic beating of their wings. He didn't know why those words got to him so much, but they did. Maybe it was the fact there was no mistaking Toby's need for him in that moment. For *him*, not his public persona, not his father's influence, but *him*.

"I'm almost done with prep, and the oven's preheated. I only need thirty minutes." Landon pressed on Toby's chest, trying to shove him away, then laughed when his hold only intensified. Why wasn't he pushing Toby away from the thought of food and toward *anything* that could alleviate the throbbing need between his legs? Oh, that's right, because he was thoroughly enjoying the torment. And more importantly, if Toby hadn't left himself on the same tremulous edge, there would be no way he'd let Landon off that easy.

While this was all new between them, he'd self-sacrifice to save Toby from himself. Just this once. "Go. Watch TV. Leave me in peace for *thirty minutes*. Then you can fill your belly *and* my ass."

Toby's shoulders drooped. "This is so unfair. I need to think this shit through better next time. I'm in hell, and you're bouncing around the damn kitchen like your only concern is channeling your inner Guy Fieri." He furrowed his brow and drew his arms across his chest when Landon finally extricated himself and returned to his cutting board. "Somewhere in this whole mess, me and my poor dick lost the reins."

Landon blew him a kiss. "*Go*. Thirty minutes."

"Yeah, yeah, thirty fuckin' minutes," Toby mumbled, throwing his hands in the air and stalking out of the kitchen.

Landon grinned as he refocused on their lunch. He had everything ready to go; he'd just needed the oven to preheat. He wrapped a towel around the lip of the casserole dish to save his hands from the heat and popped the shredded chicken enchiladas in to bake.

As he closed the door, Toby's grumbling voice called out from the living room, "Has it been thirty minutes yet?"

Landon chuckled and threw the dish towel on the counter. He surveyed the mess—something he liked to clean while the food cooked—then rolled his eyes and hollered, "You're worse than a child, Toby Carmichael. Learn some patience."

"But there's nothing on TV. I'm bored *and* horny, neither of which is doing any favors for my hangry status.

Can't I come back to the kitchen? I promise to keep my hands to myself."

Likely story. Toby might keep his hands to himself, but Landon could guess where his dick would be. Plastered against Landon's ass, no doubt, and making his own torment all the worse for it. Not that Landon would complain.

Grinning, he eyed the timer he'd set for the enchiladas. They still had twenty-eight minutes. A whole hell of a lot could be accomplished in twenty-eight minutes.

So much for saving Toby from himself. Next time, maybe.

"Hey, Tobes?" Landon started toward the bedroom, laughing to himself when Toby's bare feet smacked on the stone floor of the kitchen at a half run. He tossed a glance over his shoulder and was rewarded with the sight of Toby stalking toward him. "What can you do with twenty-eight minutes and the promise of absolute obedience?"

A snarl ripped up Toby's throat and his hands clenched into fists, causing the muscles showcased beneath his skintight white T-shirt to bunch and ripple. "Bedroom. Naked. Now."

Landon darted down the hall, tearing off his T-shirt and tossing it to the floor as he ran. Once he made it to the bedroom, he shimmied out of his pants and boxers and threw himself onto the bed, his hard cock bouncing greedily against his abdomen.

Toby prowled into the bedroom not long after, his eyes hooded, his glorious chest bare. "On your stomach, sweetheart, and spread those beautiful legs."

"Yes, sir." Landon flipped onto his belly, grinding his desperate cock into the silky caress of the bedspread.

A loud, ringing smack broke into the silence of the room about half a second before one of Landon's buttcheeks caught fire. He yelped, then worked his hips even farther into the bed, his need heightened by that delicious bite of pain mingling with his pleasure.

"Did I tell you to fuck the mattress, or did I tell you to get on your stomach and spread your legs?" Toby's hot breath appeared at Landon's throat, and his heavy, welcome weight settled over Landon's back. "What happened to the absolute obedience you promised?"

Landon bit his lip—hard—to focus his spiraling thoughts. Had he ever been this turned on? Doubtful. "I'm sorry. I'm so fuckin' horny..."

Toby placed a tender kiss over the shell of Landon's ear. "I know, sweetheart, but I don't want you to come before I have a chance to make you feel everything I want you to feel. Leave your pleasure to me, okay? I promise to take care of you."

Every muscle in Landon's body relaxed despite the clawing need to seek the release he'd been so long denied. He trusted Toby completely. He would do more than take care of him. He would cherish him and make him feel a thousand different pleasures that would far surpass any empty relief his frantic humping could bring.

"Good boy." Toby breathed the words into Landon's ear, placed another soft, sweet kiss against the flushed, sensitive skin of his throat, then levered off him.

As soon as Toby's warmth disappeared, Landon spread his legs. He remained motionless and silent, waiting for whatever gift Toby would give him next.

The nightstand drawer opened and closed, and then the bed dipped beneath Toby's weight. His strong, steady hands landed at Landon's hips. "Lift onto your knees, sweetheart, but keep your shoulders down and legs spread. There you go, like that. That's perfect." He kissed Landon's backside where a delicious sting still burnt his skin in the imprint of Toby's hand. "I'm gonna take out the plug. Just relax for me."

Landon groaned into the mattress and nodded, too entranced by his desire and anticipation to form words. Toby's deft fingers gave a gentle yank, popping the object free with one swift movement that had Landon crying out with an inexplicable mixture of pleasure and grief. He felt excessively sensitive and excruciatingly empty. Very, very empty.

But that didn't last for long. As soon as Toby removed the plug, he replaced it with his tongue. His hot, wet, wonderful tongue. Landon fisted the bedspread as a downright lascivious growl vibrated up his throat, muffled by the mattress but unmistakable in its lewd and lustful nature. He couldn't help it; his hips thrust to meet Toby's probing as he massaged the overstretched muscles and sent sparks of molten need racing along Landon's nerves.

He was so lost to the ebb and flow of desire and pleasure and sinfully delectable bliss that he barely noticed when Toby's lube-slicked fingers replaced his tongue. But when those digits disappeared and the head of Toby's cock breached his aching and ready ass, Landon yelped with hedonistic delight.

Nothing had ever, in the history of all things, felt so good.

Toby eased Landon onto his belly and stretched over his back. He nuzzled into the crook of Landon's neck to nibble and kiss, moving his hips with slow, steady perfection. His cock brushed Landon's prostate on each downward thrust, and every movement played over his sensitized opening, leaving him dizzy with the decadence those combined sensations created.

As that tightly coiled spring inside him unfurled, his orgasm imminent, panic bloomed in Landon's chest. "Toby," he moaned, desperation breaking his voice at the end, "I... I'm going to..."

"Shh, it's okay, babe." Toby slipped his hand under Landon, took his cock into the warmth of his palm, and stroked in tandem with his thrusts. "Come for me."

As if Toby's blessing was all Landon needed, a tidal wave of carnal pleasure crashed over him, stealing his senses and sending him into a maelstrom of physical and emotional turmoil. Every nerve in his body fired in a colorful hurricane that exploded across his vision and pulsated through him like bolts of lightning during a heavy summer storm.

But it was the swell of emotions slamming into his system that had his passionate cry breaking on a fragmented sob. The tumultuous feelings gripped his heart and dragged it into the pit of his stomach, where they twisted and coiled together like tendrils of acrid smoke.

Hot, thick tears poured down Landon's cheeks as he lay limp on the mattress, completely empty and utterly destroyed.

"Sweetheart?" Toby's soft, soothing voice tore through the haze clouding Landon's thoughts, and Landon curled toward the sound. "Hey, I've got you. It's okay. Come here."

Toby pulled Landon into the solid warmth of his embrace, tucking Landon's head under his chin and folding the free end of the bedspread over them both. He tangled their legs together and traced gentle, haphazard patterns over Landon's back. Whisper-soft kisses brushed over Landon's temple as Toby murmured tender, sweet words promising Landon was beautiful, that he'd made Toby proud, that he didn't ever have to do that again. That Toby was sorry.

It was that more than anything that stirred Landon to gather some semblance of sanity. What was his problem? Nothing about what they'd done felt wrong. In fact, it had felt—it *did* feel—wholly and entirely right in every sense of the word. So why had Landon shattered into a million fucking pieces immediately following what was, without a doubt, the most intense orgasm he'd ever experienced?

As Toby held him, crooning breathy pleas for forgiveness and gentle words of reassurance, realization settled over Landon like a lead blanket.

Whatever passed between them during that final exchange—right before his body found that ultimate release—

had been more than permission granted and received. It had gone far deeper than that. It satiated an unfillable void and assuaged an age-old ache he'd always known was there but could never ease.

Perhaps his discontent and frustration all these years wasn't as simple as he'd once thought. His inability to find true love, to find that connection he so craved, might have less to do with what the men he dated had sought to gain from him, and more to do with a vital, missing piece of his own mental puzzle.

Landon wasn't broken. He'd been set free. Odd that the two could feel so similar, but intense, deep-seated emotion often brought on parallel responses, no matter on which end of the spectrum it fell. The fierce, foreign feeling had left Landon confused, adrift, and grasping for direction.

Thankfully, he had Toby. His compass. His rock. The only man who had ever cared enough to dig into Landon's screwed-up psyche and help him discover a part of himself he'd never realized was missing. The only man who had ever stuck around long enough to hold him when he cried.

Landon sniffed against Toby's neck. "Sorry, that was an unsexy response to insanely hot sex."

Toby tightened his hold on Landon for a moment, then returned to his gentle caressing over Landon's shoulder blades. "Don't ever apologize for how you respond. To any-thing. Ever." He kissed the crown of Landon's head. "No response is wrong, as long as it's an honest one."

A flutter surged inside Landon's chest as Toby's words arrowed deep into his heart, setting up camp along-side the many other parts of him that were slowly, but with-out question, claiming ownership of the space.

Toby was everything Landon had ever wanted and more. From a partner. From a Dominant. *His* Dominant. His Dom.

God, had anything ever sounded better?

"You didn't do anything wrong. You didn't hurt

me." Landon pressed his lips to Toby's throat, and his Adam's apple bobbed against them on a swallow. "I'm not sure why I responded that way, but I think I was overwhelmed. That was... intense. In a very, very good way."

Toby's strong arms pulled Landon closer. "Oh, thank fuck. I thought... Jesus, I'd never forgive myself if I hurt you. If I made you feel... used or forced or..." He shook his head and buried his face in Landon's hair.

"Oh, baby." Landon shoved away so he could meet Toby's strained gaze. "I'm so sorry I made you think that. I wasn't sure what I was feeling at first, but it was a good feeling, even though it was a bit overpowering. If that makes any sense at all."

Toby carded his fingers through Landon's hair, then cupped his cheek. "It does. I'm so fuckin' thankful I didn't do something you didn't want." He brushed his thumb over Landon's cheekbone. "If we do anything like that again, we need to have a nice long talk beforehand. Set some ground rules. Safewords. Make sure we can play freely without risk of hurting each other."

"There better not be any 'ifs' about it. I so totally want to do that—and more—again." Landon grinned. "My knowledge is limited with this stuff, but I can't wait to learn. With you and your delightfully deviant ways at the helm."

Toby's cheeks crimsoned, but they tugged into that megawatt smile that never failed to weaken Landon's defenses. "Delightfully deviant ways, eh?"

"Oh yes. Wonderfully delightful and sinfully deviant." Landon chuckled. "That should be your catchphrase. It's quite fitting."

Before Toby could form a response, an obnoxious, ear-splitting ringing pealed through the air, and Landon groaned. They'd clearly been too engrossed to hear the kitchen timer, but there was no missing the high-pitched screech of the smoke alarm. "Ah, shit. There goes lunch."

Chapter Eighteen

After Landon dumped his blackened, smoking enchiladas into the trash and set the dish to soak in the sink, they ordered carryout from a Chinese restaurant down the street. They spent the rest of the afternoon and well into the evening camped out on the couch in the living room. Toby couldn't remember the last time he'd spent the day lazing around watching TV, and to be honest, this experience didn't fit the bill either.

Sure, the TV was on, and a steady stream of sitcoms, game shows, and random movies had played on the excessively large wall-mounted flat screen, but neither Toby nor Landon had paid the damn thing a bit of attention. Instead, they'd talked, kissed, laughed, and napped, their bodies intertwined, their hands touching and teasing and discovering every chance they could.

When they finally went to bed, they had sweet, languid sex, then drifted off to sleep wrapped in each other's arms.

It had been the best Sunday—the best day, period—of Toby's life.

Landon's alarm went off at half past six the next morning, and he groused under his breath as his hand shot out to smack at the offending device. When Toby yawned and stretched away—assuming the alarm meant Landon planned to get up—Landon latched on to Toby's bicep and tugged him into a snuggle hold.

"Where d'ya think yer goin'?" Landon slurred, planting a firm hand on Toby's bare ass. "Mine. Y'can't leave."

Toby chuckled and burrowed deeper into Landon's arms. "I wasn't going anywhere, but your alarm went off. I figured you had to get up."

Landon harrumphed. "Tha' thing's the devil."

"What is, the alarm?"

Nodding, Landon's jaw cracked on a yawn. "Gonna throw it away."

Toby grinned against Landon's neck. His cranky, decidedly-not-a-morning-person attitude was downright too cute for words. "You're gonna throw your alarm clock away? How will you make sure you get up on time?"

"Won't." Landon squeezed Toby's butt. "Gonna stay in bed forever."

A deep belly laugh worked its way up Toby's throat. "Oh, is that so? Gonna skirt your responsibilities and become a hermit?"

Landon nodded again and bucked his hips. "Got better things to do. Gonna spend every minute with you."

Toby's chest squeezed, and he inhaled a shaky breath. How he wished that were true. For this week, maybe, but after that?

Landon couldn't keep buying Toby's freedom indefinitely. He wouldn't let him. *Couldn't* let him. Despite Landon's valiant intentions, Toby wouldn't be free until his contract was up. There was no getting around it. His family's lives were worth far more than his, and he wouldn't do anything to put them in jeopardy. Not even for Landon.

And when those three years were over? Maybe he would look Landon up. If he happened to be single, maybe they could see if the chemistry flashing hot and bright between them now could be rekindled. But what were the chances? Would it even be worth opening that old wound when there was no guarantee it wouldn't go to complete shit?

Landon might claim he didn't mind Toby being with other guys now, but would he feel the same three years distanced with the reality of what Toby had done during that time hanging between them? Highly doubtful. And could Toby blame him? Not one fucking bit.

Which meant, even if Landon were single and Toby somehow discovered that fact, he'd never seek him out. Whatever they had this week would be it for them. They had no possibility of a future, and while Landon might not be willing to accept that, Toby had no other choice. His fate was sealed, his future guaranteed. That included his final goodbye with Landon.

Landon's alarm blared again. He growled but made no move to shut it off. Instead, he snuggled in closer to Toby and yanked the covers over both their heads, only slightly muffling the obnoxious noise.

"Fuck. You're adorable." Toby grinned into the darkness of their blanket cave and placed a smacking kiss against Landon's neck.

"I'm not adorable," Landon grumbled, giving Toby's ass another firm squeeze. "Puppies and five-year-olds with blond curls and lollipops are *adorable*. I'm a man. A man nearly a decade older than you. Didn't your parents teach you to respect your elders?"

"Too manly and geriatric to be adorable. Gotcha." Toby bit his lip to fend off his laughter. "But you're still really fuckin' cute."

Stillness… and a beeping alarm. For a good thirty seconds, that's all Toby heard. Landon didn't move or speak. Then he tossed off the covers with a growl and pounced on Toby, pinning him to the mattress and glaring him down with sleepy, grumpy eyes. His hair stood on end, and several red creases spread from beneath his thick beard where his cheek had lain against the pillow. Fuckin' adorable.

"You're gonna pay for that." Landon's voice was no longer slurred, but it retained that husky morning quality.

Toby bucked his hips and laughed when that unexpected jolt was enough to send Landon flailing, his lax, sleep-heavy arms giving out and landing him sprawled over Toby's chest, his face buried in the pillow.

Landon shoved onto an elbow, sputtering and rubbing his face. He scowled at Toby. "That wasn't very nice."

"Just trying to wake you up a bit, slugger. I figured an all-star ballplayer like you would have a bit more balance than that. I barely jostled you, and you went flying." Toby tried to keep a straight face, but the laughter won out. "Hope you didn't break a hip in the fall, Gramps. Although," Toby drew out the word, tapping his chin in thought, "you'd totally rock the walker look. Dare I say? You'd be totes adorbs."

"Oh. My. God." Landon gave an exaggerated eye roll and shoved Toby's shoulder so hard he rolled off his chest, tangling himself in the covers in the process.

As Landon tried to extricate his thrashing limbs from the burrito of blankets he'd created, Toby took the opportunity to zero in on one of the ticklish spots he'd discovered the other night. As soon as his wiggling fingers met the side of Landon's ribs, Landon howled and kicked more furiously at the covers to free himself.

"Uncle!" Landon cried as he surfaced from the snarl of sheets and blankets, gasping for breath. "Uncle, uncle, uncle!"

Toby chortled and bounced out of bed to avoid Landon's retaliatory lunge, then glanced back and laughed even harder. Landon was collapsed on his belly, his arms stretched out vainly toward the spot Toby had vacated, and a confused, disappointed frown marred those gorgeous features.

"Turn off that damn alarm—*off*, not snooze—and meet me in the shower." Toby headed for the bathroom, tossing a smirk over his shoulder. "You have until the water gets warm to join me or you don't get to come."

Before Toby could even flick on the bathroom light, the incessant beeping had stopped and Landon's sleep-warm, deliciously naked body pressed against his back. Toby chuckled and placed his arms over Landon's, which wrapped gently around Toby's bruised ribs. "There's the Turbo we all know and love."

Landon gave the tenderest of squeezes around Toby's middle and brushed a kiss over the back of his neck. "We have plans to go sightseeing today. No way in hell am I threatening those plans by being a pent-up, horn-ball mess. I'm begging you, let me come. For the sake of our day. You can do anything else you want to me... Just, please, let me come."

Toby grinned and turned in Landon's arms, planting an innocent kiss over his pouting lips. "We haven't had our talk yet. I don't plan to do anything other than make you feel very, very, *very* good. You have my word."

Landon grabbed Toby's wrist and tugged him straight to the shower. He slammed on the water before rounding on Toby and pulling him in for a ferocious kiss.

Oh yes, Toby would make Landon feel good. But not half as good as he made Toby feel simply by existing.

They spent the whole day acting like tourists, starting with breakfast at a little rooftop café overlooking the Crown Fountain in Millennium Park. Then they took a slew of goofy selfies in front of the Cloud Gate sculpture and walked hand in hand through Lurie Garden, sneaking kisses and sharing whispered conversations. They took more selfies in front of the large and opulent Buckingham Fountain, then sat on the steps of the Shedd Aquarium and wolfed down hot dogs—Chicago style, as if there was any other choice—from a street vendor.

After lunch, they hit up the Adler Planetarium, then finished the day at Navy Pier. They had dinner at a brewery with a view of Lake Michigan and the Chicago Harbor, then walked around the shops and shared a decadent banana split. As the sun set, they hopped aboard the Centennial Ferris Wheel, holding hands and pressing close as the fiery kiss of last light turned the Chicago skyline a kaleidoscope of rosy pinks, vivid oranges, and deep, rich reds.

When they arrived back at Landon's, exhausted but buzzing with the excitement and wonder of their day, they shared lazy blowjobs where the taste of Landon erupting into the back of Toby's throat sent him over his own edge. A few minutes later, he held Landon's sleepy, satiated form tucked against his side.

For the first, and very likely last time ever, Toby sent a telepathic thank-you to Joseph. As part of his drive to offer high-dollar, disease-free merchandise, Toby got tested quarterly for every disease known to man, and as soon as he'd transferred to Joseph's care and been deemed HIV-free, he'd started on pre-exposure prophylactic meds. To further assure the safety of Joseph's clients, they were all tested regularly as well.

At the very least, Toby and Landon could feel safe sharing this time together, despite the decidedly unsafe life Toby led outside these walls.

"G'night, Tobes." Landon yawned, an endearing squeak slipping out at the end. "No alarms in the morning. Tomorrow, we sleep in. And talk. Definitely talk." He snuggled in closer, and within seconds his mouth hung open, a gentle snore blowing past his lips.

Toby chuckled and kissed Landon's brow. In this moment, he was the luckiest man alive. "Sweet dreams, babe," he murmured, then drifted into the dreamless sleep of the cherished.

"You're an amazing cook." A mouthful of eggplant parmesan garbled Toby's words, but he shoved another forkful past his greedy lips anyway.

Landon rolled his eyes as he took a sip of iced tea. "You're going to choke one of these days, and I'm serious, I don't know how to Heimlich. You kinda freak me out when you eat. Can you, like, slow down?"

Toby deliberately chewed and swallowed what was in his mouth and offered a bashful half smile. Under Joseph's rule, his life was regimented. He worked out twice a day and ate specific meals geared more toward building and maintaining muscle than any kind of culinary enjoyment. These past few days with Landon, he'd been allowed to not only eat as much as he wanted, but the food had, thus far, been fantastic. It was all he could do to act human while eating when his inner hunger monster raged at him to devour every bite, lest it be his last.

His future was a gaping black hole of unknown torment that should be driving him to relish every precious minute and every delicious morsel Landon offered.

Toby's lips quirked into a full-on grin. "Sorry, I'll try to take your suffering into account and chew my food more carefully."

"That would be appreciated." Landon shook his head with a soft laugh. "So, now that we've lazed away the morning and our bellies are nice and full, I say it's time we have that talk."

Scraping his fork over the plate to get the dregs of sauce left behind, Toby angled a glance at Landon, who stared at him with a shit-eating grin stretching his lips.

"Okay, so talk." Toby returned the smile as he popped the fork into his mouth and polished off the decadent sauce, smacking his lips before setting his utensil on the empty plate.

Landon's confidence faltered, his lips sucking between his teeth, his cheeks turning pink. "Oh, ah, I thought you'd, you know, lead the discussion."

Toby rested back in the wicker patio chair, part of the dining set gracing Landon's gorgeous rooftop deck. A large red-and-white-striped umbrella blocked the early-afternoon sun from the table, but Toby stretched out his bare legs, hiking up the athletic shorts he'd borrowed from Landon to allow his pasty thighs a chance to catch a few of the unhindered rays.

"What we did the other day, that was something you're sure you enjoyed? Something you want to try again?"

Landon nodded, leaning forward on his elbows. "I've always known my, ah, sexual tastes didn't fit the norm, but I haven't had ample opportunity to experiment." Landon nibbled on his lip. "I tried a few things with Garret. Obviously, since we had those toys, but… Well, you know how that whole thing ended." He shrugged and dropped his eyes to his fidgeting hands, which were busy folding and unfolding the bloodred napkin in his lap.

Toby's heart pinched. It was clear Landon had cared for his ex at one point, and to think Garret had only been putting on an act. The very idea made Toby's stomach drop. If he had the freedom to love Landon, he would've been long lost to him by now. How could anyone pretend to love him and not, at the very least, fall by accident?

"What do you know about BDSM?" Toby smiled when Landon's flush crept up to pink the tips of his ears. "Mostly, I'm curious what it is about the practice that piques your interest. Is it the idea of the unknown? Leaving your pleasure to someone else to control, to surprise you?"

Landon licked his lips, then nodded. "Yes, but it's more than that. With you, at least." He dropped his gaze again. "I want… I want to give you complete control. Over everything. M-my pleasure a-and… and my pain. I want you to… to tie me up, a-and make me… Oh god. I'm sorry. I should stop talking."

Toby sat forward and reached across the table separating them. "Give me your hand, sweetheart, and look at me." Landon complied, placing his hand in Toby's and raising his eyes. "That trust you feel? I feel it too. Have faith in that and tell me what you want. What you need. I want to give you the world, Landon Jenks. I want to make you feel things you've never felt before. I want to test your boundaries, and I want to test mine, but I want to do it safely. I can't do that if I don't know what's in your head." Toby squeezed Landon's hand. "Would it be easier for you if I asked you questions?"

Landon nodded and exhaled through pursed lips. "I want to tell you everything, and I'm not ashamed of what I want. Not with you. Not as long as you want it too, but I…"

"Trust me, babe, I want it too." Lifting Landon's hand, Toby brushed his lips over his knuckles before releasing his hold and sitting back in his chair. "I'm no expert in this, so I'll be learning with you, but I think the best thing to do is start slow. This doesn't have to be—and shouldn't be—our only talk. I think the most important thing here is going to be open communication.

"Now, first things first. I might not think to ask you everything, or you might answer one way and realize you feel different in the heat of the moment. So, we need to establish safewords. Words you can say that will tell me if things are getting a bit too intense, or if you need whatever is happening to stop. Immediately."

Landon scrunched his brow. "I mean, why not *stop* or *no* or *don't* or whatever?"

"That's totally fine." Toby released a quivering breath. How he wished those words—*any* words—had meant something to the men who'd had him at their mercy. They'd gotten off on hearing him beg. Using those words only ensured more torment. "The only reason I brought up the idea of safewords is because—I've heard—there are some situations where the person on your end of the play enjoys sort of getting lost in the experience. Sometimes that finds them saying *no*, or *stop*, or other similar words when they don't really mean them.

"However, I'm a thousand percent down for straight communication. It's less confusing anyway, especially for beginners like us. If I were an experienced Dominant and you were an experienced submissive, it might be easier to bring those elements on board. But for us, communicating openly and honestly feels right. So, you've mentioned being interested in bondage. Is anything off-limits? Anything you can think of off the bat? Being gagged? All four appendages tied at once? Being bound in a vulnerable position? Anything?"

"I mean..." If possible, Landon's flush intensified. "Right now, that all sounds really fuckin' good."

Toby chuckled. "Okay, well, if that changes in the moment, tell me, yeah?"

Nodding, Landon grinned. "Yes, sir."

"Fuck, babe." If Toby's cock hadn't already hardened thanks to the subject matter, those two words would've had it springing to life in a heartbeat. As it was, it throbbed painfully. He fisted it through the fabric of his shorts, giving a conciliatory squeeze. "Okay. Pain. That's not anything we should jump into. I think working up to bigger things is the best way to handle that aspect." Toby's heart twisted at the thought of Landon finding another man to take that journey with him. He wouldn't be around long enough to thoroughly test those waters.

"B-but we can, like, I mean... try, right?" Landon swallowed and raked his teeth over that plump bottom lip. "I... I mean, ah... That's something I want to experiment with. Sooner, rather than later."

Toby cursed under his breath and gave his desperate cock another pacifying tug. "We can experiment, but we'll start slow, and you need to be brutally honest with me because I can't hurt you. Not won't, but can't, do you understand?"

"Yes, sir, I understand."

Landon aimed to kill Toby dead in this chair. He wasn't going to survive this conversation, let alone the actual act. Toby ran a hand through his hair to give himself a moment to collect his runaway libido. "Are you okay with me giving commands? You can always say no, but—"

"I *want* you to make me do things." Landon's entire head was bloodred, the angry color spreading down his throat and disappearing beneath the heather gray of his T-shirt. But he was adamant in his resolve. "I... I want you to have complete control. I don't want to make any decisions. I don't want to have to think. I want to feel and do and be yours, in every sense and semblance of the word."

Yep. Dead. He was dead. *Fuck*. How was he ever going to let this man go?

Chapter Nineteen

"Hey, babe?" Toby's husky drawl called over the running water Landon used to rinse the dishes. He'd gone to the rooftop to collect the plates they hadn't been able to carry on their initial trip down and walked into the kitchen balancing an armload. "You left your phone up there, and it was ringing off the hook. Whoever was calling tried back as soon as—"

The pop single acting as Landon's current ringtone cut through Toby's words, and he grinned, turning and giving his hip a bounce. "It's in my pocket."

Landon dried his hands on a dishtowel, then reached into Toby's athletic shorts, leaning in for a quick kiss before frowning down at his screen. It was an unknown number. With a shrug, he slid the answer button across the screen and held his cell to his ear. "Jenks."

"Hey, honey, we need to talk."

Landon clenched his jaw at Garret's whiny tenor. He was the last person Landon wanted to talk to. "What do you want?"

Garret sighed over the line. "Look, I know I handled everything really shitty, but I thought it was a job, ya know? But it wasn't, honey, and I realize that now. What we had... it was special. It was love. I was too blind to see it then, but it was the real thing."

"Oh, for fuck's sake." Landon cast a glance at Toby, who had taken over at the sink and was busy rinsing dishes, not paying a lick of attention to Landon or his phone call. Still, he backed out of the kitchen so Toby wouldn't have to listen to him tell off his ex-boyfriend. "Garret, we broke up—if you can even call it that—over six months ago."

"I know, but filming that movie was so exhausting. I didn't have time to realize what I was missing. But when they started airing the episodes, and I saw us together, it hit me."

Landon rolled his eyes. Even if he believed that, the timelines didn't add up. They wrapped on filming in the winter, and the first episode aired during the summer season premiere week. It was already season finale time. Why had he increased his efforts now? What was his true motive?

Garret's voice dropped an octave, shifting to the commanding growl he'd used in the bedroom. The one he'd used at the beginning, after Landon's hunger for submission first surfaced. "You know we were good together. Whoever this new guy is, he'll never be able to give you the things you need. The things you *crave.*"

"And you think you could?" Landon scoffed as he wandered into the three-season sunroom, peering out the windows at Lincoln Park. "Sad as it is to say, you broke my heart, but I'm a hundred percent over you. Not looking to repeat that travesty, thanks."

Snickering, Garret lowered his voice even further, until it took on the menacing tone Landon had mistaken one too many times as part of a consensual scene. It caused the hairs on the back of Landon's neck to stand on end as a chill shuddered down his spine. "Do you really think any-one else is going to understand you the way I do?" Garret's laugh turned sour. "You have some fucked-up kinks, honey, but I get off on giving you what you want. How many other people do you think there are in this world who would will-ingly do the things I did for you?"

Landon shook his head and pounded a fist against the tempered glass. He wouldn't let Garret shame him. Not again. Not when he'd managed to open up to Toby and they were exploring *together*. Something Garret hadn't understood. He'd never asked Landon what he *needed*, let alone took the time to set up safewords or discuss boundaries. He'd heard what he wanted to hear in Landon's late night, drunken confession and took it to mean Landon wanted to be demeaned. Debased. Used. Abused.

And at first, Landon *had* gotten off on the things they did. Maybe his kinks were fucked-up. But as soon as he'd tried to say no, and Garret only heard "more," things shifted. Had they been together even a few more days, Landon wanted to believe he would've realized it wasn't mutual pleasure driving Garret's action. And it certainly wasn't love. It never had been, and it never would be.

Not like it was with Toby.

"Lan, honey? Are you listening to me?" Garret's voice broke through Landon's thoughts, and he dropped his forehead to the glass as Garret continued. "Look, I love you, and I miss you. Don't throw this away for someone you just started dating."

"Garret, no offense, but I'm zero parts interested." Landon exhaled on an exhausted, defeated sigh. "I genuinely wish you the best, but don't call me again."

Without waiting for Garret to respond, Landon pulled the phone from his ear and hit the End button. He tossed the device onto the closest chair before planting his forehead against the glass again. Staring out over the park, he replayed his and Toby's first real date, when they'd walked hand and hand through those very trees.

A solid warmth appeared at Landon's back, and a set of strong, unyielding arms enfolded him in their tight embrace. "You okay, babe?" Toby burrowed his face into Landon's neck, planting soft kisses against the sensitive flesh behind his ear, a spot he hadn't realized he loved having kissed until Toby. "Did you get bad news?"

Landon shut his eyes and savored Toby's closeness. Garret's words washed over him a second time, and a niggling fear crept up in their wake. What if Toby didn't want the same things Landon did? Garret wasn't wrong when he said not everyone shared Landon's... *inclinations*.

He tried to remember their time in the bath when he'd first voiced his predilections. He'd been facing away from Toby, too afraid to look him in the eye when he spoke the words, which meant he had no memory of Toby's reaction to his admission. Not a firm one, at least. Toby had gone along with it, seemingly willingly and with apparent gusto, but... What if he'd done so to please Landon, not because it was something he'd wanted for himself?

Nausea swirled to life in Landon's gut as a heavy weight of realization settled over his shoulders. Landon might not see this week as a "business" transaction, but what if Toby couldn't separate the two?

After years of living under the oppressive thumb of a handler—his body and choices not his own—it might be difficult for Toby to accept the true freedom Landon had hoped to offer. And if he still believed, even subconsciously, that Landon somehow *owned* him because he'd paid for this week...

Landon's heart twisted. Toby was right. When he'd reminded Landon he was a prostitute and said that was the only way he could do things, it was because that's all he knew. It didn't matter how Landon viewed their relationship. To Toby, Landon was a paying client.

Jesus. Had anything they'd done been by Toby's choice?

Landon forced a cheerful smile on his face and pulled out of Toby's hold. He took a defensive step away so Toby wouldn't reach for him again and shoved his hands into his pockets so he wouldn't do the same. "No bad news, but, ah, I do have a bit of a headache. I might go take a nap."

"Okay, I'll come with—"

"No." The word snapped out of Landon's throat with far more vigor than he'd intended. He swallowed and amped up the wattage on his faux-happy smile. "I mean, ah, there's no need for you to waste your afternoon napping because I'm feeling crappy. Why don't you go out and do something? There's still about a million places you haven't been. You've got the debit card and cash I gave you, right? And the key to the car?"

Landon's liaison at the private investigation firm had sent a status update via email that morning. They had a few potential leads but nothing solid. It made more sense for Landon to focus his attention on figuring out a plan B in case they came up empty-handed rather than continuing to play an unwilling yet very real role in the perpetuation of Toby's captivity.

Even if Landon's feelings for Toby could never truly be returned in kind, Landon would still see his promise fulfilled. Toby would find his freedom if it was the last thing Landon did.

Toby's brows drew into a tight V, his vivid hazel eyes darkening. "Are you trying to get rid of me, Landon?"

Yes. No. "Of course not." Landon swallowed and rocked on his heels. "But I don't want to ruin your day."

"It's impossible to ruin my day so long as I get to spend it with you. Lying in bed holding you sounds a thousand times better than going into the city alone." Toby took a step forward, a soft grin pulling at his lips as he reached for Landon.

But Landon dodged his touch, trying to pull off the deliberate parry as an unfortunate coincidence by skirting around the closest chair and grabbing his phone off its seat. "No, really, you should go enjoy yourself. It's beautiful today." He motioned out the windows with his chin. "I-I won't be good company."

"Okay." Toby folded his arms in what was likely

meant to be a defiant gesture, but it came across as more of a self-protective hug, and Landon's heart constricted beneath his sternum. "You know, if you've changed your mind about having me here, I can plead your case to Joseph. He might be willing to give you a refund for what's left of the week."

"Jesus, Toby, no." Landon tossed his phone onto the chair again and speared both hands into his hair as he paced in front of the floor-to-ceiling windows. "I don't want you to leave. I just…"

"Don't want me around, either." Toby tightened his arms across his chest and lowered his gaze to the floor. "It's okay, Landon. I understand. The last thing I want is to be a burden. I can keep out of your hair until you're ready for me. And if you decide you don't want that anymore either, let me know. I'll bow out gracefully, I promise."

Landon's heart slammed into his throat. *Jesus.* He was making Toby feel like the whore he never should've been. He was hurting this beautiful man to alleviate his own guilt and unease.

What was his fucking problem? Why was he being such an ass? How was he…

It hit him like a two-ton elephant had copped a squat square in the middle of his chest. Landon turned away from Toby, his heart thundering within the hollow cavity of his chest. He dropped his forehead to the glass, then slumped to the ground.

He'd fallen in love. Sometime between the first night he'd paid for Toby's attention and now, he'd lost his heart. And yet he couldn't even be sure Toby had exercised free will in their relationship. There was a distinct possibility Landon had fallen in love with a man he'd inadvertently forced to be with him. God, what was wrong with him? He was a bigger monster than any of Toby's other "clients." At least they weren't wolves hiding in sheep's clothing.

Landon drew up his knees and hugged them to his

chest, burying his face in the space where his body hunched together. Toby's strong arms encircled his shoulders and pulled him into a tender embrace.

Selfless, brave, kindhearted Toby. He'd lived through hell and still found a way to put the world's troubles above his own.

"If I'm stepping over a line here, tell me, and I'll go." Toby's voice was thick, and his words pierced through Landon's heart like an arrow covered in poisoned brambles, leaving it fractured and bleeding.

Clutching at Toby, frightened he'd leave despite being the one pushing him away only moments before, Landon hiccupped out a sob. "I'm so sorry. I'm so, so sorry."

"Shh." Toby placed a gentle hand to Landon's temple, urging him to nestle against his chest. "Don't be sorry. I meant what I said before. No response is wrong if it's honest. It's okay to change your mind about what you want. I certainly don't blame you, and I won't make it difficult on you. I hope you'll accept my apologies if I did something wrong. If you felt pressured in some way, or overwhelmed, or... or forced. That wasn't my intent. I thought... Well, it doesn't matter what I thought. I'm sorry either way."

Landon's swollen eyes drifted open as he took in Toby's words. *Fuck.* He still thought Landon wanted to send him back to that horrible man and that terrible life. And yet, despite that belief, he was down here, on the floor, comforting Landon. He even apologized in case he'd done something wrong, for Christ's sake.

"Jenks, you're an asshole," Landon muttered the self-directed insult under his breath, then pushed out of Toby's hold. He swiped at his eyes in a vain attempt at clearing his hazy vision, but as soon as he'd wiped those tears away, more rushed in to take their place. He shifted to find Toby blinking at him with terror and hurt brightening his gaze.

"You are *such* an asshole." Landon cursed himself a second time, then widened his eyes and shook his head at the look of dejected pain flashing over Toby's face. "No, no, that was directed at *me*, not you."

Landon scooted forward to close the distance between them and took Toby's hands in his, threading their fingers together and squeezing. "*I'm* the asshole. I... I thought I was doing the right thing, but I don't know what that is anymore."

He groaned and lifted one of their joined hands to his lips so he could brush kisses over Toby's knuckles. "You were right. Way back at the beginning, you said this could never work, but I refused to believe it. I refused to see the truth."

Toby crooked his head to the side. "There's zero pressure here, Landon. You know that, right? I'm yours in whatever way you want me to be, and that includes giving you space if that's what you need. I shouldn't have pressured you to let me stay. That was wrong."

Anger shot through Landon's chest like a bolt of lightning. "Toby, why are you here?"

"Because you were generous enough to buy me this week of freedom." He wrinkled his brow. "And because there's nowhere else I'd rather be."

Landon sighed and brought one of Toby's hands up, pressing the warm palm to his own bearded cheek and holding it there. "There's nowhere else I'd rather be either. I don't want you to leave; even when I said I did, I didn't. I'm... scared."

Closing his eyes, Landon allowed himself a moment to steel his resolve before continuing. "I trust you, but I don't trust myself. And I certainly don't expect you to trust me. If I'd known the truth of your situation, that first night never would've happened. I thought I was paying someone who'd chosen that line of work. Someone who wanted to... Hell. Even then, I don't know what I was thinking. Everything about this is wrong. You deserve so much better. *So* much better. And instead of giving you the true freedom you deserve, I trapped you here. I made you... I mean, I *paid* for this. Again. God, I'm so fucking sorry."

"Oh, sweetheart." Toby's voice broke as he pulled Landon in for a sweet, passionate kiss that left Landon dizzy and off-balance. "Please don't think, for one minute, I'm not here by choice. I told you that first night, if I could have, I would've refunded you. It wasn't about the money then, and it isn't about the money now. Not with you. But no matter how much I want it to be, how much *we* want it to be, what we have can't last beyond this week. Come Saturday, I'll go back to Joseph's, and you'll move on and find someone worthy of sharing a bright, beautiful future with you."

Landon's jaw tightened. No way in hell was he going to let Toby go back to that bastard and that existence. He would find a way to fix this, no matter what it took. But in the meantime, he wouldn't press the issue. He couldn't blame Toby for being skeptical and guarding what little hope he had left. He'd lived a life of fear and pain and horrific obligation for far too long to believe it would all disappear because Landon said it would.

And if Toby said he was here by choice; Landon would believe him. Refusing to grant Toby his rightful agency in this situation would be as bad if not worse than trying to steal it away.

He'd just make sure Toby had every opportunity to say no.

"I'd like to amend one part of our earlier conversation." Landon straightened his shoulders, resolve steadying his pulse and centering his thoughts. "I think we should reconsider setting safewords. *Both* of us. And not solely for in the bedroom."

"Okay." Toby wet his lips and squinted one eye. "I'm on board with anything that makes you feel safe. Especially if it helps me to not screw up. But why would I need them?"

Landon ran a hand over his beard to give himself a moment. "Because, no matter how much I wish it weren't true, there's no escaping the fact that I paid for you to be here with me. I trust you, and I want to believe things between us haven't been impacted by that reality, but at the end of the day, it *is* our reality. So, if we're going to continue as we've started, I want there to be safeguards in place."

Toby opened his mouth to protest, but Landon held a gentle finger over his lips to silence him. "The situations are similar, really. As is the need for safewords. It's true, we might be in the middle of something where no doesn't really mean no for me, or where I need to be able to tell you where I'm at in as few words as possible. But the same could be said for you."

Pinching his brows, Toby motioned Landon to continue with a tilt of his chin.

Landon sighed and scrubbed his sweaty palms over the soft cotton of his pajama pants. "I believe you want to be here. I do. But you've also lived a life void of choice for so long I worry you might run into moments where it's difficult to say how you really feel. Or where you aren't sure *how* you really feel. I need to know, for my own sanity if nothing else, that we've put something into place to combat that possibility. Even if it isn't the best answer, at least it's *something*."

With a shake of his head, Toby leaned over to plant a chaste kiss at the corner of Landon's mouth. "You're amazing, you know that? It's hardly necessary, but the fact that you care enough to worry means more than I can possibly say."

Landon dropped his eyes and curled his lips in to hide a smile. "Trust me, I care."

"I know you do." Toby knuckled under Landon's chin to drag his gaze back up. "And so do I."

This time, Landon allowed the smile to freely stretch his lips. "So, what'll your safewords be, big guy?"

A short, quick laugh brightened Toby's face. "Well, if we want them to exist outside the bedroom too..." He tapped a finger over his lips and squinted an eye. "How about *bourbon* for stop—because I despise the smell of that liquor, so you can bet your ass I won't be saying it in casual conversation—and..." He twisted his mouth and hummed in thought. "Maybe *wintergreen* for slow down?"

A flash of Garret, downing his favored bourbon sour before crowding into Landon's space, drew his lips into a sneer. Paired with a memory of his father, who always chewed wintergreen gum to cover the scent of his evening cigar so Landon's mother would kiss him good-night... Yeah. He was sold. "Mind if I use yours too? I'm rather opposed to both smells myself."

Toby chuckled. "Well, that's handy."

"Okay, so, safewords. Check." Landon popped his brows three times in quick succession. "I wouldn't be opposed to putting them to the test. You know, maybe find us a situation where there's a slightly higher probability that one of them might prove useful?"

To Landon's utter delight, Toby's megawatt grin illuminated his face. "You trying to start something, Jenks?"

Landon pursed his lips in a pathetic attempt at hiding his smirk. "Oh yeah, Carmichael, I'm trying to start something."

Toby ran his tongue over his top lip, then cocked a brow. "In that case, why don't we move this party to the bedroom? While I'm all about spontaneity, there are certain *tools* our current locale lacks." He shot a wink in Landon's direction, then stood and held out his hand. "Come on, babe, let's go see how limber you are."

Landon took Toby's proffered hand and allowed Toby to pull him to his feet. A thousand butterflies danced in his belly, the erratic rhythm of their wings tickling his ribs.

Oh yes, he'd been a fool. Not for falling in love, but

for fighting it. For questioning not only his own heart, but the unfailing trust Toby inspired. Their future wasn't certain, and Landon couldn't guarantee Toby would return the love he felt, but none of that mattered. Not really. What mattered most was, in this moment, Toby was his, and he was Toby's.

For now, Landon would relish every minute he had with the man he loved. Starting with the delectable scene about to unfold.

Chapter Twenty

Toby bent over Landon and nibbled at his earlobe. "So far, so good, sweetheart?"

Landon's breath escaped his lungs on short, quick, panting exhales, and he nodded. "So far, s-so very, *very* good."

"You up for more?"

Again, Landon jerked his head to the affirmative. "Pl-please."

"As you wish, handsome. Spread your legs." Toby levered off the bed so he could admire the beauty bared before him. Landon was bent forward over the mattress, his feet planted on the floor. That glorious ass exposed. His hands were secured behind his back in the traditional hand-cuff style but using a length of the bondage rope Toby found in the nightstand drawer.

Toby crouched by Landon's left leg, trailing kisses from the crease of his behind all the way to the top of his foot. He retrieved another length of rope draped around his neck and secured a two-column tie around Landon's ankle and the footboard. Landon writhed his hips in response. Toby stood and landed a cracking spank on Landon's left buttcheek. "Stay. Still. No grinding on the bed. Your pleasure belongs to me, remember?"

Landon whimpered but stilled his hips. "Yes, sir."

Toby rubbed a palm over Landon's reddened cheek as a reward for good behavior, then shifted his attention to his right foot. Again, he rained kisses down Landon's leg before nudging the inside of his ankle. "Here's where we test your flexibility, sweetheart. Think you can go a little wider?"

Landon was nearly stretched to the limit, but he didn't hesitate to comply. Toby helped him move the needed distance, then tied his ankle to the bedpost closest to the headboard, leaving him splendidly spread and deliciously vulnerable. He tested the bindings to be sure they were secure but not too tight and then ran his fingers up the backs of Landon's thighs and massaged his magnificent ass. "Okay?"

"More than." Landon huffed out a breath. "Just... Fuck. Will you touch me? Please? Everywhere. Anywhere. I need to feel you right now."

Toby had zero qualms fulfilling that request. "Anything for you, babe."

By the time he finished leisurely suckling and licking and teasing, Landon was a mewling mess. But he kept his hips still, leaving his pleasure to Toby as he'd been ordered. The thrill of that blind, all-in deference had Toby's dick throbbing, but it also did something unexpected to his insides.

A rolling wave of longing for *more*—for more than the week they had, for more of this man he couldn't get enough of—clashed with an unexpected current of genuine, honest-to-goodness self-confidence. Not the manufactured kind Toby put on as a front to protect his bruised and battered psyche, but an authentic swell of emotion. Maybe he really could be what this beautiful man needed. Somehow worthy of that gilded future so far outside his grasp.

The need for intimacy and closeness with Landon—whose stunning body was only surpassed by the kindness of his heart, the cleverness of his mind, and the gentleness of his soul—nearly suffocated Toby with its intensity. If his future wasn't mapped out with striking clarity and irrevocable certitude, there was little doubt what he would choose for himself.

He would choose Landon. He would open his heart and offer it freely without fear or insecurity. Landon would understand the vulnerability attached to an action that big, and he wouldn't tread on Toby's offering, even if he himself couldn't return the words in kind.

But something deep inside Toby knew that wasn't true. Not his conviction that Landon would never hurt him, but that Landon could never love him.

Because as Toby draped his naked body over Landon's and locked their lips in a kiss filled with yearning, promise, and connection, that last thread of protection encasing his heart was obliterated. And when he opened his lids and caught Landon staring at him, he knew he wasn't alone in this tempest of emotional turmoil.

He loved this man, and he believed—with every fiber of his raw, exposed heart—Landon could love him too. Someday.

At least he'd have this warmth in his heart and these sweet, wonderful memories to get him through the darkness ahead. It was far more than he'd had a week ago and far more than he could've ever hoped to find.

Toby trailed kisses and licks and nips down the skin of Landon's back, over his bound arms, and around each perfectly curved globe of his backside. He let his fingers follow in the wake of his lips, kneading and stroking and loving every inch of Landon's flesh.

When he traced his tongue up the seam of Landon's ass, swirling it in gentle circles over that sensitive opening, Landon whined. "T-Toby, please, I... I need... I-I can't..."

Toby placed a kiss at the center of each cheek before rising to his feet. "What do you need, sweetheart? Talk to me."

"*You*." The word was spoken with such force and assertion, Toby grinned.

"You already have me. You have *all* of me. I'm yours." If only he could tell Landon how true those words were. They weren't sexual banter. Joseph might own his body for now, but Landon owned his heart. Forever. Toby pressed his cock into the crevice of Landon's ass, sliding it back and forth between his clenched cheeks. "Can you take a little more? Or do you need me to stop?"

Landon turned into the mattress and nodded, his fists clasping tighter behind his back.

Toby tilted Landon's chin with a gentle nudge. Once their eyes connected, he brushed those dark, damp bangs from his forehead. "I asked two distinctly different questions, sweetheart. Which are you saying yes to?"

"M-more. I... This... It's good, Tobes. It's so good." Landon squeezed his lids closed and blew out a quivering breath. "I feel... safe. Protected. Understood. *Insanely* turned on. It's... it's perfect."

Another rush of conflicting emotions warred inside Toby, and his dick wept for attention. He wanted to give Landon the world and then some. He wanted to make him squirm and cry and moan and beg. He wanted to make him feel... *everything*.

Deciding Landon had suffered enough indirect teasing—for now—Toby snatched the items he'd set aside on the dresser, out of Landon's view, and settled back between his legs. He snicked open the bottle of lube and coated the necessary bits of the first item before placing another dollop on two of his fingers.

When Toby's cool, goop-covered digits pressed against Landon's opening, he bucked into the mattress, earning him another sharp thwack across the butt. He groaned, the sound amplifying when Toby inserted his first finger and sought out his prostate. At the first stroke, a slew of colorful curses spilled past those exquisite lips.

Toby took his time working his second finger inside, teasing Landon's sweet spot with each inward thrust. Once satisfied with the prep, he pushed the tip of the slim vibrator into the well-lubed opening. He guided the object in until it was flush with Landon's backside, its secondary appendage pressed against his perineum for added stimulation.

Landon went still as Toby situated the device, then trembled in anticipation. Toby took hold of his own throbbing dick, giving himself a few conciliatory strokes with his lube-coated hand before switching on the vibrator.

A low, pulsating growl emitted from Landon, and his hips swiveled.

"Ah, ah, ah, sweetheart, what did I tell you about keeping still?" Toby cracked a sharp slap across one cheek, then placed a matching blow to his other. When the stinging smacks only spurred on Landon's helpless moaning and grinding, Toby made a tsking noise at the back of his throat. "Well, this won't do, will it?"

He wandered into the bathroom and wet a washcloth, then cleaned the lube from his dick. When he returned to the bedroom, Landon had buried his face in the bedspread. An incessant rumbling of muffled curses and whimpering cries floated through the space, but his body had stilled.

Climbing onto the mattress, Toby guided Landon up by the shoulders so he leaned—albeit with his legs very, very far apart—against the side of the bed. On his knees facing Landon, Toby was taller than him. He angled his gaze to meet those pleading eyes mired in abject desperation with a soft smile.

Toby stroked his own cock once, twice, then let go. He was almost positive those tears welling in Landon's eyes stemmed from sexual frustration—something he insisted he enjoyed, and Toby thrived on giving him—but he refused to leave it to chance. "This all good, babe?"

In a transfixed haze, Landon glanced away from Toby's dick and latched his hungry gaze on Toby. "So totally good." He licked his lips, then let his lids drift shut. "I've never been so miserably happy in all my life. I mean, I'm n-not miserable… Well, I kind of am… but, like, in the best, most amazing way possible and…"

Landon opened his eyes and returned his pleading stare to Toby's. "Please tell me you're about to make me suck your cock, because if not, I'll totally beg for the privilege."

It was Toby's turn to groan. He fisted a hand into Landon's hair and guided him—gently—to his dick. Landon took him straight down in one fell swoop. Toby's head tipped back on a growling moan, and he released his grip on Landon, allowing him the freedom to suck, lick, and tease at his own pace.

Pressure—a sweet, delicious pressure—built at Toby's core. As he was about to pull away, Landon's breath hitched, and his eyes squeezed closed. Toby slipped his cock free and cupped Landon's chin. "I don't want you to come until I'm buried inside you, understood? Focus, sweetheart, and *breathe*. Don't. Come."

Landon nodded but kept his eyes closed, a bleating whimper rolling up his throat.

Toby climbed off the bed and returned to his little pile of naughty paraphernalia. He extricated the lube as well as a condom and dressed his dick. He massaged Landon's reddened cheeks, giving each a perfunctory slap that had Landon mewling as Toby pressed his lower back and eased him to his belly.

He flicked off the humming vibrator, and Landon cried out in surprise and bitter relief. When Toby pulled the device free, a sob broke through the air in the shape of Toby's name. He placed his dick at Landon's opening and slipped the tip inside, kneading his ass as he did. "It's okay, babe. I'm gonna take care of you. I'm gonna make you feel *so good*. I promise."

Landon jerked his head, then pressed against Toby's cock until it slid the rest of the way home. "I need you, To-bes. Pl-please, fuck me."

A warmth stole through Toby that was partially due to Landon's glorious begging but had more to do with an overwhelming realization. For the first time in his life, he wasn't going to "fuck." He was going to make love.

That thought heated Toby's blood and sent a shiver of delectable longing over his sweat-slickened flesh as he draped over Landon's back and dove into his mouth, plundering every inch of its sweet depths. His hips drove forward in a methodical rhythm, aimed to strike Landon's prostate. They climbed the tandem peaks of their release, and in a moment so breathtakingly superb it nearly shattered Toby with its perfection, they came. Together.

Landon's soft snores were the only thing disturbing the early-evening stillness. They both lay on their sides, facing each other, and Toby held him pressed close to his chest, stroking his soft black hair with reverent fingers.

After their shared, earth-shattering orgasms, Toby had untied Landon, one limb at a time, and massaged the pins and needles from his stiff, aching muscles. He'd kissed every inch of flesh he could reach as he did and cooed soft, loving words filled with promise and pride and adoration. Once he'd been sure Landon's body no longer pained him, he'd gone to the bathroom, discarded the condom, hastily cleaned himself, then returned to Landon with a warm washcloth. He wiped him down, then drew back the covers, lifted Landon's lax form into his arms, and tucked them both beneath the sheets.

Within minutes of snuggling into Toby's embrace, while Toby continued his soft stroking and gentle words of affirmation, Landon drifted off.

Toby's mind was too cluttered and his heart too full to join Landon in sleep. Far too aware of the impermanence of it all, he savored every breath fanning over his chest, every inch of soft, warm skin pressing against his own.

Eventually, Landon stirred. He nuzzled his bearded cheek into Toby's neck, placing breathy kisses against his pulse point. "Hi."

That single word drew a smile to Toby's lips. "Hi. Did you sleep well?"

Landon nodded into Toby's throat. "I slept like the dead. I'm not sure I've ever felt so well rested and so bone-deep exhausted all at once. It's... fantastic."

Toby chuckled. "Why don't you stay in bed for a bit longer? If you don't mind me poking around your kitchen unattended, I'll go make us something to eat."

"What's mine is yours, Tobes." Landon shoved away so he could catch his gaze with Toby's. "I mean it. You don't ever have to ask permission or feel like you're intruding. Take whatever you want, do whatever you want."

Toby smirked to cover the twinge of pain at those words. He wasn't going to be around long enough to make use of such a grandiose offer. "All right, I'll go whip us up some din—"

"Oh shit... What time is it?" Landon sat bolt upright, his eyes seeking out the alarm clock. A squeak of distress escaped his throat, and he jumped out of bed. "Oh my god! It's after six. How is it after six?"

"Ah, because you took a nap?"

"A *three-hour nap*?" Landon slapped his hands to his cheeks in the most devastatingly adorable way and stared at Toby with his mouth hanging open. "Why did you let me sleep for so long?"

Toby scratched his eyebrow with a thumbnail and squinted at Landon. "Because you needed it?"

Landon grabbed Toby's wrist and tugged. "Get up. We have to shower. We're gonna be late. Shit, shit, shit."

"Late? For what?" Toby let Landon drag him into the bathroom, then leaned against the doorframe. He fought a grin as Landon raced around the room, turning on the shower, flicking on the towel warmer, and initiating an avalanche of toiletries in his attempt at freeing their toothbrushes.

Releasing a breathy chuckle, Toby strode over to Landon, who stared at the pile of personal products that lay at his feet with a deep frown. Toby took Landon's jaw in both hands, forcing their eyes to meet. "Landon, breathe. It's gonna be okay. Let me help you." He ran a thumb over Landon's trembling bottom lip. "What are we gonna be late for, sweetheart?"

"The g-game." Landon huffed out a breath. "It was supposed to be a surprise. I fucked it up."

"You didn't fuck anything up." Toby drew Landon in for a kiss, thankful when he melted against him and deepened the kiss of his own accord. Toby hummed in appreciation before pulling away. "I'd say I'm thoroughly surprised, wouldn't you? What game are we going to, exactly?"

"Oh, ah, I called in a few favors." Landon's cheeks tinged pink, but a sweet smile lifted his lips. "I got us tickets to the players' Club Box on the lower level between the dugouts. Best seats in the house. And the guys said we could hit up the locker room afterwards if, you know, you wanted to meet anyone."

Toby's eyes widened, and he grinned so hard his cheeks hurt. "You're taking me to Wrigley Field? To see the Cubbies?"

"Well, yeah, I mean... you mentioned being a fan, I thought maybe—"

Landon cut off with whooping laughter as Toby lifted him by the hips and spun him in a circle, heedless to the screaming in his ribs. He set him down beside the steaming volley of water and gave his bare butt a hard, ringing smack. "Get that fine ass in the shower, babe. We've got stadium dogs and foamy beer in our future."

Chapter Twenty-One

Landon drifted awake to the smell of freshly brewed coffee. He threw out an arm, seeking the solid warmth of Toby, and frowned the rest of the way to consciousness when he found nothing but cold, empty sheets. He bolted upright, blinking around the dimly lit room, but saw no sign of Toby. The only hint he wasn't far away was the lingering bite of coffee in the air and, when Landon strained his ear, a faint baritone rumble coming from the kitchen.

He scrambled out of bed, emptied his bladder, brushed his teeth, then threw on a pair of athletic shorts and headed toward the sound of Toby's voice. Landon found him in the kitchen—bare-ass naked aside from the *Kiss the Cook* apron he'd tied around his front—slicing peppers and belting out, of all things, a show tune. Like, a sixty-plus-year-old show tune.

Landon grinned. He cocked a hip against the hallway wall and folded his arms over his chest, settling in to enjoy the show. Toby's voice was made for music, its vibrato spot-on, and the low, rumbling bass smooth as silk and perfectly on pitch. Why hadn't Toby mentioned he could sing? Like, *sing*-sing. Really fucking well.

When Toby angled around to turn on the gas stovetop, his eyes caught Landon's lurking form, and his melodic crooning halted. His face flamed red, and the cutting board he held, piled high with sliced peppers and onions, clattered to the floor. "Shit," he grumbled, scowling at the mess. "I thought you'd sleep another hour, at least. Did I wake you?"

Smacking a hand over his mouth, Landon lurched forward. "I'm so sorry. I didn't mean to startle you like that. I should've announced my presence sooner." When Toby offered a crooked grin and waved him off, tossing the cutting board into the sink before bending to start scooping the veggies into a pile, Landon hurried over to the small closet that held his cleaning supplies and retrieved the broom and dustpan. Before he could start sweeping up the spill, Toby snatched the broom from his hands and pointed to a stool.

"Sit. I've got this."

Landon hesitated a beat, until Toby raised a brow and pointed—again—at the stool.

"Ah, yes, sir." Clearing his throat, Landon leaned in to kiss Toby on the cheek, then skirted out of his way and took up residence at the kitchen island as instructed. He propped his chin on his fist and enjoyed the view while Toby swept up the spilled veggies. His gorgeous, fully exposed back and butt muscles bunched and rippled with the task. "I didn't know you could sing."

Toby shrugged. "I did musical theater in high school, alongside football and hockey. Kept me insanely busy, but I loved it. All of it." He dumped the ruined vegetables into the trash and returned the broom to the closet. "I think that's what tipped everyone off. You know, before I even told them."

"Before you told them what?"

"That I was gay." Toby peeked at Landon over his shoulder before grabbing a clean cutting board. He moved to the spot he'd stood before and pulled out a fresh green pepper. "I'm not exactly effeminate or anything, and I tried really hard to keep my wandering eyes off the boys at first, but everyone seemed to know already when I told them. My parents, my little sister, my friends. I was expecting some big shock-and-awe moment, but mostly I got pats on the back and a few 'it's about time' comments. A few of my classmates started avoiding me after I came out, but most everyone was super welcoming and chill about it."

Landon's gaze dropped to the marble countertop, and he traced the varied grains with his eyes. "I'm really glad you had a positive experience."

"Yeah, well, looking back, I'm guessing some of it had to do with my size. I've always been into lifting, so I was ripped even as a junior in high school. Plus, I'd fallen into the, for lack of a better term, *popular crowd*, since I did sports, so that acted as a buffer too." Toby appeared at Landon's side and threaded their fingers together. "I wish you'd had a similar experience. I hate knowing how horrible yours was."

Landon offered a flat-lipped smile. "I only came out to my folks. And, later, Steffon. Plus, you know, the handful of guys I tried, and failed, to have clandestine relationships with. No one else knew. I made damn sure of that. Well, I mean, until I allowed an internationally aired TV show to broadcast the news to all the world at the ripe old age of thirty-five." He groaned and dropped his forehead to the cool granite. "I'm such a tool."

Toby squeezed their hands together. "Look at me, sweetheart." When Landon obeyed, Toby offered a soft smile. "We all have our stories, some better, some worse. Until being queer is considered as normal and acceptable as being cishet, coming out will be something people across the gender and sexuality spectrum will have to face. But what you did? It was brave and strong, and it *helps*. Having a well-respected professional athlete come out as gay normalizes it, and anything that brings the LGBTQ+ community into a positive light is a step in the right direction."

"Normalizes?" Landon snorted. "Hardly. That episode got a lot of backlash. There was support too, but... definitely hate. I just wish I'd had the balls to come out earlier in life. I've always idolized strong-willed advocates like Xavier Wolfe for giving the middle finger to everyone, including the homophobes in the sports world who didn't think him worthy because of who he chooses to warm his sheets."

"But the more people like Xavier Wolfe who aren't afraid to come out and tell the world, loud and proud, that they don't fit society's norms, the better. Especially those who hold influential positions in our fame-hungry society, like certain famous, sexy baseball players turned entrepreneurs." Toby kissed Landon's knuckles before returning to his chopping. "Got any plans for today?"

"Well, ah, actually..." Landon blew out a breath and massaged a hand into his tense neck muscles. While their experience at the ballpark the night before had been filled with laughter and excitement and countless stolen kisses, ass grabs, and hand holding, Landon had also caught Toby's veiled discomfort.

It was something he'd worried about, and something Toby did quite an impressive job of hiding, but it was clear as day the night before. During several different instances.

Toby didn't like Landon paying for everything, and who could blame him? Money for any couple held a fundamental thread of power and control that could lead to issues. Money for them? It went even deeper than that. It hinted at bastardized ownership and played around the edges of questionable consent and distrust.

Toby had bent over backward to thank Landon for his grand gesture and seemed genuinely gracious and thrilled, but Landon hadn't missed the underlying unease at the expense entailed. He had no intention of adding to that discomfort, so his original plans to continue their tour of Chicago's finest—and, in many cases, quite expensive—tourist spots fizzled on the spot.

An idea wriggled into his mind as Toby tossed him a quizzical glance over his shoulder.

Landon sat up a little straighter as the thought bloomed brighter. "What would you say to a day trip?"

That unease crept over Toby's face but was quickly replaced with a smile. "Sure, I'm down for whatever, as long as I get to spend it with you. Where we headed?"

"Nowhere in particular."

Toby cocked a brow as he turned on the gas and placed a frying pan over the open flame to preheat. "We gonna hop on a train and see where it takes us?"

"No." Landon grinned. "I was thinking more like hopping on a motorcycle. One of my favorite things to do is to take long meandering rides into the country. There's nothing quite like the feel of the wind on your cheeks while the beauty of nature whips by your periphery."

Toby's smile kicked up a few notches into a genuine megawatt Toby-grin. "That sounds fan-fuckin'-tastic."

"Good." Landon pursed his lips to hide his smirk and leaned onto his elbows. "So, you're cooking me breakfast."

If possible, that grin cranked up another level. "I am. I'm no Landon Jenks, chef extraordinaire, but I can find my way around a kitchen. I figured it was the least I could do after… well, after everything you've done for me." His smile faded a little, replaced with that disquiet Landon had hoped to assuage with the thrifty bike trip. But Toby shook it off, the grin returned, and he refocused on his omelets. "Why don't you grab a shower? I've already had mine. Breakfast should be ready and waiting by the time you're done. Then we can hit the road."

Landon hopped off his stool. "Sounds perfect." He swung past Toby to steal a kiss before heading into the bedroom to get cleaned up. He pulled up his email app while the water heated, and frowned when he found the email he was looking for. That morning's update from the PI.

They only had a few days until Toby was due back at that bastard's prison, yet the most expensive and respected private investigation firm in the country was still coming up short on answers. They'd sprung an infinite well of questions but couldn't manage to answer a single fucking one. At least, none Landon could leverage to free Toby from his captive hell.

Resolve flooded through Landon as he stepped under the punishing spray of the shower alone—and surprisingly lonely—for the first time in days. Today would be about Toby, in all ways and in all things. And while they pressed close and enjoyed the beauty of the open road together, something Landon couldn't wait to share with Toby, he would think.

After all, he did his best thinking on the seat of a bike, with the whole world stretched before him. Today would be the day he figured out how to save the man he loved. With or without the damn law on his side.

It was the perfect weather for a ride. Puffy white clouds muted the heat but didn't promise rain, allowing them to wear the necessary safety gear—jeans, lightweight but long-sleeved biker jackets, and helmets—without the discomfort of a punishing sun.

Landon had already stopped once for gas, but mostly as an excuse to check on Toby. Having him pressed against his back while he rode kept a permagrin tilting Landon's lips, but he had to be sure Toby was enjoying himself before they got much farther out. The longer they rode in one direction, the longer it would take to get home, and he didn't want Toby miserable.

He was pleasantly surprised by Toby's enthusiasm. He'd bounced around the gas station like a five-year-old on Christmas morning, chattering about the rush he'd felt on the bike and how charming he'd found the picturesque scenery. Then he'd waggled his eyebrows and admitted to having a hard-on the entire trip, thanks to the vibration of the motor and Landon's "sexy ass."

It was getting to be lunchtime, so Landon headed for an entrance ramp to the expressway. The two-lane road they'd been traveling was mostly scenic. They would have better luck finding food off the main drag. Plus, it was time to think about heading home. They'd been on the road for four hours already, which meant they had at least that much to look forward to before getting back to the city.

"Keep your eyes peeled for somewhere you might like to grab lunch." Landon's voice echoed in his own ears as he spoke into the helmet communication system.

"Roger that, good buddy. Ten-four. Over and out."

Landon rolled his eyes. Toby had treated their talks over the comm like a child might treat his first walkie-talkie experience. Like an adorable little asshole. Rather than verbally responding, Landon bumped his butt back into—*yep*—Toby's hard cock and snickered when he groaned through the speakers.

They decided on a fast-food joint and scarfed their burgers in the parking lot. Landon twisted in the seat so he could face Toby, draping his legs over Toby's and leaning against the dash. "Your ass handling the long ride okay, baby?"

Toby quirked a brow as he chewed and swallowed his blessedly normal-sized bite. To Landon's delight, he'd made a concerted effort to eat in a less frightening fashion after his plea the day before.

"My butt's fine. It's my dick that's crying. Being perpetually turned on is brutal, man." He pouted out that full lower lip and pinched his brows. "The real question is, how are *you* holding up? Your sexy ass was still rocking pink cheeks when we made love last night." He popped his brows a few times before tearing off another bite.

Landon froze with his burger halfway to his mouth. Had Toby really referred to the sweet, sensuous sex they'd had after the game last night as making love? He swallowed air. It had to be a slip of the tongue. No way he'd meant it the way Landon so fucking wished he'd meant it. His heart ached, but he forced himself to take a bite before Toby caught on to his unhinged response to that casual turn of phrase.

"Babe?" Toby knuckled a finger under Landon's chin, forcing his gaze to meet those gorgeous hazel eyes. "You're worrying me. Are you okay with what happened yesterday? You can tell me the truth. I'm so totally, a thousand percent okay with sticking to vanilla for what's left of our time together. Just being with you rocks my world. I don't need any spicy extras. I promise."

Landon's stomach roiled, and the greasy food threatened to make a reappearance. It broke his heart to know Toby still believed there was no hope. That he still thought he'd be sent back to Joseph's on Saturday, and that would be that.

No fuckin' way that was happening. An idea had kernelized in Landon's brain, but he wanted to talk it through with Steffon before broaching the topic with Toby. He needed to figure out the logistics first. So, for now, he wouldn't touch on that part of Toby's statement.

"I'm more than okay with what happened, Tobes." Landon leaned forward and brushed a knuckle down Toby's stubbled cheek. "I meant it when I said that was fuckin' amazing. I loved every minute of it. I'm sorry if I seemed a little distant there. It had *nothing* to do with that, okay? I promise. My brain's busy calculating our return time if we swing home now. We'd be hitting the city at rush hour."

Toby pursed his lips to the side in thought, thankfully buying Landon's excuse. "We could drive a little farther so our return trip falls later."

Landon nodded, but a little niggling of a thought had him grinning and shaking his head instead. "No, I have a better idea."

"Oh? And what's that?"

Landon winked and swung his legs off Toby's so he could hop to the ground. He stuffed their trash into the bag and headed toward the trash can, calling over his shoulder, "You'll just have to wait and see."

Toby's rumbling laughter echoed through Landon's helmet, bringing a grin to his lips as he pulled onto the off-ramp. Clearly, Toby spotted the same sign Landon had noticed earlier when they passed by this exit going the opposite direction.

Oversized letters on a giant billboard in garish neon pink and gaudy glittery gold proclaimed the words ADULT, ADULT, ADULT, with a big red flashing arrow pointing straight down at a ramshackle little building off an exit to Nowheresville. Landon pulled into the gravel lot and dropped the kickstand. He yanked off his helmet and angled a glance to catch Toby's Cheshire-cat grin as he tugged his own free.

Landon smirked. "I thought we could get into a little trouble here for a while. Kill some time. What do you say?"

"I knew you were smart, but this is bloody brilliant." Toby levered off the bike and proffered a hand to help Landon. He tugged him in for a lascivious kiss, then intertwined their fingers and pulled him toward the door.

When they stepped inside the run-down building, Landon's eyes popped. The interior looked nothing like the outside. It was surprisingly well-kept and packed to the gills with every possible sex toy, bondage device, and kinky costume a deviant, newly minted D/s couple could ever want.

They spent longer than planned roaming the aisles and filling their basket with far more items than they could possibly make use of in the two and a half days they had left before Toby was supposed to return to Joseph's. Even if they spent every waking moment experimenting with something new, it would be a stretch.

Landon relished that Toby didn't notice that fact, nor did his disquiet over money surface despite the excessive amount their bill would be. Perhaps, deep down inside that magnificent brain of his, the trust they shared was beating some sense into Toby's subconscious. Maybe he was starting to believe, as Landon did, that this life they were building wasn't transient, but could very well be their forever reality.

As they finished checking out, Toby tilted his head to the side. "You guys got a public restroom by chance?"

The cashier—a thin man in his early twenties sporting a faded '80s' hairband T-shirt—sneered at Toby, then rolled his eyes. "Yeah, in the back." He sniggered as he handed off a paddle with the word *bitch* cut into its face, presumably so it would leave that behind as an imprint on whatever buttcheek it smacked. A key dangled from the end. "It's for paying customers only, so it's locked."

Toby accepted the paddle with a graceful smile, then gathered up their purchases and guided Landon toward the back of the store. He unlocked the door and peeked inside, then tugged Landon in and snicked the door closed.

"Gotta pee, babe?" Toby leaned against the door and crossed his arms with a grin.

"Ah, no, I went after lunch, remember?"

"Just checking." Toby waggled his brows. "Drop your pants."

Landon's eyes drifted from Toby's smirking grin to the bag of sex toys at his feet. Anticipation coiled thick and heavy in his gut, and his cock stirred to life. Without a word, he undid his belt, popped the line of buttons on his fly, and pushed his jeans and boxer briefs around his knees.

"Good boy." Toby dug into the bag, rooting around for a minute before angling a glance at Landon. "Turn around and lean on the sink. Let me see that beautiful ass."

Again, without question, Landon obeyed. Toby gave his backside a few gentle caresses before landing an open-palmed smack that covered both cheeks and rang into the silence of the private bathroom. There was no doubt anyone standing outside could hear both that and Landon's follow-up groan. But he didn't care. Not one fucking bit.

Toby spread Landon's cheeks, and then something cold and wet appeared at his hole. "Brace yourself, babe. I don't have time for a thorough prep. Don't wanna get kicked out before I do what needs doing."

Landon nodded and focused on relaxing his muscles as Toby inserted what he guessed was a lubed-up butt plug. It stretched and burned but was clearly one of the smaller ones, as it hit home with no pain. Toby pressed his rock-hard, jeans-clad cock against Landon's butt, forcing the plug farther inside until it nudged his prostate. He bit his lip and canted his hips to guide it deeper still.

"Pants back on, sweetheart." Toby stepped away, digging through their purchases again as Landon complied. He stood up a moment later and turned to Landon with a lopsided, cocky grin in place. "Now, lift your shirt."

Landon swallowed at the sight of the nipple clamps. He unzipped his jacket and pulled up the T-shirt beneath with trembling hands. Toby noticed and placed one of his own steady palms over Landon's clenched fist. "This okay?"

Nodding with as much force as he could muster without bobbling his head off his shoulders, Landon tugged his shirt the rest of the way up. "So totally more than okay."

Toby wet his lips, then laved at Landon's left nipple. He sucked and nibbled and licked until it pebbled up, leaving Landon weak-kneed. Then he attached one of the clamps. It nipped at the sensitive flesh with a delicious bite that arrowed a jolt of electric desire straight into Landon's dick. Toby repeated the process on the right side, then ordered Landon to lower his shirt. The fabric brushed his now oversensitized nipples.

"All right, sweetheart, if you don't have to actually use the bathroom, we should probably vacate the premises before they kick us out."

Landon nodded and zipped his jacket, following Toby as he led them out of the store. The cashier smirked at Landon, and a flash of delicious heat flushed his skin. The kid might not know the specifics, but he could guess the gist of what went down in the bathroom. He would know Toby made use of their new purchases to satisfy Landon's hedonistic cravings. He would probably assume—and rightly so—that Landon's clothing hid an adornment or two.

It should bother him, shouldn't it? Knowing a stranger possessed such intimate, personal knowledge about things he'd always been taught to associate with disgrace and immoral debauchery.

But it didn't.

Sure, humiliation sizzled over his skin, but it fed something in him akin to the satisfaction he derived from pain. He couldn't explain how those seemingly negative feelings—physical agony and public shame—could twist and coil and morph to produce such heightened, pleasurable experiences. But for Landon, they did.

When Toby used a loving, trusting touch to offer such delicious torment, Landon soared. And when Toby held him close as he freefell into the abyss of emotional upheaval following his release, cooing and stroking and praising Landon until all he knew was *Toby* and the safety and care he provided, Landon was reborn. Over and over and over again.

So why *wouldn't* his chest swell with pride at the thought of facing a mortification orchestrated by Toby? There was no doubt he would've known as well as Landon did that the cashier could guess at the less-than-innocent nature of their shared bathroom time. Which meant Toby wanted Landon to feel this swell of gratification resulting from nothing more than the wicked idea that his misery pleased Toby.

At any other point in his life, Landon might've balked at the direction of his thoughts. But not now. Not when he was under Toby's careful control and caring command. He'd never felt so free to be himself or so safe to give in to his deepest, darkest desires. Because he knew Toby would be there to guide him and to pick up the pieces that might need to be mended and reshaped on their mutual path to discovery.

Toby packed their prizes into the saddlebags, then gave Landon space to climb awkwardly onto his bike. The second he sat down, the plug shoved farther in. He hissed through his teeth and levered off his backside. Toby hopped on behind him and pressed close, purring into his ear, "Rev this baby up. I can't wait to see what the rumble of that engine does if you're already getting squirmy."

Groaning, Landon cranked the starter and immediately regretted his eager compliance as the vibration not only hummed through the plug, but also the clips attached to his nipples.

Fuck. This was going to be one hell of a long ride.

Chapter Twenty-Two

Toby cursed and squeezed his arms tighter around Landon's waist. That heavy breathing over the comm, along with the occasional groan or whimper, was almost as torturous as Landon's lithe body squirming against his. The constant friction against his cock—enough to drive him fucking crazy, but not enough to finish the job—drew out moans and grumbles of his own.

He couldn't take another damn second. "Hey, babe?"

Landon grunted in response, wriggling his ass in the way that sent Toby's heart rate skyrocketing to match the throbbing beat in his desperate dick.

"Mind finding us somewhere to pull over?" Toby loosened his grip around Landon's middle and trailed a hand down to cup between his legs, thrilling at the hard bulge that kicked against his palm at the contact. "Somewhere with a little... privacy?"

"Oh god," Landon groaned, the speed of the bike picking up to complement his erratic breathing. "Yes, please."

It only took about ten minutes to find a field with a clump of oak trees at its center. Landon steered off the road and drove through the high grass and wildflowers, the added jostling causing them both to swear in tandem.

As soon as the bike slowed to a stop, Toby leapt off, not even waiting for Landon to cut the engine. He gave his needy cock a few mollifying rubs while he waited for Landon to settle the kickstand into the soft earth. Once he had, Toby grabbed his hips, helping to ease him off the bike and into his arms.

When Landon pressed flush against Toby's chest, his pelvis shot forward, grinding their cocks together with licentious abandon. "Holy. Fuck. I've n-never been so horny in my life." Landon gripped Toby's shoulders and panted against his ear.

"Tell me about it." Toby dug his fingers into Landon's hips. "Take your jacket and shirt off."

Landon scrambled to obey, his frenzied hands shaking as he fumbled with the zipper. As soon as he worked it free, he tore off his jacket, then made to tug his shirt over his head but paused when the fabric caught on the clamps. "Oh my fucking *god*. I never knew my nipples held this much power over my dick."

Toby reached under Landon's shirt and palmed his clamped nipples to protect them. Landon's eyes fluttered closed at the contact, and he tugged his shirt free without further aggravation. Once he'd gotten the tight white cotton over his head and flung it to the ground, Toby removed his hands and took in the magnificent sight of Landon's inked chest adorned with the metal clips.

"You're so fucking gorgeous, sweetheart." Toby traced a circle around Landon's left nipple, careful to avoid touching either it or the clamp, and was rewarded with a guttural groan. Landon's knees gave out for the briefest of moments, and Toby wrapped an arm around his waist to support him, then eased them both to the ground. He guided Landon onto his back among a bed of wildflowers and grinned at the ridiculously picturesque scene it made.

Then he removed the left clamp. Landon gasped and clutched at the foliage surrounding him. Knowing full well what Landon was experiencing—that sharp pain as blood flow returned in earnest to the tingling tissue that, for Toby, had been unnervingly erotic in those unwanted situations— he laved attention on the reddened nub. He suckled and licked and kissed while he worked to free Landon's cock, then encouraged Landon to grind into his fist as he writhed against the double-edged sword of pleasure and pain.

When Landon's frenetic movements slowed, Toby placed one last kiss over his freed nipple and traced his tongue across his chest to pull the still-clamped bud into his mouth. Landon fisted his hands further into the grass and dirt beneath him. "One more, babe. Are you ready?"

Landon took a few heavy, panting breaths, then sucked the last one in and held it, nodding his agreement moments before Toby liberated his flesh and employed the same soothing, worshipping actions he'd done for the other side. Landon thrashed against the sensation, a ravaged growl filling the air around them.

"T-Tobes..." Landon gasped. "I-I'm going to c-come... Please... Stop..."

Toby traced a few more comforting circles around Landon's nipple before lifting his head to look down at his beautiful man. "You don't want to come?"

Landon's shook his head. "N-no. Not yet. Please, n-not yet."

Obliging, Toby removed his hand so the wanton roll of Landon's hips could no longer find purchase. He placed his thumbs over Landon's inflamed nipples and brushed gentle strokes over the raised skin. Landon mewled and writhed and trembled with barely banked desperation.

Toby's own dick screamed for release, but savoring Landon took priority. He moved his hands across Landon's overheated skin, sketching the ink with his fingertips and enjoying the tremors humming beneath his touch.

Slowly, as Toby soothed and calmed, Landon quieted. His cock lay swollen and heavy against his belly, but the frenzied bucking of his hips subsided, and his breathing moved toward normal. Toby continued to run his hands over Landon's exposed flesh, shifting from his torso to trail light fingers over the quivering muscles of his arms.

He paused and retraced an area of Landon's forearm he'd skated over, narrowing his gaze. There were scars there. Rows and rows of interlacing marks, each one cleverly interwoven into the tribal tattoos covering his arm. But they were there. Clear as day, their silvery raised surfaces drawn out by the glaring afternoon sun.

In disbelief, Toby's gaze drifted over the rest of Landon's visible skin, seeking hidden damage camouflaged by ink. With a nauseating chill, Toby spotted more of the intricately designed tattoos curling and looping to mirror faintly visible mars on the tender flesh of Landon's other arm.

"Sweetheart?"

Landon hummed in response, turning his head toward Toby and squinting at him with a little half smile.

Toby ran his thumb over the marks on Landon's arm once again, cursing himself for not noticing them before. The tattoo artist who covered them was a genius, to say the least. "Where did you get these scars?"

Landon jerked free of Toby's grasp and sat up. He folded his arms tight across his chest. "It's not a big deal." He swallowed, then released his self-hug and stuffed his dick into his pants. "We should probably get going. It's, ah, getting late."

Before Landon could push to a standing position, Toby gripped his shoulders. "You don't have to tell me anything you're uncomfortable discussing." He moved a hand to cup Landon's bearded jaw. "But I'm here, sweetheart. If you need to talk, I'm here."

A single tear slid down Landon's cheek, but he kept his gaze locked on Toby's. Minutes stretched by, but his stare never wavered. Finally, his eyes drifted closed. "I was a cutter. I did it to myself. For years."

Toby wasn't sure what he'd expected Landon to say, but it hadn't been... that.

Before he could collect himself enough to come up with a response, Landon extricated himself from Toby's hold. His shoulders slumped as he traced the lines of a tattoo on his right forearm. "It didn't start until I was in middle school. Not until after I, ah, you know... after I told my mom I was gay."

Toby's stomach heaved, and his lunch threatened a reappearance.

Landon cast him a sidelong glance and a flat-lipped smile, as if he already knew the effect his words would have on Toby.

"My parents were never huge fans of mine. Especially my dad. But after that? Things kind of... deteriorated. It wasn't healthy, and I'm not proud, but it was the only coping mechanism I had to get me through some difficult times. Hell, I still fight the urge today when life gets tough. I probably always will." Landon shrugged, then leaned across the grass for his T-shirt. He slipped it over his head before standing. "Anyway, it really is getting late. We should get on the road. We still have three hours before we hit the city."

Toby stood and pulled Landon into a tender embrace. He pressed his mouth against Landon's ear. "You are a beautiful man, Landon Jenks. A beautiful man who has led a difficult, heartbreaking life. If I could take all your pain and make it my own, I would. The fact you've become the person you are today—kindhearted, generous, sweet, strong-willed, and endlessly good-natured—is a feat that defies all odds. Don't you dare believe anything anyone has ever said to the contrary. Promise me, when I'm gone, you won't settle for another asshole. You deserve so much better. You deserve to be treated like the king among men you are."

Landon clung to Toby and buried his face in the crook of his neck. Toby rubbed his back and murmured quiet words of comfort and encouragement, laced with the love he didn't dare voice.

When Landon finally pulled away, he snatched his jacket and pulled it on without looking at Toby.

Sucking in a steadying breath, Toby dropped his own gaze to the area of trampled grass where Landon had writhed beneath his touch. A single white daisy had survived, its stem standing tall and proud among its crushed brethren. He plucked it from the ground, playing his fingers over the velvety petals.

"Tobes?" Landon's voice drew Toby's attention. He stood beside the bike, helmet in hand. "You, ah, ready?"

Toby nodded and closed the distance between them. He tucked the flower into the open collar of Landon's jacket and placed a chaste kiss on the tip of his nose. How he wished he could proclaim his true feelings. The words itched to fall from his lips, but he held them back.

It wouldn't be fair to profess his love. Knowing Landon, he'd wait for Toby if those words were spoken, and Toby couldn't let that happen. Landon needed a clean break when this was over. He needed the freedom to find his future with a man who deserved him and all the happiness he offered.

Landon pulled the daisy free of his jacket and spun the petals over his lips. He offered a crooked smile. "My favorite flower has always been tulips, but that might change now."

Toby brushed a knuckle down the soft beard covering Landon's cheek and returned his smile with a soft one of his own. "Do you want to take out the plug before we leave? It might make for a more comfortable ride." He fingered the nipple clips in his pocket, but his cock lay dormant in his pants.

Landon shook his head. "No. I... I know this sounds

ridiculous, but it… I mean… it makes me…" He speared a hand through his hair. "When I'm under your control, I feel safe. Cherished. Protected. I kind of need that right now. I need that reminder. It's silly, I know, but…" He sighed and darted his eyes to the ground.

"Oh, sweetheart." Toby's chest tightened. "Nothing about that is even remotely silly. I truly believe what you're feeling is part of the package. I have some intense emotions intertwined with the things we've done I never would've guessed at before we did them. This isn't just about kinky sex. It goes so much deeper than that, and I can assure you, you are absolutely cherished. You're mine, and I'm yours, and I'd give you the world if I could."

Landon bit his lip, then smiled, the action tugging at the flesh trapped between his teeth. "You're a very, very good Dom, Tobes."

That brought a chuckle to Toby's lips. "Oh yeah? This from the guy who's as clueless as I am?"

Landon lifted a shoulder, his smile pulling into a grin. "I know more than you think."

"Oh, do you now? Had more experience in this department than you let on, have you?"

Laughing, Landon pulled on his helmet and hopped onto the bike. He flipped the visor up and turned to Toby. "It's called the internet, baby. It knows all. Now come on; we've got a long trip ahead of us and two saddlebags full of toys to try out when we get home."

About an hour into their ride, Landon's desperation returned and his wiggling resumed. In full force. As a direct result, Toby's erection was back, pressing painfully against the fly of his jeans and suffering periodic molestation by Landon's gyrating backside.

In retaliation, he rubbed Landon's dick each time he

humped into his. Which sounded great on paper but resulted in even more relentless grinding against Toby's cock. He switched to tweaking Landon's tender nipples instead, which worked much better. After the second time, Landon groused, "Am I being punished for something?"

"Yes, you are."

"What did I do?"

Toby rubbed his cock against Landon's surprisingly still behind. "Do I need to remind you I've endured many, many hours on the back of a motorcycle that vibrates like a damn sex toy while pressed against your delectable body? Toss in the shopping spree at an adult sex shop, you rocking a plug *this entire time*, those damn nipple clamps, and that hot little scene set against a backdrop of wildflowers? Voila. You've got one very grumpy, very horny Dom. Then, to up the ante, you keep bumping your gorgeous plugged ass into my deprived dick. What do you *think* I'm punishing you for?"

"Oh, um… for being delectable and gorgeous?"

Toby latched on to both nipples and pinched. Hard. Landon yelped, then hooted with laughter. "I'm sorry, I'm sorry. I'll keep my butt firmly planted on the seat. No humping."

Rolling his eyes, Toby gripped Landon's cock through the painted-on fabric of his jeans. "I'll believe that when I see it."

"That's not fair," Landon whined. "How am I supposed to keep still if you're touching my dick? That only makes me wanna squirm even more."

"I'm testing your mettle, sweetheart. Let's see how well you do with a little added challenge."

Landon growled, his knuckles whitening on the handlebars. "I already have an added challenge, thank you. My ass is plugged. Oh, and lest we forget, I have a sexy hunk of man flesh pressed into my back—within easy grinding distance."

"Sexy hunk of man flesh?" Toby barked out a laugh. He gave Landon's cock a perfunctory squeeze before hugging both arms around his waist. "Okay, okay, I won't add to your torment. But if you so much as *think* about grinding into me one more time on this trip, I'll be forced to break out the flogger."

"Promises, promises," Landon purred, then deliberately wriggled into Toby's crotch.

"Oh, for fucking Christ's sake." Toby dropped his helmeted head to rest on Landon's shoulder. "How much longer must I endure this torture?"

"Only about two more hours." Landon didn't even try to hide the mirth in his words.

Toby sighed. "I'll never make it. I'll implode long before then. We might have to stop again."

"Nope, ain't happening... Unless you demand it, of course. But a certain kind and generous Dom promised me he'd try out our new flogger. I want him good and horny so he doesn't hold back. I'm craving a hot, red ass and a good, hard fuck."

"Are you trying to kill me?"

Landon laughed. "No, baby, I'm trying out that open communication thing. Works quite well, if I do say so myself." His laughter shifted to a cackle, and he humped Toby's dick. Again. "Yes. Quite well indeed."

Chapter Twenty-Three

A loud clatter echoed through the foyer when Toby dropped the bag filled with their kinky treasures inside the door. He pulled Landon in for a heart-stopping kiss, complete with groping hands that tugged and ripped at his clothing. He marched Landon backward toward the bedroom without separating their mouths. They crashed into the wall once or twice, neither caring as they yanked articles of clothing free and left them strewn in their wake.

By the time they fell onto the bed, they were both naked, and their desperate bodies collided with shared groans of long-denied pleasure. Their hands roamed free, touching and teasing and taking without question or qualm.

"I need you. Now. Please, I c-can't wait any longer." Landon whimpered when Toby's skilled mouth latched on to an exquisitely tender nipple. "Oh god, please, baby, I need you inside me."

Toby traced his tongue in circles around Landon's nipple before biting down, sending a jolt of delicious pleasure straight into Landon's groin. He cried out and grabbed on to Toby's shoulders.

Lifting his eyes, Toby lapped at the abused flesh to soothe and torment anew. "I thought you wanted to try out the flogger?"

"Later." Landon mewled, bucking his hips. "We have forever to try out our toys. I need *you* right now."

A dark look passed over Toby's face before he angled off Landon. "Flip onto your belly, sweetheart."

"No." Landon shook his head. "Not this time. I need to see you."

Toby smiled—a precious lopsided grin that stole Landon's already shallow breath. "All right. Lift your legs for me?"

Landon obeyed, guiding his legs up and back, then placing his hands behind his knees to keep them spread wide. Toby scooted closer until their thighs rested together, then took Landon's cock in the soft warmth of his fist. He gave a few pumps, drawing a whimper from Landon before moving his other hand to the plug. "Take a deep breath, babe."

When Toby removed the intruding metal object, Landon ached from the loss, but Toby was quick to ease his anguish. His deft, lube-coated fingers appeared at Landon's opening, massaging and calming the overstretched muscles with gentle strokes.

No one had ever treated him with such reverence. Every time they were together, Toby made the experience about Landon. He worshipped him with every touch, with every kiss, with every movement of his body. It was always about Landon's pleasure; Toby's was always secondary.

Resolve firmed Landon's jaw, and he let his legs fall, draping them over Toby's, who glanced up from his intent ministrations and cocked his head. "You okay?"

Landon nodded, then pushed to his elbows. "I want you on your back."

Toby arched a brow. "I thought I was supposed to be the one giving orders."

"Oh, you absolutely are." Landon grinned and scooted away, biting back a whimper when those probing fingers pulled free, leaving him desperately empty. "This is more of a request, if you'll indulge me."

Chuckling, Toby held up his hands in mock defeat. "Your wish is my command. On my back, you say?"

Landon hummed in agreement. When Toby positioned himself as requested, stretching those thick, gorgeous arms up to prop under his head—the muscles bulging and rippling beneath his skin—Landon swallowed a moan. *Fuck.* He was beautiful. And his. *All his.*

He spotted the lube and a condom lying on the bed and grinned. His man was always prepared. He snatched them up and moved between Toby's legs, and Toby immediately shifted into the same position Landon had been—legs up and spread wide.

"Ah, that's not what I want, baby."

Toby scrunched his brow. "I thought you wanted to fuck me."

"I do." Landon eased Toby's legs back to the bed, then moved to straddle them. "But not like that. I told you, I don't top. Never have, never will. Not my thing."

"But I—" Toby cut off when Landon took his cock in hand and rolled the condom down its thick, heavy length. When he filled his palm with lube and stroked Toby's rubber-covered dick, Toby gripped the sheets. "Careful, sweetheart. I want to be inside you when I blow."

Laughing, Landon shimmied forward. He positioned Toby's cock at his entrance, then sank down, relishing the low rumbling growl that followed each inch of descent. As soon as Toby was fully inside, he rocked his hips, and Toby dug his grip into Landon's thighs.

After the long day of riding that edge and the sweet agony of the plug vacating his body, having Toby inside him felt like heaven. Landon tipped back his head, closed his eyes, and worked his hips in a deep, satisfying grind.

"Fuck, babe, I'm not gonna last very long." Toby rolled his pelvis to meet Landon's downward momentum. "You feel goddamn amazing."

Toby's palm closed around Landon's dick, stroking in rhythm with their joint thrusting. His other hand cupped Landon's balls, tugging gently as he kneaded and rolled them between his skilled fingers. It felt so good to have every part of him surrounded by Toby that Landon's orgasm slammed through him without warning. An electric pulse of long-awaited release exploded in his groin, traveling the length of every nerve in his body to fire off mini bursts of decadent delight.

He fell forward, trapping Toby's hands between their sticky bodies, and trembled as the aftershocks of that mind-fuck of a release rolled through his noodle-limp body. Beneath him, Toby's heart raced against his chest, and his hot breath panted over Landon's sweat-slickened skin.

Determined to do for Toby what he always did for him, Landon pried away from his body, groaning as that glorious cock slipped free and left him once again empty. "I'll be right back. Don't move."

He went to the bathroom, cleaned himself with a few quick swipes of a cool washcloth as he waited for the water to heat, then wet a warm one for Toby. He frowned when he opened the door and found Toby waiting for him outside the bathroom rather than sprawled on the bed.

Toby planted a kiss on the tip of his nose, then tried to slip by him, but Landon latched on to his bicep before he made it all the way past. He wasn't sure what made him glance down, but he did. A fist of guilt and despair drove straight into his gut.

Toby was still rock-hard, and the condom he wore held no proof of his own release.

Fuckin' great. Landon's first attempt at taking control of Toby's pleasure—aside from that one blowjob—and he'd screwed it up.

"Oh my god, Tobes, I—"

"Shh, sweetheart." He shut Landon up with a kiss. "I'm gonna clean up. You have a guest."

"Wait, what?" Landon pinched his brow. "A guest? Who?"

Toby chuckled and smoothed his thumb over Landon's forehead to erase the wrinkles. "Steffon. At least, I think that was his cackling I heard. I'm guessing he came across our forgotten bag of toys and breadcrumb trail of clothes."

Landon squeezed his lids shut and cursed. "I'm going to kill him."

"You go on out. I'll meet you in a few minutes, okay?"

"Fuck no." Landon's eyes flew open. "Steff can wait. I have bigger and far better things that require my undivided attention." He fisted Toby's cock. "Get back on the bed."

Toby groaned and fucked into Landon's hand with a desperate thrust of his hips. "You don't have to—"

"Oh my god, as if it's even a question whether I want to or not." Landon shoved Toby toward the bed but didn't release his grip on his dick. "For starters, the idea of getting to watch you come apart while not distracted by my own, ah, *reactions* sounds like the best thing ever."

Toby fell on the bed when Landon gave him one final push, a laugh bubbling up his throat right beside a moan when Landon freed his cock from the condom. "I'm supposed to be focused on you, not the other way around. I don't mind cranking one out in the bathroom while you—"

"Are you serious with this right now?" Landon glared down at Toby. "I don't care what context that obligation stems from—whether you think that's how this whole Dom/sub thing works or if it's something even more fucked-up I don't want to get into right now—but that is absolutely *not* the truth. Everything we do is about *us*, not about *me*."

Toby sighed and levered onto his elbows, wincing as the action twinged his bruised ribs. "Would it make you feel better if I didn't touch myself?"

"Jesus, Tobes, you're kinda missing the point here."

A loud crash sounded from the kitchen, and Steffon's high-pitched screech of surprise echoed through the condo. No follow-up wailing ensued, so Landon was fairly certain he hadn't hurt himself.

"You should check on him." Toby slipped off the bed, careful not to touch Landon as he did. "I'll meet you out there in a minute. Promise."

Landon angled a narrowed-eye glance at Toby's deflating dick as he stepped around him and headed toward the bathroom. He shoved the heels of both hands into his eyes. How had he fucked this up so badly?

"You're pissed at me." Steffon cocked a hip against the bar beside Landon where he worked on mixing their second round of drinks that evening. "Admit it so I can start groveling."

Landon blew out a measured breath and worked his jaw from side to side. "I'm not pissed at you."

"Bullshit. I can read you like a book, Lan, and you're pissed. What's worse, I can sense tension between you and Mr. Hot-as-Hades. I did that, didn't I? Because I bum-fucked into the middle of your sexy time." Steffon frowned. "I'm sorry. I know you asked me not to show up unannounced. I screwed up."

"Steffon, seriously, I'm not pissed at you. Yeah, your timing wasn't perfect, but there's other shit at play here. So... drop it, okay? I don't feel like talking about it."

"Is it the finale that's got you on edge?" Steffon placed a hand over Landon's shaking one. "Talk to me, sweetie."

Landon had forgotten the stupid fucking finale aired tonight, which was why Steffon had made an appearance in the first place. He understood Landon well enough to know he'd be out of sorts over the whole thing, had he even remembered it was happening. But that was the last thing on his mind today. He passed Steffon his drink. "I don't want to talk about it."

Steffon accepted the glass and pursed his lips. "Do I need to kick Toby's ass? Did he hurt you?"

"Steff." Landon closed his lids to fend off the urge to shake his best friend into silence. "Toby didn't do a damn thing wrong. I did. And I don't want to talk about it, okay?"

"Does this have anything to do with those sexy toys I found strewn across the foyer when I came home tonight?" Steffon squeezed Landon's hand. "Did you guys bite off a bit more than you could chew this early in the relationship?"

Landon glanced over his shoulder at Toby. He'd all but followed Landon into the kitchen earlier, so there was no doubt he hadn't taken care of himself. And when Steffon offered to leave after cleaning up the water glass he'd broken, Toby insisted—vehemently—he stay. But he wasn't being his outgoing, charming Toby self. He'd barely said two words since his adamant refusal to let Steffon leave, and he'd kept his gaze lowered most of the evening.

The only time he'd looked up was when Steffon said, a second time, he was going to head out. Toby had fought, a second time, for him to stay. Clearly, he didn't want to be alone with Landon, and that hurt worse than anything else.

"Look, I know we usually talk about everything, but right now, this topic is off the table, okay? Let's try to enjoy the evening."

"Lan, do you want me to leave? I feel like my presence is only making things worse between you two. I think you guys should talk. Whatever happened, I'm sure you can work it out."

Landon was about to toss out a weak argument as to why Steffon shouldn't leave—for Toby's sake—when his intercom buzzed. He frowned and handed Toby's drink to Steffon. "Here, I'm gonna see who the hell that is."

He strolled to the door and hit the button to answer

the call. "Hello?"

"Good evening, Mr. Jenks." The warm, weathered voice of Thomas—Landon's favorite doorman—sounded through the speaker. "There's a delivery here for you."

Rubbing at the tense muscles in his neck, Landon schooled his voice to remain calm and polite. "Thanks, Thomas. Could you have the front desk sign for it? I'll pick it up tomorrow."

"Pardon me if I'm stepping out of place, sir, but…" Thomas dropped the volume of his voice to just above audible. "I believe this is one package you might prefer delivered straight to your door."

Landon stifled a groan. He didn't need any more surprises tonight.

"Mr. Jenks? Sir?"

Before responding, Landon glanced over his shoulder to be sure Toby hadn't moved into eyeshot of the door. "Ah, yeah, that's… that's fine, Thomas. Go ahead and have it sent up. Thank you."

Landon rested his forehead against the doorframe until a clipped knock broke the silence a few short moments later. He braced himself for god-knew-what might be on the other side, then punched in his unlock code and gave the handle a tug.

A giant bouquet of long-stemmed orchids filled the doorway, obscuring the delivery person with their extravagant bulk. Without seeing the card, Landon knew who they were from, and his stomach dipped to his knees. He darted another quick glance behind him, then hissed out a whispered, "Garret? Is that you?"

The massive flowers shifted, and a familiar face popped over their tops. But it wasn't Garret.

"Oh my g-god." Landon took a step back, his mouth going dry. Of all the people in all the world he might've expected to show up at his door, the one grinning at him from behind the soft white petals of an orchid would've topped his "least likely to ever happen" list.

"Landon?" The husky tenor was recognizable even in the out-of-place surroundings. "Of course you are; who else would you be? Sorry, I'd shake your hand, but mine are a bit full. I'm Xavier—"

"—Wolfe. You're Xavier Wolfe." Landon shook his head and blew out a single self-deprecating huff. "I'm sorry. You obviously know that already. I mean, you're... you."

Xavier laughed. "I do, and I am, but it's nice to be recognized either way. Not a lot of people know who I am these days."

Landon scoffed. "You're a legend. Everyone knows who you are."

Which was mostly true. Xavier Wolfe was the youngest ever Golden Glove winning shortstop for the Chicago Cubs. He was Landon's predecessor and his greatest inspiration. The raw talent Xavier possessed in a single pinky would've kept Landon benched and second-string had Xavier not suffered a career-ending injury during a home invasion just prior to spring training of Landon's first season in the big leagues.

It was entirely possible Landon owed every ounce of his success to Xavier's extreme misfortune. But that wasn't why Landon idolized him. Not only was he an enviable ballplayer Landon had strived to emulate, Xavier had also gone on to become a spokesperson and advocate for LGBTQ+ rights. It came out that the home invasion and subsequent injuries he'd suffered were a hate crime carried out by angry bigots who didn't like a gay man being awarded the coveted Golden Glove. Once that hit the news, Xavier used his experience to bring awareness to the cause during a volatile and intolerant period of American history.

Perhaps not as volatile and intolerant as it was today, unfortunately, but Xavier had never stopped using his voice for good. Even when he'd found a new career as an ESPN anchor, he'd continued to champion the LGBTQ+

community on and off camera.

But despite all the goodness in his heart, it still made no sense why Xavier Wolfe would be standing at Landon's door with a giant bouquet of flowers. And with things between Landon and Toby at such a rocky point, Landon wasn't sure whether to be thrilled or terrified at the unexpected appearance of his greatest hero.

"I guess you're probably wondering what I'm doing here." Xavier held the flowers out to Landon, who accepted them with a smile of gratitude and a shrug of curious agreement. "Your fiancé wanted to do something special to celebrate the big season finale and the freedom to finally announce your engagement. His agent got in touch with mine, and when I heard one of my own heroes wanted to meet me, I was more than willing to play delivery boy. Especially for such a once-in-a-lifetime occasion."

Landon's brain stuttered on the word *fiancé* and stalled out completely when Xavier hit *engagement*. By the time he dropped the *hero* bomb, Landon's processors were no longer computing English, and all he could do was stare, agape and rooted to the spot.

So it *was* Garret. Just... vicariously so.

Chuckling, Xavier reached into the inside pocket of his jacket and withdrew a fat envelope. "In addition to those gorgeous flowers, Garret also asked me to deliver the tickets for the first leg of your engagement trip around Europe. He'll be meeting you in Paris once his promotional tour is over next week; then you two lovebirds can travel the continent together. Sounds like he's got quite the romantic trip planned."

Stumbling forward, Landon set the vase of orchids on the hall table with a resounding clink-*thud* as glass banged against marble. He willed his brain to produce a response beyond the whole wide-eyed fish-out-of-water thing he had going on, but before he could, a sound drew his attention to the two men standing stock-still in the parlor behind him.

Landon froze, the very blood in his veins slowing to a crawl. Steffon eyed Xavier like a predator who hadn't eaten a meal in days and just spotted their prey of choice. Toby, on the other hand, wore a closed-off expression as his gaze bounced between Landon, Xavier, and the giant spray of orchids.

Reading the room entirely wrong, Xavier took a step forward and stuck out his hand toward the new arrivals. He introduced himself and managed to achieve a stiff nod and brisk return shake from Toby, and a fawning welcome from Steffon.

"Sorry to interrupt your evening. I won't keep you guys any longer. I only came to deliver an engagement present from the doting groom-to-be." Xavier handed off the envelope to Landon, who accepted it with numb fingers. "You're a lucky man, Landon. I'll admit I watched the show. The chemistry and affection between you two were enviable. I consider myself fortunate to be one of the few let in on the romantic secret engagement before it aired to the rest of the world. I wish you both the happiest of futures together."

Xavier tipped the bill of his cap as he said farewell to the room before heading for the elevator.

Steffon gave Landon's elbow a squeeze before disappearing after Xavier, but Landon only had one goal in mind. When he turned and found Toby en route to the bar to refill the drink that only moments before sat full in his hand, Landon knew things between them had gone from bad to worse.

Landon went straight for the bar, leaving Steffon to handle seeing Xavier off with a proper—or more likely, *improper*—goodbye.

"Tobes?" Landon placed a hand on Toby's forearm, his heart skipping a beat when Toby met his gaze with a heady mixture of desire and what could only be called the epitome of green-eyed envy darkening his irises. Landon couldn't remember the last time—if ever there had been one—where a man cared enough for him to get *jealous*.

It was the wrong time to smile, but Landon couldn't help it. He faked a cough just to cover his mouth before Toby misinterpreted the response as anything other than the rush of ecstatic joy it was.

But there was no need to fear a misunderstanding, because after that brief glance, Toby returned to the task at hand. His knuckles whitened as he clutched the ice cube tongs and deliberately placed one after another in his glass.

Landon suppressed a sigh and tried again. "Tobes? Please, I—"

Leaving his glass only half-filled with ice and nothing more, Toby stepped away from the bar. "You don't have to say anything, Landon. I appreciate everything you've done for me, but there's no obligation between us. I've told you before, whatever you need from me, that's what I'm here for. End of story."

A heavy weight crushed Landon's chest. "I *want* obligation between us. Please don't say there isn't any." Toby shoved his hands into the front pockets of his jeans and stared at the floor rather than meeting Landon's pleading gaze. "I meant it when I said my relationship with Garret ended months ago. Tonight was the season finale of that stupid fucking show. I'm sure this had something to do with that. A promotional stunt or something. Nothing more. It's—"

Toby held up a hand to stop Landon's continued groveling but still didn't meet his eyes. "It's okay. Really. But I think I'm gonna go to bed."

"Tobes, you can do whatever you want, but if you're going to bed, I'm coming with you."

"No, you don't have to. You should spend some time with Steffon. Don't let me ruin your night by dragging you to bed early."

Landon clenched his fists to stop himself from reaching out. "Toby Carmichael, look at me." When that intense hazel gaze finally shifted to meet his, Landon drew his brows into a frown. "I know I don't have to, but I *want* to. There's nowhere else I'd rather be than with you."

Toby dropped his stare again. "I don't deserve you."

Guffawing, Landon dared to trace a finger over Toby's jaw. "You deserve better, actually, but I'm not going to let 'better' have you. You're mine, and I'm not letting you go."

Chapter Twenty-Four

Toby eased into bed, concentrating on maintaining a neutral expression. His ribs screamed at the disservice of bending and stretching to accommodate his stiff movements, but he clenched his jaw and kept the hiss of pain from slipping past his lips as he settled onto his back.

Landon slid in beside him and snuggled up to Toby's side, the scent of minty toothpaste mingling with his eucalyptus face wash. It was amazing how those distinctly Landon smells had worked their way into Toby's brain. Any time they hit his nose, memories of the man he loved washed over him in a wave of euphoric bliss. He hoped those mental connections would never fade.

Nuzzling his soft, bearded cheek against Toby's neck, Landon planted butterfly kisses over his nearest pulse point. "I'm so sorry, Tobes."

Toby gave Landon's shoulder a brief squeeze. "No need to be."

Landon draped a leg over Toby's. "Yes, there is. Having my ex pull a stunt like that when things with us had been left... *unresolved* was hardly the end to the evening we needed."

Absurd mortification electrified the nerves under Toby's skin like live wires frayed by Landon's words. It killed Toby that Landon harbored guilt over the experience they'd shared that afternoon just because Toby hadn't come, meaning Toby's biological failure had ruined one of their last chances to be together before his week of faux freedom came to an end.

He only had so many chances to make memories, and he'd royally fucked that one up.

"Nothing was *unresolved*, sweetheart." Toby quelled a sigh. If Landon could understand his pleasure was the only thing that mattered to Toby, and thus Toby considered their afternoon a resounding success, he might shed the guilt weighing him down.

But how to explain his feelings without revealing the much deeper emotion he didn't dare speak aloud? If he told Landon he didn't care about his own release as long as Landon was satisfied, Landon would assume Toby was pushing him away. Which, in a way, he was. But not by choice, and not because his love for Landon had faded. Not one single bit.

When Landon harrumphed in response to Toby's statement, Toby smiled into the dark. "I mean it, babe. I enjoyed watching you come apart. There's nothing wrong with a little one-sidedness among friends, remember? I believe it was you who said that to me on my first day here."

Landon sighed, his warm breath feathering over Toby's bare chest. "Tell me you at least believe it when I say that stunt Garret pulled was just that—a stunt."

Toby brushed the sweep of bangs from Landon's brow. "Of course I believe you. But it doesn't matter—"

"Yes, it *does* matter." Landon pushed to an elbow, his eyes glittering in the faint moonlight spilling in from the curtains they'd forgotten to close. "I know our situation is complicated, but Garret isn't one of our obstacles. He's barely a blip on the radar of issues right now."

"I know, sweetheart." And he did. For the most part. But it wasn't the belief Landon was still affianced to Garret that had Toby's chest twisting in despair. It was the reminder Garret's little show of "affection" had drawn to the front of Toby's mind. The reminder that he was, and always would be, a penniless whore who possessed few to no viable options for a successful future. He could never give Landon the things a man like Garret Ramsey had to offer. The money. The respectable reputation and gilded persona. The all-expenses paid trips abroad and access to Landon's greatest heroes to carry out grandiose romantic gestures.

All Toby had was a shitload of baggage and three more years of rough use before he could offer whatever was left to Landon without the marionette strings of his contract attached.

Not exactly Dominant material, let alone worthy of owning Landon's heart.

Landon's warm palm drifted whisper-soft over Toby's abdomen, then dipped beneath the band of Toby's boxer briefs. "Will you let me fix my mistake from earlier? Please?" He stroked, slow and languid. "I want to focus on us right now. That's all that matters. I want to lose myself in you and forget everything else."

Toby shifted so he could seek out Landon's mouth, but the awkward angle of the movement sent an arrow of pain through his damaged ribs. He lay back on the pillow, unable to mask the growl of frustration lancing up his throat.

Just another reminder of all the ways he was undeserving of the man he loved.

Landon's hand stilled. "Jesus, Tobes, I'm sorry. Are you okay? Can I get you anything? Some ibuprofen maybe?"

Biting his tongue to fend off another reaction that would only further confirm his weakness in Landon's eyes, Toby shook his head. "I'm fine, but I'm not really in the mood, babe. Can we go to sleep? I'm exhausted."

"Oh." Landon's hand disappeared, and he pulled bodily away. As much as it hurt, Toby let him go. "I-I'm sorry."

"Don't be. I'm tired, that's all." Toby drew the covers up to compensate for the loss of Landon's heat now that he lay on the other side of the massive king-sized bed.

Landon was silent for a moment, and then he rolled over, facing the opposite wall, and mumbled softly, "Good night, Toby."

When Landon padded into the bathroom the next morning, Toby caught his sleep-heavy eyes in the mirror and offered a small smile. He rinsed off his razor under the running water before lifting it to his neck again. As he stroked the blades up the underside of his jaw, Landon sighed and stepped to the second sink. He cranked on the faucet, grabbed his toothbrush, and for a few minutes, they stood side by side, performing mundane morning rituals. As if they'd been doing it for years. As if they'd be doing it for years to come.

Heart twisting, Toby rinsed his face. He glanced in the mirror to be sure the line around his jaw was even, then dried off with the same towel he'd used to shower.

"Growing a beard?" Landon's voice was tentative, but a cautious smile tugged at his lips as he wiped his mouth with a hand towel.

"Haven't been allowed to for so long. Thought I'd give my face a break." Toby frowned and ran his hand down the two-day growth. "If you don't like it, I can shave it off."

"No, I like it. Really. It's crazy sexy on you." Landon dropped the towel on the counter. "You're free to do whatever you want, Tobes. You don't have to answer to me. You don't have to answer to *anyone*."

Free. The word rattled through Toby's brain like an electrified bowling ball, barreling over every other thought in his mind and replacing them with painful jolts of memories best left forgotten. He wasn't free, even if the mirage he'd stumbled into told him otherwise. It was only temporary and far from real.

"I'll give you some privacy to shower." Toby turned toward the door, then forced a cheerful half grin as he locked gazes with Landon. "You hungry? I can whip up some breakfast if you'd like."

Rather than a verbal reply or a simple nod, Landon fell to his knees.

Toby's heart slammed to a halt. It kicked sluggishly back to life with thick, heavy beats that shuddered through his pulse points and sent the room spinning.

With desperation darkening the smoky gray of his irises, Landon blinked up at Toby. "I don't want privacy. Not from you. I want you immersed in every aspect of my life. I want... No, I *need* you to tell me what to do. I need to know how to fix this. I'll do anything, be anything, *say* anything. You can do whatever you want to me. Use me to make this better. I'm yours, in whatever way you need me."

Those words crashed into Toby like a wall of hot, sticky summer air after leaving the cocoon of an air-conditioned building. They clung to his skin and crawled into his brain until their power all but consumed him.

His world shifted, tilting on its axis until what was once wrong felt right and there was nothing but Landon. He yearned to reach out and touch those soft black waves, to murmur words of praise and adoration. He ached to give the man at his feet everything and anything his heart desired until he wanted for nothing and they became so intertwined—heart, body, and soul—there would be no telling them apart.

Toby hungered to share the love in his heart and craved to find it returned. But that was idiocy and nothing more. They only had two more days together, and then harsh reality would remind them of the foolishness surrounding this perceived bubble of perfection.

Even as he struggled to suck air into his constricted lungs, his cock thickened and throbbed within his briefs. He'd almost touched himself in the shower, but one wandering thought about an expensive bouquet of orchids and a thick padded envelope filled with promises far beyond anything Toby had to offer set him off the idea. Still, after that long day of teasing and deprivation, followed by insanely hot sex where he got to enjoy Landon taking control of his own pleasure, he was useless to dampen his reaction now. No matter how much he strived for prudence.

Remembering Landon riding him threw another wrench into the works, and a groan slipped past his lips. But what he wanted didn't matter. In the end, no matter how much Toby wished they were living the dream Landon offered, he was still the whore and Landon was still his client. He couldn't let himself forget that.

Even if it broke him to remember.

"Sweetheart," Toby cooed the word, placing an innocent touch to Landon's shoulder but stifling his baser urges. "I don't need you to fix anything. It's fine, really. But I'm hungry and already showered, so I'm going to leave you to yours while I make us breakfast."

Landon's face pulled into a frown. "But I d-don't…" He released a quivering breath, his chin falling to his chest. "Okay. I'll, ah, I'll meet you in the kitchen." With that, he pushed to his feet and strode to the shower without lifting his gaze.

Toby backed out of the room as Landon turned on the shower and slipped out of his boxer briefs. He stepped under the freezing spray without waiting for it to warm and stood there, head hanging, as the water beat down on his sagging form.

There was nothing in this world Toby wanted more than to believe Landon might share the intense feelings all but swallowing him whole. But that would be impossible and, quite frankly, ridiculous. Landon was a brilliant, beautiful man who would see the error in logic behind trying to turn a whore into a boyfriend. Especially one like Toby, who couldn't walk away and leave that part behind no matter how desperately he wanted to.

If he truly wanted to give Landon a gift, he would make sure, when they parted ways, Landon held no desire to see Toby again.

Threading his fingers through his damp hair, Toby steeled his resolve. That's exactly what he'd do. He'd allow them one last day of perfection. But tomorrow? He'd make sure Landon Jenks never thought twice about seeking his company again.

He'd break his own heart to save Landon's.

Chapter Twenty-Five

❝Okay, sweetie, time to spill.❞ Steffon snicked Landon's office door closed and pointed to his chair. "Sit."

Landon dragged his feet to the swivel barrel he'd opted for in place of a traditional rolling office chair. He sank into its soft leather opulence and dropped his head—hard—to meet the cluttered mahogany desk. "I'm losing him, Steff. In more ways than one."

"Cryptic much?" Steffon flopped into a cream-colored, overstuffed leather armchair opposite Landon's desk, kicked off his flip-flops, and tossed his legs over the side. "I assume you're talking about Mr. Tall, Sandy Brown, and Insanely Gorgeous, but I need you to be a bit more specific. Nothing about what I saw last night indicates that boy has *any* plans to vacate your vicinity any time soon."

"Seriously? Were you in the same room I was?" Landon lifted his head to cock a brow at Steffon. "He was practically begging you to stay and act as a buffer between us. All because I royally fucked up. And that was only the first in a long line of screwups that are going to lose me the first man I've ever really loved."

Steffon swung his legs back to the floor and faced Landon square-on. "Well, that's a lot of shit to unpack. Let's start at the beginning, shall we? What happened that had him so quiet? What was I 'buffering,' exactly?"

"You mean what did I royally fuck up?" Landon sneered, but his lips quickly fell into a pout. "I tried to take control in the bedroom—a role I do *not* belong in—and managed to have an epic orgasm that left Toby... unsatisfied. I didn't even realize he hadn't come until I came out of the bathroom to clean him up and there wasn't anything to clean."

"Oh, sweetie." Steffon placed a gentle hand over Landon's clenched fist. "That's a normal part of sex. Those moments happen. It can't always be screaming O's and mutually timed explosions. Toby's a smart man. He understands that."

"Yeah, but how many times do you think he's been left like that? I guarantee his *clients* don't put a lot of effort into getting him off." Landon pinched the bridge of his nose and whistled out a breath. "I've been trying so hard to make him see I want more. I'm not another 'paying customer.' Then I go and do *that*. When I tried to fix it? He... he didn't want me to."

Steffon leaned back in the chair, tapping his painted black nails over his pursed lips. "Maybe the guy has some baggage there. You're right... He's been an escort for a long time. Sex for him is going to hold some difficulties you two will have to work through together. If you think he's worth the trouble, of course."

Landon scoffed and slammed a fist on the desk. "I'd do fucking *anything* for Toby."

"Good." Steffon nodded and dropped his hand. "Because I think the feeling's mutual."

Squeezing his eyes closed, Landon huffed out a breath. "I know he cares for me, Steff. But I'm not sure I'm what he needs right now, let alone what he wants." The raw ache in Landon's chest that had taken up residence after his failed attempt at offering his heart to Toby in every way but the literal spilling of those three little words had only intensified since that morning. "I can't blame him, even if it does hurt to know we're in two very different places right now. He's dealing with a situation so far out of my sphere of understanding we're barely living on the same planet. I can't expect him to put all that aside like it hasn't been a completely life-changing mind-fuck for the past five years. Just so I can feel *appreciated* and *seen* or whatever the hell it is I feel like I'm missing that I have no right to demand. Not from Toby. Not when he's facing the return to a hell far worse than either of us could ever imagine."

Steffon rolled his eyes in a dramatic fashion befitting a stage actor trying to ensure even those in the nose-bleeds could sense his exasperation. "You didn't see what I saw last night, Lan. If you had, you'd be singing a different tune."

Landon scrunched his brow. "What exactly is it you think I missed?"

Tapping the side of his nose, Steffon bounced his brows and smirked. "You shoulda seen that boy's face when he first caught sight of those flowers. I thought the green-eyed monster was gonna turn literal Hulk on us."

"Wait, what?" Landon had seen the glint of jealousy in Toby's eye, but it had come and gone so quick he'd second-guessed the validity of his assumptions. Especially when Toby refused his fumbling attempts at initiating a connection before bed.

Steffon whistled and shook his head. "When he caught wind it was *the* Xavier Wolfe hand-delivering an *engagement* trip abroad as a favor to your newly announced fiancé? Lan, I swear, the ground shook beneath our feet. He was ready to rumble." Steffon shuddered, but a mischievous spark lit his eye. "I almost ran for the hills, and that jealous anger wasn't even aimed my way."

Crossing his legs at the knees, Steffon settled into the chair. "That wasn't the reaction of a man who's in this only balls-deep, sweetie. You've got those cute little hooks of yours lodged smack dab in the center of his big, muscly heart."

Landon dropped his head into his hands, resting his elbows on the desk. It didn't matter if Toby had a flare of jealous rage two heavily poured drinks into a high-stress evening. That didn't mean he was ready to share the magnitude of Landon's emotions. And that was okay. Landon couldn't lie to himself and say it didn't hurt, but he also couldn't blame Toby for protecting himself when his future was so uncertain and his world so unstable. He had bigger and much more important things to expend his energy on than falling in love.

Over breakfast, Toby had been quiet and withdrawn, his attention far from the silent meal they'd shared. Unsure of how to reach Toby behind the defensive walls he'd thrown up, Landon eventually murmured some lame excuse about having to check in at the shop to give Toby the space he so clearly needed. Toby had barely offered a nod before scooping up their dishes and heading for the sink.

Landon selfishly wished things could have ended differently between them. He'd always known he was reaching a bit, being greedy and self-centered in his dreams for their relationship. But he'd hoped maybe, just maybe, if he gave enough of himself, Toby might find a few moments of happiness. To that end, he'd allowed their time together—erroneously—to focus more on distraction rather than healing or even helping Toby find hope. Landon had worked in the background to find a solution rather than discussing it with Toby or inviting him to take an active role because he hadn't wanted to burden Toby or add more stress to his plate.

But he'd made a mistake, and the closer it got to the end of Toby's faux freedom, the more obvious it was. He should've told Toby from the beginning about the PI firm. He should've been brainstorming ideas with him rather than stewing on them alone.

He'd pushed Toby to the brink, then left him clinging to that edge without any hope of a safe landing on the other side. But that would change. Today. After Landon talked things through with Steffon—and Toby had a bit of much-needed time to himself, away from the demands Landon's very presence put on his overtly selfless shoulders—Landon would sit him down and tell him everything. Then they would prepare. Together. And after they liberated Toby from his life of servitude and fear, Landon would be sure to release him from any unfounded responsibilities that might drive him to stay with Landon as an ill-conceived obligatory repayment for that freedom.

"None of that matters right now, Steff." Landon sat up straighter, running both hands through his hair before folding them on the desk. "I need your help. I have an idea about how I might be able to set Toby free, but I need someone to work through the logistics with."

Steffon smacked an open palm on the desk, excitement flashing in his chocolate-brown gaze. "Hell yeah. I'm just the girl for the job. Let's get this shit done, Lan. Then when he's free, you two can go on being too fuckin' hot for words, and I'll find my own place." He waggled his brows. "Then you can spread your legs and let him thank you all proper like. Maybe with a ball gag in your mouth and a nice cherry-red ass for him to hold on to."

Landon rolled his lips to fend off a bark of laughter. "Hey, who says I'd be the one with a red ass?"

Steffon pulled off another of those epic eye rolls that had his whole head lolling side to side. "Buddy, we've been friends for far too long for that to even be a question. Sorry, but you're total sub material. Known it for years. Been waiting for you to catch up. And Toby? He positively *reeks* of Dom energy."

Landon's eyes widened. "You sound awfully knowledgeable."

Without missing a beat, Steffon's grin cranked up a few notches, and he recrossed his legs. "Do you think the guys I bring home scream so loud and so often because I've got a magic cock wand or something? Come on, Lan. Use that big, beautiful brain."

"You're not..." Landon's jaw dropped, and all he could do was shake his head.

Steffon smirked. "The boys under my control call me Master, and I wield a mean cat-o'-nine-tails."

"Well, hell." Landon let his head fall to rest against the chair. "I really am a clueless asshole, aren't I?"

"No, you haven't been with the right person before now. I don't give a fuck if the right person turned out to be an escort, or that you're *technically* paying for the pleasure of his company. It's the real deal between you two. I can tell. It takes trust to open yourself to this world, especially when you've spent most of your life trying to hide from who you really are. The few guys you've been with have been such well-kept secrets, I'm surprised you've managed to have sex period, let alone delve into the kinkier side of things."

Landon opened his mouth to retort, but before he could, there was a loud crash outside his office. He leapt to his feet and bolted to the door, then yanked it open in time to see—of all fucking people—Garret Ramsey untangling himself from a pile of freshly painted body pieces no longer drying unscathed on the rack outside Landon's door.

"What the fuck, Garret?" Landon stormed out of his office and scooped up one of the plum-faded-to-black moldings his painter had spent so much time perfecting. Dents and scratches marred the paint's glossed surface. "What are you doing here?"

Garret shoved to his feet, brushing at his jeans with a scowl. "I came to see you, obviously."

Steffon's fingers dug into Landon's bicep as he peeked around his shoulder. "Were you eavesdropping, Ramsey?"

"No." Garret's eyes flashed wide before they dropped away. "I was waiting here for you to finish."

"Who even told you I was in the shop today?" Landon narrowed his gaze. It had to be one of his technicians. He'd done a sweep through the shop to check in on things and put out a few fires before holing up with Steffon in his office. One of them could've called Garret when he first arrived, which would've given him plenty of time to get here. "You know what, I don't even care. I told you on the phone the other day I'm done. I'm not interested. And that show you put on last night? It doesn't change a damn thing."

"But honey, we're so good together. I miss what we had, and clearly you aren't happy with that... with that *whore*, so why stay with him?"

"Oh my god, you *were* listening in on our conversation." Steffon stormed forward, stabbing a finger into Garret's chest. "Get the fuck out of here, dirtbag, before I tie your ass to the rafters and get creative. Since you were snooping, you know I've got years of experience finding people's pain threshold without going over it, but for you? I'd make a special exception and forget all that knowledge right alongside my good Dom manners."

A squeak fell from Garret's slack-jawed mouth. He took a step back, nearly landing on his butt when his foot slipped off the sloped surface of a custom stretched gas tank in the same plum-faded-to-black design scheme. It left a streak in the topcoat. The whole damn bike would need repainting.

Landon allowed himself a moment to close his eyes and pray the Hollywood starlet who ordered the custom chopper as a birthday present for her current beau hadn't agreed to a delivery date too close to the big day. Thanks to Garret, they would likely miss the deadline.

"Get lost, Garret. Just... *get lost*." Landon sighed, then turned to Steffon. "How about lunch? We have plans to make."

Steffon threw a fist-pump into the air and hopped lithely over a tailpipe whose matte black paint appeared— from Landon's current vantage point—blessedly unharmed. He stuck his tongue out at Garret as he passed, then weaved his arm through Landon's. "Yes, we do. How's our Mexican place sound?"

Landon hummed in appreciation. "Sounds perfect. You parked out back?"

"Duh. My baby needs space to breathe. No way am I risking her getting hit by those crazy assholes who think they're the only ones on the road."

"Wanna ride with me, then? Or meet there?"

Steffon slipped his arm free and kissed Landon on the cheek before backing toward the rear entrance. "I'll drive myself. You'll need freedom to act when we're done. Whether that be to get home to your hunk o' burnin' love or to hop on your white steed and ride into battle."

Landon grinned as Steffon disappeared around the corner. He patted his pockets to be sure he had his keys, phone, and wallet, then headed for the side entrance. Before he could shove the heavy metal door open, thick fingers landed at his shoulders and squeezed. "Can I at least walk you out, honey?"

Gritting his teeth, Landon shrugged Garret's hands off and pushed through the door.

Dozens of bright flashbulbs went off at once, followed by a barrage of shouting voices all talking over one another. Rapid-fire questions overlapped with pleas for Landon and Garret to "Look this way!" or "Over here!"

Garret's meaty hands once again grabbed at Landon, wrapping a protective arm over his chest before barking at the throng of paparazzi. "No comment. Can't my fiancé and I have a little privacy?"

"Mr. Ramsey, has a date been set for the big day?"

"Has it been difficult to keep this private from your friends and family all this time?"

"How did your father respond to the news, Landon?"

"Will there be a second season? Your fans are dying to see inside the wedding plans and get more of you two. You're America's favorite couple right now."

Landon took a momentary pause as he tried to work out the best way to handle this situation without causing a bigger scene than necessary. Per the contract, they were technically free to discuss the truth about their current relationship status, but he'd agreed to wait until they did the official reunion "epilogue" on some random talk show he'd never heard of, before coming clean.

Garret took advantage of Landon's frozen indecision and pulled him close, placing a soft kiss at his temple before holding a hand up to the increasing swarm. "No final decisions have been made, but there have been talks of a season two. For now, we kindly ask that you allow us time to enjoy some privacy in our relationship."

With a barely restrained growl, Landon jerked free of Garret's hold. He offered the media a flat-lipped smile and curt nod before shoving through the horde of flashing lights and crushing assault of questions. As he cleared the initial throng of paparazzi, he ran into a small group of fans who had gathered on the sidewalk. Their high-pitched shrieking rang through his ears as dozens of hands pawed at his clothing and scratched at his exposed skin.

"It's okay, honey," Garret cooed into Landon's ear, latching on to his elbow and attempting to steer him toward their bikes, parked side by side. "I'll drive you home."

But before Landon could follow through on his gut reaction to elbow Garret in the balls, a horn blared from a few feet away. He glanced up and caught Steffon's behemoth of an SUV stopped in the middle of the street, the passenger door flung open and Steffon's narrowed gaze locked on him and Garret. "Come on, sweetie, we've got a lunch date, remember?"

Garret's grip tightened, but Steffon's presence—and the safety of his looming vehicle—knocked some sense into Landon, and he tugged free without inflicting any scene-inducing injuries. He made a quick break for the open door, tossed himself inside, and barely had it closed before Steffon sped away.

Rolling his eyes, Steffon gave Landon's arm a squeeze. "We need to figure out how to rescue your Dom. I'm tired of being the only one keeping your ass protected and in line. It's exhausting."

Chapter Twenty-Six

After Landon left that morning, Toby kicked himself in the proverbial balls. He'd wanted one last perfect day, and what had he done? He'd shut down. He'd holed up inside his head, drowning in his own stupid fears and misgivings rather than fixing the mess he'd made with Landon.

He'd hurt Landon, and yet he hadn't apologized. He hadn't drawn him in for that much-needed physical contact they both craved, nor had he whispered the words of reassurance and affirmation itching to fall from his lips. Instead, he'd sat there. Like the lump of nothing he was.

For over an hour, Toby wandered through the empty condo, praying Landon would return so he could throw himself at his feet and beg for the forgiveness he didn't deserve.

Eventually, he'd gone to the building's fitness center. After working his body into submission twice a day for most of the past three years, his lack of gym time over the last week had been both liberating and suffocating. Once surrounded by the familiar equipment, he fell into a state of zoned out determination, ignoring the agonized screams pulsing from his ribs and giving his body the beating it deserved. For what he'd done to Landon. For his weakness. For his inability to properly protect and care for the man he loved.

After a cold shower to unwind from the gym and shift his desperate cock to neutral, Toby flopped onto a stool at the kitchen island and dropped his forehead to the cool granite counter. It was going on lunchtime and Landon hadn't returned. Hell, he hadn't even called. Not that he could; Toby didn't exactly have a phone of his own.

Unease churned through Toby's stomach. He'd royally screwed up. When Landon fell to his knees, it all but broke Toby with its perfection. What if it meant as much to Landon as it had to him?

Even if it only meant half as much, Toby's rejection would've crushed him.

Fuck, he was such an asshole. He wanted so desperately to rewind time and give them both what they'd needed in that moment. But he couldn't. He had to sit here and hope, wish, and pray Landon could find it in his heart to forgive him so they could savor whatever was left of their time together.

A shadow of an idea wiggled its way into Toby's brain, and he sat up straight. He slid off the stool and went to the refrigerator, snatching the notepad Landon and Steffon used to leave notes for each other off the magnetic surface. Yanking the doors open, he took stock of what was there and what he'd need.

Landon had taken him on a slew of breathtaking dates over the past week. Toby didn't have any money, nor did he know the city, so he'd been forced to sit back and let Landon do all the work, something that hurt far more than he was willing to admit. It was time he returned the favor in the only way he could. He'd cook Landon dinner. Even though he'd still have to use Landon's money to pull it off, at least it was something he *could* do.

Once he had a list together, Toby grabbed the keycard to gain him entrance to the front of the building, scribbled a note in case Landon beat him home, and left. The closest grocery store was a short walk away, and by early afternoon he'd returned, laden with his purchases, to a still empty condo.

He dropped the bags on the kitchen island and glanced at the wall clock. He had no clue when Landon would be home, but the meal he'd planned took a while to prep. He wanted at least that much done before Landon arrived so he could spend every second possible making up for being an asshole.

Out of the first bag, Toby removed the modest bouquet of cherry-red tulips he'd splurged on. More of Landon's money he hadn't needed to spend, but when he saw them at the flower stand, he couldn't pass them up. It was childish and self-indulgent, serving more as a personal reminder that, while he could never give Landon everything he deserved, at least he listened well enough to remember his favorite flower.

Something Garret Ramsey with all his fame, wealth, and freedom had failed to do.

Toby rustled around the kitchen until he found a handblown glass vase weaved through with smoky tendrils of teal and purple. He cut the stems, filled the vase with water, and carried it to the bedroom.

After dinner—or before, depending on when Landon got home—Toby would bring him to bed and show him how much he cared. He'd apologize, voice every word he'd held back during that stunning moment Landon had taken to his knees, and then he'd worship him, drawing every last scrap of pleasure from that beautiful body he could.

After all, everything—for Toby—was about Landon. It always had been, and whether he was present in Toby's life or not, it always would be.

He set the tulips on the nightstand, brushing a finger over their soft petals as he imagined Landon teasing them over his lips as he had the daisy only a day prior. Toby's mouth tingled at the thought of that mouth covering his, a smile nudging up his cheeks as he headed to the kitchen to start dinner preparations.

Toby had his head buried in the refrigerator a few minutes later when firm hands landed at his waist and drew his ass against an unmistakably hard cock. A wave of relief coursed through his system, and he grinned, dropping the butter he'd been searching for on the shelf and straightening. But before he could turn to pull Landon in for the kiss he craved, the fingers at his waist dug into his hipbones and an unfamiliar voice rasped into his ear, "You're a delicious morsel, aren't you? No surprise Landon picked you."

Unease slithered into Toby's gut. He pulled free of the brutal hold, the refrigerator door swinging shut as he backed into the kitchen island and took in the man before him. He reminded Toby in many ways of Joseph. Both were blond, and each was easily six-foot-four if not taller. His shoulders were as broad and muscled as Joseph's, his dark-brown eyes as cold.

"I'm sorry, but who are you? And how did you get in here?" Toby scowled, schooling his voice to hide the apprehension constricting his throat.

The man guffawed as he leaned against the counter opposite Toby, crossing his ankles in a casual, nonchalant pose. "I'm Landon's fiancé, Garret. I'm sure he told you about me, although he might've kept a few of the key details to himself."

This was the asshat who had broken Landon's heart? Toby's lips curled into a sneer. "Yeah, he told me about you. What the fuck are you doing here?"

Again, Garret laughed. "Landon sent me. It seems his foray into sexual exploration has come to an end. He's gotten the bug out of his system and is ready to focus his full attention on us and our future."

It was Toby's turn to laugh, and he did. Loud and hard. "Yeah, right, asshole."

Garret raised a brow and pursed his lips into a snarky

grin. "Quite bold of you to speak to a client that way, isn't it? What would your handler say if he knew you were using such language?"

Ice-cold dread dripped into Toby's veins, freezing their contents into a slush that pumped lethargically through his pounding heart. He opened his mouth to respond, but no words would come.

"What, you thought Landon wouldn't tell me? Honey, I've been in on it from the start. I agreed to let him blow off a little steam before we tied the knot. It's only fair after the sheltered sexual existence the poor boy lived for so many years of his life." Garret folded his arms across his broad chest. "Honestly, I thought I'd be more resentful, but the stories he's told have been far too entertaining to warrant jealousy. To think he managed to convince a whore they had a future together. I bet you even fell in love with him, didn't you?"

A fist of humiliation and disbelief gripped Toby's stomach with a merciless twist. "Where's Landon?" It was a pathetic question, but it was all Toby could get past his lips.

"Do you really think he's the type for confrontation?" Garret shook his head and chuckled. "I mean, honestly, as one Dominant to another, do you think our little sub—excuse me, *my* sub—has it in him to stand up and tell the truth? That he's just been goading you on for a taste of something different before settling down? Not sure what you did, but he's ready to end this fantasy. He asked me to get rid of you."

Toby's heart squeezed, and the air left his lungs on a painful whoosh. It couldn't be. Landon would never... But maybe he had? How else would Garret know Toby was a whore? How else would he know about their dip into the Dom/sub waters?

How else would he know they'd fought?

"Don't believe me?" Garret tilted his hip free of the counter, then reached into his back pocket. He unearthed a cell phone, swiped at the screen a few times, then held it up for Toby to see.

It was one of those gossip magazine websites. A bold headline read, "Out, Proud, and Desperately in Love," with a picture of Landon—wearing the same outfit he'd left the house in that morning—nestled into Garret's arms. A caption beneath the photo stated, "In a rare moment of public affection between America's favorite sweethearts, Landon Jenks was caught snuggling his fiancé, Garret Ramsey. They teased a possible season two portraying their much-anticipated wedding plans and nuptials. Looks like these two aren't done sharing their love with the world just yet!"

"No." The word fell past Toby's trembling lips. He slapped a hand over his mouth and shook his head. *No.* It couldn't be true. It couldn't... and yet it was. The proof was right there, wasn't it?

Garret tossed his phone on the island, then pressed into Toby's space. He placed his arms on either side of Toby, blocking him against the counter. "I'd apologize on behalf of my fiancé, but quite frankly, you should've known better. You're a whore. Did you really think someone like *Landon Jenks* would fall for someone like you?"

Those words sliced through Toby's heart, nearly flaying him alive. Garret was right. Of course he was right. Toby wasn't worthy of a man like Landon. He'd questioned it a thousand times, hadn't he? If only he'd examined it a little harder. If only he hadn't been stupid enough to lose his heart to a man he'd known, deep down, was far too good for him.

But did any of that really matter? Wasn't it better that Landon didn't have feelings for him? Toby was so worried he'd hurt him when he left. Now that wasn't an issue. He could walk away today and know, without doubt, he wasn't leaving Landon behind hurting and alone. In fact, he'd be anything but. He had a fiancé and continued fame, fortune, and happiness in his future.

Toby attempted to slip free of the unwelcome close-ness, but Garret firmed his hold by pressing his large, intimidating frame flush against Toby's.

"Where do you think you're going?"

Clearing his throat, Toby forced his gaze to meet Garret's narrowed stare. "To pack my things. I'll leave right away."

"Did I say you could go yet?" Garret pressed closer, his hard cock rubbing against Toby's hip. "Landon says you're an excellent fuck. I plan to get a taste before you leave. Your time's already been paid for. It certainly doesn't matter who it is you're fucking."

Dread lanced into Toby's core, drawing a cold sweat to his brow. Garret was right. Again. Joseph put forth precious few rules for the time his whores spent under the command of clients. Landon had paid for him, but there was nothing to say he couldn't pass Toby off to someone else, as long as all parties wore condoms. Sure, Joseph screened his primary clients for STDs and the like, but once his whores were under their control, only standard precautions were required. It would be up to Toby to report any contact with an untested john so Joseph could take the necessary steps to assure the safety of future clients, and as a happy coincidence, Toby's continued good health.

"I know Landon had you fucking him, but I don't bottom. So, drop 'em and spin."

Toby closed his eyes, and for the first time in years prayed for a reprieve. It proved far easier to accept his lot in life than to fight it, and over time, he'd stopped hoping for salvation. But in this moment, he'd give damn near anything to escape the inevitable.

Too stunned and heartbroken to contest the brutal treatment, Toby allowed Garret to grab his shoulders and shove until he stumbled in a half circle and faced the island. His palms landed on the counter with a loud smack as he sucked in a breath against the bite of pain lancing through his ribs.

"Pants off. Now."

A wave of frigid nausea swirled through Toby's belly. He let his head fall between his shoulders and pinched his eyes shut. He couldn't do it. He couldn't willingly give himself to Landon's true love. It would shatter him into a million irreparable pieces.

If Garret wanted a piece of his ass, he would have to take it. Toby refused to aid or abet his own destruction.

When Toby didn't reach for his belt as instructed, Garret's patience snapped, and he did it for him. Within seconds, Toby's pants were around his ankles, Garret's heavy body pressing him into the unforgiving counter as a rough hand grabbed his dick.

"Not as impressive as I thought it'd be in your line of work," Garret growled into his ear. "But then, you aren't hard yet. Let's see where you measure up when you are."

A roar of frustration and heartache ripped up Toby's throat. He shoved away from the counter, sending the unsuspecting Garret stumbling backward as he yanked up his pants.

"Where the fuck do you think you're going?" Garret rounded on Toby, his eyes flashing with an anger so akin to Joseph's that Toby took an involuntary step back.

"Protection." Toby eased toward Landon's bedroom. "Gonna grab a condom and lube, that's all."

Garret rubbed a hand over the fly of his jeans. "Fine. Hurry the fuck up."

Toby bolted for the bedroom. He closed himself inside, leaning against the door as he fought for the breath Garret had stolen. This was a whole new level of messed up. He couldn't hide behind that wall of cocky disinterest he'd built to protect himself from clients. Not with Landon involved. Not with every last one of his defenses stripped and bared to the man he loved. The man whose fiancé was about to destroy every last drop of hope and humanity Toby had left.

But he couldn't say no. His family's safety depended on him doing what he was told, no matter how little of himself would be left when it was over.

He walked stiffly to the bedside table and retrieved a condom and the bottle of lube he and Landon had used to make love so many times. The feeling hadn't been mutual, but that's what it was for Toby. Whether Landon felt the same way or not, Toby would always love him.

His eyes drifted to his suitcase, propped in the corner of the room, then fell to the items in his hand.

A niggling thought wormed into Toby's brain. He'd fucked up in the past, but Joseph always forgave him. His body always paid the price, as Joseph liked to use his fists to ease his frustrations, but Toby's family had never come to harm.

Clinging to the only hope he had left, Toby tossed the condom and lube onto the bed and went instead for his suitcase. Thankfully, he'd refused Landon's insistence that he unpack, so all he had to do was stuff his pile of dirty clothes inside, grab the handle, and exit the bedroom with as much purpose as possible.

"Where the hell do you think you're going?"

Toby clenched his jaw. "I'm not having sex with you. I'm leaving."

"That's precious." Garret tossed back his head on a laugh. "Can't handle fucking your 'boyfriend's' fiancé, can you?"

Too distressed to respond, Toby opened the front door and left without another word. Echoing laughter shadowed him onto the elevator, but Garret didn't follow.

Toby fingered the cash and prepaid debit card he hadn't removed from his pocket following the grocery-store excursion. He half considered taking a cab to the little beat-up motel he still held the key for and holing up for the night. The only oasis he had left. But would one night even make a difference? Would it be enough to heal the damage wrought by the loss of Landon and the painful truth of Garret's words?

Doubtful. Very fucking doubtful.

But the decision wasn't his to make anyway. After all, what were the chances Garret hadn't called his handler and reported his desertion already?

Joseph had never chosen to go after Khloe or their family when Toby misbehaved before. He'd always taken it out of Toby's hide instead. But what if this time was different?

There was no other option than to get his ass back to Joseph's.

Spending more of Landon's money to get there would be a difficult pill to swallow, but at that point, there wasn't a way to return it. Showing back up at Landon's door and finding it answered by Garret—or worse, having it slammed in his face by Landon—was about the last thing Toby wanted to do. He wasn't sure his shredded and bleeding heart could handle any further abuse.

Fuck, what had he done? How could he be so weak that he chose his own pathetic heart over his family's safety? He'd walked out of that condo knowing full well it put them at risk. But he hadn't cared. He'd been so afraid of his own heartbreak he'd endangered their lives.

And there would be no going back now. He was well and truly fucked.

Chapter Twenty-Seven

For the second time in their relationship, Landon broke countless traffic laws as he sped to see Toby. When he burst through the front door with a spring in his step and a grin on his face, he couldn't have cared less how they'd left things that morning. He'd finally done something right. If he showed Toby he was trying, that he'd be willing to do anything to make himself the man Toby deserved, maybe he would forgive him his failures and offer a second chance.

A second chance that might last forever.

His heart was full to bursting with happiness, love, and the promise of a future he'd only ever dreamt of as he called out in a singsong voice, "Honey, I'm home."

He wasn't surprised when Toby didn't respond. Toby was likely a bit sour with him, considering he'd taken off that morning, hadn't gotten in touch all day, then failed to come home until midafternoon. But again, he didn't care. Once Landon told him why he'd been gone so long, Toby would join him in his triumphant glee, and they'd make crazy, passionate love right there on the spot.

Or so he really, really hoped.

"Tobes?" Landon swung through the kitchen, his grin widening when he saw the bags of groceries cluttering the island. He peeked inside one and groaned in anticipation even as his stomach growled its own eager delight.

Toby had gone to the store and bought filet mignon for dinner.

Landon practically skipped out of the kitchen, peeking into the living room to be sure Toby wasn't napping on the couch, then hurried toward the bedroom. No Toby, but there was something else that hadn't been there that morning. A vase of bright red tulips.

His favorite flower. Toby remembered one off-handed comment when Garret couldn't remember a dozen purposeful conversations.

Landon hadn't thought it possible, but his heart swelled even further as he plucked one of the tulips free of its brethren and brushed it over his lips. An elated shiver raced over Landon's skin when his eyes caught on the condom and lube laid out on the bed. Ready and waiting.

Perhaps Toby wanted a second chance as badly as Landon did.

Too thrilled to contain himself, Landon did a half-twirl before bolting from the room, tulip clutched firmly in hand. If Toby wasn't inside the condo, he must be on the roof. Landon raced for the door, nearly ripping it from its hinges in his effort to get to Toby.

But when he rushed out of the stairwell, there was no sign of Toby, nor any indication he'd even been up there.

Fear wiggled in to take up residence beside a flutter of panic. Landon's gut churned in a nauseating wave that sent acrid bile rising up his throat. He hurried back to the kitchen, then dived into the bags still spread over the counter, removing one item after another that should've been refrigerated. One held a soupy mess of melted vanilla ice cream.

"Oh god, Toby." Landon sank to the kitchen floor, still gripping the tub of liquefied ice cream in his trembling hands. He didn't even care when it oozed out of the carton and puddled in his lap.

Where had Toby gone in such a hurry? And why hadn't he come back?

He was an idiot.

Landon slammed the door with far more force than necessary. The paper-thin walls rattled, and powdery dirt fell from the ceiling like a sprinkling of moldy fairy dust. It drove him to sneeze once, then twice, and a slew of curses followed as he stalked toward the closest bed.

Had he really thought Toby would be here? That he'd purchased the fixings for dinner and bought flowers, then at the last minute decided, *nah*, let's leave all this here and run off to that derelict motel?

Utter stupidity.

Landon fell on the mattress and stared at the ceiling. The last time his gaze had rested on that water-stained off-white surface, he'd been in Toby's arms. He closed his eyes and hugged himself, trying to burn that feeling into his long-term memory.

The fact of the matter was, he didn't know where else to look for Toby. He'd left detailed instructions with the front desk to contact him if Toby's keycard was used to access the building or elevator, and hadn't left until he'd checked every possible place he could think to look. The gym. The pool. Hell, he'd even looked in the business center, the rental hall, and every one of the boutique shops and cafés that made up the ground floor of the building.

No sign of Toby anywhere.

The debit card and cash Landon had left for Toby were gone, as were his keycard to the building and his suitcase. But Landon couldn't believe Toby would just bail. Even if something out of his control had come up and he'd been forced to leave for some unforeseen reason, he would've left Landon a note.

Which, he had. Before he'd gone grocery shopping. Landon had found a balled-up note from Toby in the trash can, simply saying he'd gone to the market and would be back by noon at the latest.

When Landon got home, it was pushing three. And considering Toby had been there long enough to start to put the groceries away but not finish—there were items dotting Landon's refrigerator shelves that hadn't been there that morning—it was safe to assume whatever caused Toby to leave had happened sometime around noon.

Landon had checked with the front desk when he'd left instructions to monitor Toby's keycard. He'd asked if they noticed anything suspicious before, during, or after the timeframe of Toby's departure. Only one person manned the desk during the slow business hours, and today it had been a perky young redhead who insisted she hadn't seen anything out of the ordinary. She remembered spotting Toby come and go a few times, the last of which he'd sported a suitcase-on-wheels, but nothing about his demeanor had set alarm bells ringing for her.

When Landon pressed further to see if she'd noticed anything else amiss—any comings and goings not typical to the residents or their common guests—the woman had tensed a bit, thinning her lips into a straight line and losing her friendly chattiness. She'd stated matter-of-factly, "We're not in the business of sharing personal information about our residents, and that includes their arrivals and departures or chosen guest lists. As a celebrity yourself, you should be appreciative of that fact, Mr. Jenks."

Too focused on finding Toby to press the issue further, Landon had thanked the woman and bolted for the garage. The only thought spiraling through his mind was Toby had to be in trouble. He never would've left like that if he wasn't. But what the hell could have happened? And where could Landon possibly start looking for him?

If he called Joseph to see if that bastard had some

hand in this, and he *hadn't*, then Landon risked not only Toby's family's safety, but also put on the chopping block his almost sure-fire plan to rescue Toby. He covered his face, and a roar erupted from the very center of his being, rumbling up his throat and ending on a drawn-out scream of frustration and pain.

He'd never felt so helpless in his life.

A heavy knock had Landon bolting upright mere seconds later. He scrambled to his feet and yanked the door open, a whimper of relief dying in his throat when he saw who awaited him on the other side. "Garret, what the *hell* are you doing here?"

Putting on his best faux concerned act—one Landon had caught the bullshit behind early in their relationship—Garret pulled Landon against his solid chest. "I heard your boyfriend left you, honey. I thought you might need a shoulder to cry on."

Landon stood, stunned, in Garret's massive arms as his anguish-drenched brain tried to chug into gear. No one, not even Steffon, knew Toby had left him. Nor had he told anyone where he was going.

"Get off me." He shoved away from Garret, taking a stumbling step backward. "How did you know where I was? Have you been following me again?"

Dawning realization had Landon scrubbing both hands over his face and turning away on a groan. It made sense. If Garret had been watching his building, he probably saw Toby fleeing. But why wait until Landon came to this piss-stain of a motel to approach him?

Garret stepped the rest of the way into the room and closed the door behind him. "Look, honey, Toby said—"

"*Toby said*?" Landon's shattered heart kicked to sudden life, the many scattered pieces working together to create a pounding pulse that made the room spin with its ferocity. "You talked to him? When? Why? *How*?"

Garret drew his lips into a flat-lipped, toothless

smile. "I happened across him."

Landon narrowed his eyes, clenching his fists until his knuckles cracked. "So help me, Garret, if you had *anything* to do with him leaving..."

The smug flash flitting over Garret's face was quickly replaced by yet another mask Landon had learned to disbelieve. A grin, bright as his beachy blond waves, drew up Garret's cheeks, and those dark eyes sparkled with syrupy sweet and achingly false charm. "I'd never—"

"The fuck you wouldn't." Landon chuffed out a growl. "You did, didn't you? You've got 'I'm guilty' written all over you. What the fuck did you do?" He stormed forward, fisting his hands into Garret's ribbed tank and giving him an adrenaline-fueled shake. "*What the fuck did you do?*"

"I did what you should've done." Garret knocked Landon's hands away and crossed his arms.

Why had Landon ever thought he was attractive? Compared to Toby's sculpted physique, Garret looked like a steroid-induced nightmare. "And what, exactly, do you think I should have done?" He shook with suppressed rage, which was a blessing, because in any other state he'd be quaking in fear at the cold glare Garret aimed his way.

"He's a fuckin' whore, Landon. I can't blame you for getting your sexual kicks with the guy—he was quite gorgeous, I'll admit—but that's where it stops. For your future, and in the public eye, you need a man by your side who'll bolster your reputation and success, not drag it into the murky pits of shame and defamation. And we can do that for each other, Lan. We *did* do that for each other. Look at how successful our show was. We belong together, honey. Together, no one can stop us. We'll be a powerhouse couple."

Landon schooled his voice into a calm, even cadence, enunciating each word with precision and care. "I repeat, what the fuck did you do?"

Garret threw his arms in the air and barked out a frustrated laugh. "What do you think I did? I sent the little slut packing. I told him you were done sowing your oats of sexual exploration and that you and I were together—which we will be once you calm down enough to see reason. You'll thank me for this. I promise. We're going to do big things together, Lan. Big. Things."

Landon covered his face with both hands, squeezing his lids shut as a wave of white-hot agony rolled through his system, bringing jolts of painful awareness in its wake. Toby had left because of Garret. Because Garret had told him lies. Lies that—if Toby felt even half of what Landon did—would've crushed him.

He let his hands fall as a frigid storm of fury and hatred swirled within his mind. "Why won't you just *leave me the fuck alone*? I don't want you. I've told you that a thousand times now, but I'm done playing nice. You hurt the man I love—the man who showed me what *real* love feels like. Do you think I'm going to let you get away with that and, what, come crawling back to you? What is your fucking problem, Garret?"

Landon surged forward, shoving the stony wall of Garret's chest with every ounce of his strength, causing the asshole to stumble backward with a yelp of surprise.

"Answer me, you piece of shit. *Answer me.*"

Garret solidified his stance and glared down at Landon, a sneer contorting his features. "You're my ticket to success. That's all you've ever been to me. Did I get off on tying you up, ordering you around, and having free rein to beat the shit out of you and fuck you any time I wanted in the name of your kinky little desires? Fuck yeah, I did, but not because I *trusted* you or *loved* you or any of that other bullshit you lapped up like a lost little puppy."

His rage and continued fear and concern for Toby were the only things standing between Landon and one hell of an epic emotional meltdown, so he clung to them with every ounce of mental strength he had left. When this was all over—when Landon knew Toby was safe and Garret had fucked off to whatever rock he'd crawled out from under in the first place—Landon would allow those words to land the blow Garret had meant for them to achieve.

But not now. A frenzy of electricity traveled the length of every nerve in Landon's body, lighting him up like a power grid fueled by a fury unlike any he'd felt before. For himself, but mostly for Toby.

"Your career—brief and pathetic as it was—is over." Landon spat the words, his fingers curled into fists vibrating with the urge to let loose on Garret's smug countenance. "If you think I'm going to keep quiet about this, you're wrong. You're dead fucking wrong."

Garret's head fell back on a hoot of laughter before he dropped his gaze to Landon, seething with palpable disdain. "That's where you're wrong, Lan, *honey*. Because you're going to do exactly as I tell you. You're going to appear by my side with a smile on your face at every media event I schedule. You're going to tell the world we're madly in love, and we're going to *do* that second season."

It was Landon's turn to hiss out a scathing laugh. "Like hell I am."

"No?" Garret tsked and shook his head. "That's a shame, because if you don't? I bet all those paparazzi who couldn't get enough of us today would just *love* to hear how you cheated on me with a whore. A whore who then threatened to expose your relationship, so I kindly stepped in and handled it to save your reputation. A whore whose name I wouldn't hesitate to leak to those same ravenous reporters. Tell me, Lan, would Toby like the world to know he's a slut-for-hire responsible for breaking up America's sweetheart couple? Do you think that would sit well with him or his family and friends?"

Landon deflated, his fists falling limp at his sides. Garret beamed, fully aware he'd struck the only possible weak spot in Landon's otherwise bulwarked defenses.

"That's what I thought." Satisfied with his complete and utter destruction of Landon's emotional fortifications, Garret headed for the door. "Don't even think about trying to worm your way out of this, honey. I'll run to the press so fast your head will spin. And if you think I won't be able to find you when I need you, think again. I always know *exactly* where you are."

When the door slammed closed, Landon sank to the bed and dropped his head into his sweaty, shaking palms. He didn't have the energy to worry about Garret's final statement or what he could've possibly meant by it.

He would give himself exactly five minutes to collect himself, and then he had work to do. If Garret had chased Toby off, and Toby hadn't come *here*, then there was a good possibility he'd gone back to Joseph's. And if he'd gone back there before Landon had a chance to set the gears of his plan into motion...

Fuck his five minutes. Landon had to get moving. *Now.*

Chapter Twenty-Eight

When he first arrived back at Joseph's, Toby hadn't even tried slipping in unnoticed. There was little doubt Joseph would have his ears pricked for Toby's arrival, and even if Toby had managed to sneak in, what then? If Joseph wasn't aware he'd returned, the danger to his family would continue to mount.

He'd expected Joseph to be waiting for him, ready to dole out his much-deserved punishment before shipping him off to Howard Mayson with a shiny red bow on his bare ass. But Joseph acted shocked to see him, and rather than pounding him into the marble floor, he'd tossed Toby into his room and all but disappeared. For days.

If Toby's calculations were correct—and he wouldn't be surprised if he'd lost a day in there somewhere—it was Thursday again. A week had passed since his return, and he hadn't seen a single client. Including Mayson.

Even more baffling was Joseph's continued absence. He hadn't let Toby out once to use the gym or wash his clothes, and the strict diet Toby always maintained was reduced to two protein shakes a day. Joseph delivered neither, and when Caden—another of the contracted prostitutes—brought the premixed bottled drinks, he wouldn't meet Toby's eye and refused to speak.

Toby's gut cramped for real food, and his mind deteriorated to a state of near-psychosis in the endless, silent darkness of his room. His feverish dreams and whirling thoughts drifted to beautiful memories and impossible fantasies that found him far from there and safe within Landon's embrace.

He was too weak with dread and fear not to grasp at any sliver of hope, even though there truly were none. Because that would never happen. Landon would be snuggled up to Garret and sharing laughs at Toby's expense, not dumping his movie star fiancé for the whore he'd played pretend with.

There was no salvation, only this endless, waiting hell. Because eventually, Joseph would return. And when he did, it would only be to shift him from one prison to another.

The deadbolt slid back, and Toby turned toward the noise, fully expecting Caden's hunched and quiet form to set another plastic bottle on his nightstand before scurrying out the door. But it wasn't Caden this time.

Toby sat bolt upright, his heart pounding in his ears as he strained his eyes against the blinding afternoon sun spilling into the space around Joseph's hulking form.

"Get cleaned up and put on something of your own. When you're done, throw all your shit—*your* shit, nothing I bought you—into this bag." Joseph tossed a black nylon duffle on the floor beside the bed.

Toby blinked at the bag, his eyes still adjusting to the change in lighting, then squinted up at Joseph's shadowed face. "Why am I packing my stuff?"

"You've been sold. You're no longer my problem." With that, he turned on his heel and slammed the door, then clicked the deadbolt into place.

A hollow ache settled into Toby's chest and crept outward. Somehow, he wasn't surprised. Part of him had known this was coming. He'd worn out his welcome with Joseph. The man was tired of dealing with his shit, and the brief "reprieve" had likely been due to some sort of bidding war. Toby had been through this before. He knew the ropes.

He could also guess who had forked over the obscene amount of money it would cost to buy out his contract. The same man who had never been a fan of sharing his toys and who'd recently gotten so *excited* about the thought of a solid week with Toby under his roof.

Howard Mayson.

Toby's foray into the darkest pits of hell had finally arrived.

Toby stood by the entryway, clutching the duffle bag in his white-knuckled fists. The heavy weight of fear and dread twisted his guts. Joseph wasn't a nice man, but at least Toby had known what to expect. There was routine, and he had his own room. That hadn't been the case during his first few years. He'd lived in a brothel and slept on a cold stone floor with zero privacy, even while servicing clients.

Why hadn't he appreciated what he had while he had it? Why did he push his boundaries and anger Joseph enough that it became easier to sell him than deal with his insubordination? No matter what Toby's future held, it was guaranteed to be worse than this.

He blew out a shaky breath. There wasn't a question whether he'd do it all again. He'd done it for Landon, and he would never regret the opportunity to know what it was like to love a man as pure of heart and kind of soul as Landon Jenks. Even if Landon hadn't felt the same.

Shoes squeaked on the marble floor, and Toby dropped his gaze. Mayson preferred him submissive, and there was no sense starting things off on the wrong foot on day one.

"He's all yours, Mr. Jenks. Do you need any help getting him to your car?"

Mr. Jenks? Toby's head snapped up, and he sucked in a stuttered gasp. *Landon?* It couldn't be... How...?

"No, thank you." Landon's lips pulled into a soft smile as he stepped around Joseph. "We'll be just fine, Mr. Coulier."

Toby stood rooted to the spot, his heart nearly beating free of his body. What was going on? Why was Landon here? He couldn't be the one who'd bought him... Could he? What happened to Mayson?

Landon closed the short distance between them and placed a hand over Toby's tightened fists. "Let's get out of here."

When Toby darted his eyes to Joseph—expecting him to wear an evil, mirthful smirk that would prove this was the cruel joke it had to be—he was already disappearing down the hallway. Toby swallowed and shifted his gaze to Landon's. "I don't understand."

"Does any part of you still trust me?"

A shiver wound up Toby's spine, but he nodded.

"Then come with me." Landon opened the door and angled a sidelong glance at Toby. "I'll tell you everything in the car."

Toby blindly followed Landon out of the house, down the familiar walkway, and straight into the passenger seat of Landon's sleek black sports car. He clutched his bag in his lap while Landon circled the hood, slid into the driver's seat, and gunned the engine. Landon tossed a thick envelope into the back seat before shooting Toby another nervous smile and pulling away from the curb.

Once Joseph's house was out of view, Landon huffed out a breath and rubbed at one of his temples. "I'm sure you have a lot of questions."

That was the understatement of a lifetime. Toby caught Landon's side-eyed stare and shrugged. He didn't know what to think, let alone what to ask. If Landon had bought his contract, what did that mean?

Maybe this was the "worse" he'd prepared for. Maybe being owned by the man he loved would be his final, darkest hour.

Nausea coiled through his belly, and acrid bile rose up his throat. How could he survive three years like this? He'd rather be locked in Mayson's basement than free to roam Landon's condo, witnessing the idyllic life he'd dreamt of sharing with Landon playing out around him without his involvement. Or the wrong kind of involvement.

Landon shifted gears as they eased onto Lake Shore Drive, then moved his hand to rest over Toby's. When Toby spread his fingers, he marveled at the warmth that seeped into his churning gut as Landon interlaced their hands and drew them to his lips, brushing a soft kiss across their joined knuckles.

"I didn't *buy* your contract, Toby. I bought it out. It's gone. Done. Over." Landon shot another look at Toby and squeezed their palms together. "I need to know you understand that. I-I need to know you understand what's happening. You're free, and you have no obligation to me. *None.*"

An odd mix of cold heat washed over Toby's skin, drawing a sweat to his brow and a shiver to his core. Goose bumps crept up his arms, and a dizzying rush forced him to close his eyes and drop his head against the seat.

"Tobes, can you look at me? P-please?"

Landon's desperate plea had Toby lolling his head to the side. He fluttered his eyes open and caught Landon's panicked, glistening gaze before Landon had to shift it back to the road.

"I'll take you wherever you want to go. You don't ever have to see me again if you don't want to, okay? I-I can drive you to the airport. I'll buy you a ticket home. Back to Ph-Phoenix. Or… or wherever you want to go. I didn't… I didn't *buy you*. Not like that. Not for… not for that. Please, *please* tell me you understand."

A numb disconnect prevented Toby from making sense of Landon's words. They jumbled through his mind like pinballs, lighting up areas of his brain he couldn't quite reach with conscious thought, yet leaving him confused and bereft.

Landon pulled his fingers from Toby's grasp, and the grief intensified. But then the car came to a stop and strong arms pulled Toby against a hard, warm chest. Landon's beard scratched over his cheek as he spoke softly against Toby's ear. "I'm so sorry, baby. P-please believe me, whatever that asshole said to you, it was all a lie. H-he overheard me talking to Steffon, and he used what he heard to make you think... t-to make you think things that aren't true. I would *never* go back to him, and I would never... Jesus, Tobes, I would *never* put you on blast like that.

"I'm not ashamed of you or what you've been forced to do. I hate that this started because I *bought* you, but I'll never regret that I did. Because if I hadn't, I never would've met you. But it was never like that. Not to me, not even that first time. You were never just a body to me. N-never. I don't want you to think for one second that I... that I expect anything from you. I want you to find happiness again, that's all."

Clarity settled over Toby, and the anxious minutes he'd lost within his frightened anguish clicked into bright, beautiful focus. Landon's words slammed through that barrier in his consciousness, and their meaning wrapped around him with warm tendrils of promise and love. A dry sob escaped his lips, ending on a bubble of laughter.

Landon clutched Toby tighter. "Tell me what to do to make this better. I'll do anything."

Toby pulled away. He tilted his stare, his heart pinching at the proof of Landon's suffering glistening off his lashes and flushed cheeks.

"There's only one place I want to go right now."

Landon licked his lips and nodded. "Anywhere. I'll

take you anywhere."

The corners of Toby's mouth stretched into a full, genuine grin. "I wanna go to our room."

Toby ran his fingers over the worn surface of the desk. He hadn't known it then, but the last time he'd stood in this exact spot had been the final mental preparation he'd ever have to make for the arrival of a client. And that final client had been Landon.

But as Landon had said before, even that very first night, it hadn't been about Toby's obligation to perform. Not really. It had been about more than the contract or his fear of Joseph or his need to protect Khloe and his parents. He'd pushed all that aside, and he'd given *himself* to Landon. For the first time in all the years he'd used his body to slake the needs of others, he'd allowed himself to take an active role—mind, body, and soul.

"So, I'm free."

Landon straightened against the door, his Adam's apple bobbing beneath his well-trimmed beard. "Khloe's safe. Your parents are safe. The contract is paid off, and I'm going to burn the thing the first chance I get. Or you can burn it. Or shred it into a million pieces. Or do whatever you want to with it. B-but, yes, it's done. Gone."

Toby cocked a hip on the desk. "Is that what was in the envelope? The one you threw into the back seat?"

Landon winced but nodded, shoving his hands into his jeans pockets.

"And you and Garret...?"

"Oh, Tobes, I'm s-so sorry." Landon's eyes flashed with a mixture of anger and grief. "He's tried to convince me to get back with him multiple times, but I've never said yes. He... he thinks I can somehow help boost his career, so I'm pretty sure I haven't seen the last of him, but even if you aren't in my life, I'll *never* go back to him. Things between us were hardly as rosy as they appeared on TV, but that's neither here nor there. I'm so, so sorry. For everything. For *anything* I did to make this all s-so much worse."

Toby shifted so he could spread his legs a bit and gave his chin a tilt. "Come 'ere."

Landon wet his lips and pulled his hands from his pockets. He stepped slowly forward. As soon as he was within grabbing distance, Toby pulled him between his legs. He speared his fingers into the thick, dark tousle of hair at Landon's nape and wrapped his other arm around his leanly muscled back, tugging him close.

Toby inclined the hairsbreadth necessary to plant a chaste kiss over Landon's deliciously soft lips. "I believe you, sweetheart. But I've got another problem."

"O-oh?" Landon trembled in Toby's arms, his hands drifting to rest on Toby's shoulders. "I might be able to help. If you want me to."

"Well, see, it's not that easy of a fix." Toby trailed a line of whisper-soft kisses over Landon's cheekbone and across the shell of his ear. "But you do seem to have a knack for solving the unsolvable."

The hands gripping Toby's shoulders tightened when he traced the line of Landon's ear with the tip of his tongue.

"I'm always, ah, up for a challenge." Landon breathed the words, ending on a whimper when Toby's ministrations moved down his neck.

"This is a biggie. I'm talking life-altering stuff here." Toby slipped his hand beneath Landon's shirt and pressed his palm against bare flesh. "Think you can handle squaring off against two mountains in such a short period of time?"

Landon's hands strayed from Toby's shoulders to relocate against his cheeks. The move drew Toby's eyes up.

"For you, I'd do anything."

Toby slid his tongue across the closed seam of Landon's mouth and moaned along with him when those luscious lips fell open. Their tongues met, and Toby's eyes drifted closed from the utter perfection of it all. Landon's hips shoved forward, his cock pressing against Toby's greedy arousal, and another joint groan filled the air.

"I love you, Landon Jenks."

Landon froze in Toby's arms, his entire body going rigid, and Toby's heart cramped. He never should've said anything. What was he thinking? They barely knew each other. Landon didn't mind that Toby was a prostitute, but his understanding could only go so far. Toby was the kind of guy you fucked, not fell in love with.

"You... Tobes, I..."

"No, it's okay. I'm sorry." Toby dropped his hands from Landon's body. "It's my problem, not yours. I shouldn't've said anything."

"That... *that's* your problem?" Landon still hadn't moved. His palms rested against Toby's cheeks, his body stiff between Toby's legs.

Toby tried to angle away, but Landon clamped his hands tighter along Toby's jaw and planted his feet, keeping him anchored in place.

"Don't. Please." Landon placed his thumbs under Toby's chin and tilted it up so their eyes connected again. "I... I never thought... You a-aren't saying that because you feel like you have to, are you? I meant it when I said you owe me nothing."

"I said it because it's true." Toby sighed and placed his hands over Landon's. "I'll never be able to find words to thank you for what you did, but I'll try every day. Telling you I love you isn't some cop-out. No one has ever gotten under my skin the way you have. Not even before all this. You saw *me*—and made me see myself—in a way I've never experienced before. I don't expect you to feel the same way. I... I just needed to say it. It's so much bigger than anything I've ever felt before. I thought maybe it would be less suffocating if I could say the words out loud."

"Is it? I mean, you know, less suffocating?"

Toby laughed and shook his head. "'Fraid not. But it was worth a shot."

Landon's lips pulled into a crooked smile. "I don't have a solution to your problem, but I do have the perfect way to make it worse."

"Ah… Not sure I'm looking to make it worse." Toby rubbed at the center of his chest with a chuckle. "It's plenty painful as is."

Landon's fingers traveled down Toby's stubbled neck, over his collarbone, and covered the hand Toby held over his sternum. "I love you too, Toby Carmichael." Landon grinned when Toby's eyes widened and sought out his gaze. "There. I hope your heart exploded the same way mine did when you said it. Fair's fair and all that."

It had. It absolutely had. "Say it again."

That gorgeous grin widened. "I love you, Tobes."

"Fuck." Toby tugged his hand from beneath Landon's and wrapped him in a desperate embrace. "I love you, sweetheart. I love you so fucking much I can feel it like a living thing inside me."

Landon buried his face in Toby's neck and melted into his arms.

"I want to forget everything before you." Toby let out a shaky exhale and squeezed his eyes shut. "I want to be yours. Not because of some stupid fucking contract, but because I *want* to belong to you. Wholly and completely. In every sense of the word."

Landon leaned back and locked eyes with Toby. "I want that too. I want to be yours as much as you're mine. Maybe even more."

A painful memory flashed through Toby's mind, and he hugged Landon closer. "When you went to your knees that morning… Fuck, sweetheart, I about lost it. It was the most beautiful, most powerful moment of my life. I would've given you anything you asked for and more right then, but I…" Toby pressed his forehead to Landon's. "I failed you. I'm too weak to be the Dom you're looking for. And in that moment? I panicked. I realized I wasn't good enough for you and never would be, and I—"

Rumbling laughter filled the space around them, and Toby leaned back, cocking his head at the unexpected mirth lighting Landon's grinning face.

Landon shook his head, his amusement dying into a soft chuckle. "Remember how we decided, if we were going to do this thing, communication would be key?"

Toby swallowed and nodded. "I know, I should've said something instead of running. I promise, if you're willing to give me a second chance to at least attempt to be what you need, I'll try to do better in the future."

"Oh, baby, you're already everything I need and more." Landon quirked his lips in that adorable, lopsided grin Toby loved so much. "But here's the thing. I was just as guilty of hiding my feelings. And you know what's really stupid? We were both thinking the same damn thing."

Toby drew back his chin and frowned. How could a man like Landon doubt his worth? Especially when it came to someone like Toby? There was no comparison.

"Why would you think you weren't good enough for me? Fuck, you're perfect. If I could, I'd spend every minute of every day worshiping at your feet."

Landon waggled his brows. "That's my place, baby. You can worship me from a standing position. Maybe with a flogger in your hand. Or a riding crop. Or a bottle of lube and one of those damn plugs you seem to like so much." He winked and rolled his hips into Toby. "But you're… Jesus, Tobes, you're the ultimate dream all rolled into one delectably sweet package. I've spent most of my life hiding from my sexuality, so I haven't, you know, had the best experiences with men. I've given myself to some shitty guys just to feel a connection. Any connection. Even if it was one-sided and left me feeling worse and more alone when it was over."

He toyed with the hair at Toby's nape, avoiding eye contact. "You're the first guy who's ever cared enough to make sex feel good for me." He huffed out a breath. "*So fucking good*, by the way. You're also the first guy I've ever been so uncontrollably horny for. But the sex isn't all there is for me. Sure, I mean, that's part of it, but..."

Landon sighed and finally shifted his gaze to meet Toby's. "You make me laugh. From that very first day we met, you've drawn out some silly part of me that never existed before. And you make me smile. Not the kind of smile you put on to maintain a socially acceptable veneer, but the real kind. The kind you can't stop even if you wanted to. The kind that makes your belly do flips and your heart pound in your ears. And you make me want to be a better man. Not so you'll keep me, but because you inspire me to be all I can be and more. I..."

He blew out another long exhale and squeezed Toby's neck. "Fuck, I love you so much. And while, yes, you're breathtakingly gorgeous, you're so much more than a pretty face. You're insanely brilliant and witty and clever. You have a heart the size of Texas, and your generosity and kindness know no bounds. You're the strongest, bravest, most fearless man I've ever known, and, I mean, you've survived things most of the population couldn't even imagine enduring, yet you're still *you*. You still manage to find the courage to put yourself out there and to take care of my needy ass to boot.

"And, ah, moment of brutal honesty?" Pink colored Landon's cheeks, but his gaze didn't waver. "I'm terrified you're going to realize how amazing you are and how much better you could do than an aging ex-baseball player reality star who's lived a nearly celibate life. I have nothing to contribute to a relationship with a man as wonderful as you. There are literally millions of men out there with more to offer, both with their younger bodies and physical attractiveness, as well as in the sexual knowledge and skill department."

Toby's emotions pinged through him like erratic electrical currents, setting off a volley of small explosions at the end of each nerve that left him shuddering in their wake. How did he even begin to respond to all that?

"First of all, thank you." He pulled Landon closer, guiding his head down to rest on his shoulder. He stroked his soft hair as Landon nuzzled into his throat. "Thank you for loving me despite my many flaws. Thank you for seeing past my weaknesses and finding strengths where I can't see them. Thank you for believing in me to be what you need, and for trusting I'm adept enough not to royally fuck this all up. Again."

Landon tried to lift his head, but Toby pressed gently to keep him in place, brushing a kiss over his temple. "And I don't give a shit about age. To me, you're beautiful. Exquisitely so. Inside and out. But here's the thing... I hold the same fears you do, sweetheart. I'm petrified it's going to sink in I'm nothing but a used-up whore, and you're going to realize what that really means. And for all the sex I've had over the years? I'm no better versed in it than you are. I only had a few partners before I became a prostitute, and trust me, I didn't pick up any usable knowledge or skills lying on my back or bending over."

This time, when Landon pulled away, Toby let him. But he didn't merely lift his head, he stepped clear out of Toby's arms. Thankfully, before Toby's heart could grind to a halt at the sudden chill of Landon's absence, Landon did something that had it kicking to life at twice the normal speed.

He dropped to his knees.

Blood roared in Toby's ears even as the air caught in his lungs. He lifted off the desk and stood with the toes of his shoes mere inches from Landon's spread knees.

Unlike the last time he found himself in this position,

Toby carded his fingers through those luscious black waves without hesitation.

This beautiful man—this man he loved, and who incomprehensibly loved him in return—was on his knees, at Toby's feet, because he chose to be there. Not because he'd been forced or felt obligated, but because he wanted to give Toby the ultimate gift. The gift of him, in all his awkwardly adorable, inconceivably wonderful glory.

Landon whimpered and pressed into Toby's touch. "I meant it that first night when I said I didn't care. But that feeling of complete not-giving-a-fuck was amplified by about a million and six when I found out it wasn't your choice." Landon lifted his head, and those smoky gray eyes—misted with tears Toby could only hope were from happiness—locked on to his. "Everything that happened before this moment doesn't matter. Our future starts now. And you know what? I kind of adore the idea of discovering things together. I never thought I'd find a man to love, let alone one who would love me back so completely."

"Oh, sweetheart." Touched beyond what words could say, Toby fell to his own knees and wrapped Landon in a fierce embrace. He wasn't sure if a Dom was supposed to join his sub on the floor, but he didn't give two fucks what the guidelines might say or not say about the subject. Landon was right. They could figure things out together and make their own rules. Who said they had to abide by a script? They just had to be safe, happy, and in love.

"You know..." Toby's voice turned grave with a hinting lilt of humor. "You're kind of stuck with me now. I hope that isn't going to be a problem."

A bubble of laughter fell past Landon's lips. "I've never been so thrilled by words meant as a threat in all my life."

"Yeah?" Toby chuckled and pressed Landon closer. "Does that mean I can keep you?"

Landon was still a moment, and then he nuzzled into

Toby's neck. "Is that even a question? You own my heart, Toby Carmichael. I'm already yours."

Until Next Time...

This is the first book in the Owned Heart, Body, & Soul trilogy. Be sure to keep an eye out for He Owns My Body—*the next installment in Toby and Landon's story—due to be released Winter 2020!*

About the Author

Evie Drae (ze/hir/hirs) is a registered nurse by day and a bestselling, award-winning MM romance writer by night. Ze has won first place in seven Romance Writers of America® (RWA®) competitions, including the prestigious title "Best of the Best" in the 2018 Golden Opportunity Contest. Ze was also a double finalist in the 2019 Golden Heart®, in both the Contemporary Romance and Romantic Suspense categories.

One of Evie's favorite things to do is encourage hir fellow writers. To that end, ze started the #writeLGBTQ, #promoLGBTQ, and #DailyWriteLGBTQ hashtags on Twitter to support and promote LGBTQ+ authors and allies while providing a safe space to connect and grow as a community. Ze is married to the love of her life, is the parent of two wonderful fur babies, and runs almost entirely on coffee and good vibes.

Evie loves to link up with fellow writers and readers. You can reach hir directly at EvieDrae@gmail.com or find hir on hir social media accounts listed below. Twitter is where ze's most active but be sure to check out hir blog too. Ze focuses on reviews for LGBTQ+ authors and allies with the occasional quirky advice/recommendation post just to toss things up.

Website/Blog: https://www.eviedrae.com/
Twitter: https://twitter.com/eviedrae
Goodreads: https://www.goodreads.com/eviedrae
BookBub: https://www.bookbub.com/authors/evie-drae
Facebook: https://www.facebook.com/eviedrae
Instagram: https://www.instagram.com/eviedrae/
Pinterest: https://www.pinterest.com/eviedrae/

Also Available From

BEAUREGARD AND THE BEAST

AN MM ROMANCE FAIRY TALE RETELLING